THE TASTE OF DATURA

Also by Lorenzo

The Love Fool
A Mistake Incomplete

THE TASTE OF DATURA

An alluring affair in Napoli.

A Novel By
Lorenzo Petruzziello

Published by Magnusmade, www.magnusmade.com

Interior design by Elizabeth Bonadies

ISBN: 978-1735065441

e-ISBN: 978-1735065458

Library of Congress Control Number: 2023919795

First edition

Printed in the United States of America

*For my parents and grandparents for giving me the opportunity to
make this region of Italy an important part of my life.*

This book is also dedicated to myself.
For committing to this work, and pushing through to the end.

Datura stramonium, also known as jimson weed, is a poisonous plant that belongs to the deadly nightshade family. Known to produce a mind-altering and amnesia-like effect, its taste is both bitter and nauseating.

INTRODUCTION

Prepare to be allured by some of the myths and legends that surround Naples (Napoli)—the City of the Sun. I always knew I was going to write a story set in the Campania region of Italy, as it is the region where I spent a lot of my summers growing up. Although I didn't travel to Naples often when I was in the area, I was still intrigued by the history and legends that surrounded it.

I hesitated to base my story here, however, because I didn't feel like I knew the city and its culture enough. Sure, I was familiar with Avellino, the area I spent my time in, but not Naples itself. So, before I put pen to paper, I needed to go there. I needed to become more acquainted with the city. I needed to see her, feel her, and understand her in order to know what to write.

As I continued to visit Italy, I began to take time to visit Naples. But, every time I went, it wasn't for long—maybe a day trip or less, with my visits being mostly limited to the historic center or the university area; I was thrown off and jarred by the chaos that is the heart of the city.

Eventually, I visited other neighborhoods like the beautiful Chiaia, up the hill to quieter Vomero, and to the elegant neighborhoods of Margellina and Posillipo. But it wasn't until a few years ago, that I booked myself a hotel and actually stayed a couple of nights in Naples, beginning my research for my story. I visited the churches, saw the sculptures, perused the museums, and walked along the *lungomare* (waterfront).

In my investigations, in addition to the religious hold on the city—which, I personally found excessive and boring—I discovered something that was more fascinating to me: the myths and legends that surrounded Naples; stories about Virgil, Greek mythology, ghosts, and mediums. Once I discovered this, the burst of creativity came to me. I was inspired.

As I wrote my story and invented my characters, I continued my research, finding myself connected to a specific plant; the datura, which was the plant named in the title. So, I needed to write a character who was an expert in horticulture. That character ended up being Lavinia, the florist.

During my research of flowers and the practice of being a florist to make Lavinia believable, I discovered the Victorian language of flowers. A message could be delivered just by the selection of flowers one puts into a bouquet. I tried incorporating this into Lavinia's scenes. When she gifted a flower or a bouquet, I sometimes described the flower, giving myself that hint of a message she was inadvertently, or maybe intentionally, conveying. It was a little game for myself.

As far as the title of this book, I struggled a bit. I came up with a great title originally, but I was concerned it gave away a big part of this story. While I continued to consider the pros and cons of that title, I came up with one that focused on tone, while using the flower and plant theme: *The Taste of Datura*. I thought the tone of this title fit seamlessly into the genre of noir fiction. It reminded me of great noir films, and it was intriguing enough to make a reader wonder what datura could be. It's a poisonous plant with a nauseous and bitter taste. Perfect. It was eerie, suspenseful, and cringeworthy.

So, sit back and enjoy *The Taste of Datura*, and be allured.

PARTENOPE'S SORROW

Darkness loomed over me.
As wonder sailed nearer.
Like a cloud of lead, I did not see.
Through the perilous waters I mirror.

I sat and watched you,
but you wouldn't see.
What were we to do?
Was this sorrow; my new eternity?

Was it the scent of a flower,
that lured with its charm?
Or the taste of the herb,
that caused you this harm?

Like an elixir to lips,
in a cup made of clay.
Your slight shattered walls,
brought to a fog of grey.

Your heart saw through it;
the spirals of smoke.
But my heart wanted love,
and a promise spoke.

See me, hear me.
I sing. I cry.
You brought this sorrow,
and my tears, by and by.

— Lorenzo Petruzziello

PROLOGUE

Naples, Italy
December 1890

The crisp breeze trickled in from the bay, across the piazza, through the narrow buildings, and brushed along the back of the neck of the elderly German archaeologist. He was determined to have his afternoon walk through the Spanish Quarter. Being out of the hotel room and in the open air made him feel a lot better.

He'll get back to Athens soon enough. Sure, he should have been celebrating the holidays, surrounded by his family and fellow archaeologists, but his health kept him from continuing on his journey. A special gift he bought in Naples was ready to be picked up, so he wanted to go get it and bring it with him to Athens. He imagined showing the piece to everyone waiting for him. If only his infection hadn't come back, he would have been allowed to take the ship to Greece and be in Athens for Christmas as he had planned.

But being stuck in Naples was a consolation, though. While he had spent some of the time in bed recovering, he had made the most of his time until the doctors could clear him to continue on his travels. For example, he was able to return to Pompeii and examine the ruins with more detail—something one cannot do during the summer holiday with the influx of tourists crowding around.

So, he couldn't really complain. After all, he was absolutely fine staying in the comforts of the wonderous and luxurious Grand Hotel, with its incredible view of the bay. Not a bad place to recover from his lung infection.

As Christmas was getting closer, the visits from the doctors had diminished. Of course, the old man understood doctors had families too. Besides, they did see improvement in his condition, and said they would check in on him after the holiday.

When he was feeling better, he bathed and dressed and focused his time on visiting the artifacts in the museums of Naples, including that excursion to museum and ruins of Pompeii.

On Christmas Day, however, the museums were closed, so the old man had agreed to participate in the hotel's abundant holiday lunch with other guests. The staff were kind enough to understand his condition and seat him alone at a private table, so he didn't risk getting anyone else sick.

After the meal, he had decided to take a walk to the church. A young concierge procured the old man a driver as he helped him put on his coat and handed him his gloves and hat.

As he walked across the front gardens and onto the main street along the bay, the old man greeted the staff and some of the other guests he had met while he was stuck recovering in the hotel. He looked at the water, took a deep breath, and allowed the crisp, salty air to fill his lungs, immediately feeling the renowned healing powers of the Mediterranean Sea.

He turned away from the bay and crossed back to the car that was waiting to take him to Piazza Plebiscito. It was not his destination, but he figured he'd take a walk to the church he had in mind. He was somewhat familiar with the area, but not enough to take himself directly to the church. It was not a problem, though, he knew he'd find it strolling around.

He asked the driver to return in a couple of hours, then walked across the round piazza, onto Via Toledo. Halfway up the climbing street, he felt his body become weaker than his ambition. He forced himself to slow his steps as he continued his climb.

He paused at a shop window and admired the Christmas decorations. Really, he felt his heartbeat racing and needed to catch his breath. He needed to rest. He examined the miniature figurines displayed in a religious scene, finally presented with the miracle baby they had been eagerly awaiting. Ignoring the reflection of his old face staring back at him, he looked away and saw a clearing further ahead.

Deducing it to be another piazza, he would rest at a café and sort out his route to the church. He gathered his strength and continued on.

He reached piazza Santa Claritá and looked around for any open café. He felt the space spinning as he turned and turned. His head felt numb, the sounds around him were garbled, as if underwater. He blinked heavily before everything turned to black…

CHAPTER 1

Cairo, Egypt
Present Day

NICK FOLLOWED THE transportation concierge out of the airport, down to a group of drivers, who were chatting and smoking cigarettes while waiting for their next passengers. He stood by as the concierge called out to one of the drivers—a plump man with a stoic look. The concierge put his arm around the driver and whispered instructions. The driver kept looking back, glaring at Nick up and down. The concierge unfolded the document Nick had handed him, and after some resistance, and some bribery, the driver relented with hands raised in surrender, taking the paperwork. The concierge nodded and put up his finger— appearing to give the driver a warning. The driver responded with a frustrated nod.

The concierge then proudly turned back to Nick. "This is your driver," he said, leading Nick toward the vehicle. "He will take you straight to your hotel in Giza. He is instructed not to stop anywhere else. Do not pay him." He pointed to the copy of the receipt on his clipboard. "I just showed him the address and the payment receipt. He understands your fee was already paid in full, and," he added, "it already included his tip. A generous one too."

"Thank you," Nick responded but with some hesitancy. That driver just didn't seem at all happy about this particular drive.

"Listen to me," the concierge said, leaning in and speaking softly and sternly, but still with a smile, "do not give him any more money. He has already been tipped." Then, he pointed to the small white van and indicated for Nick to board.

Nick climbed onto the cushioned, bouncy seat covered in yellow velour stripes, which matched the thick, yellow curtains drawn closed on all of the vehicle's windows. The evening sunlight still managed to make its way through, giving the interior of the van a warm, orange glow. An opened sliding glass window separated him from the driver. Nick turned back to the concierge and thanked him.

"Farewell, Mr. Terenzi," the concierge replied, and then closed the van door. Before the door was completely closed, Nick was certain he saw the concierge's smile disappear as the driver squabbled with him one last time.

The little, white van bolted toward the flux of red lights heading away from the airport. Nick held onto his overly-bouncy seat as the driver maneuvered his way through traffic onto the major motorway. Nick looked every which way and tried to register the surroundings: landmarks, signs, exit numbers, etc. It was his first time in Cairo, and with no time to prepare or research the city, he felt out of his comfort zone.

The instructions were clear: get to the hotel in Giza and deliver the bundle to a man named "Mo"—he would be found in the shipping and receiving office. Once the transfer was complete, it was suggested, strongly suggested, that Nick leave immediately and return to Naples. Nick didn't ask any questions; he just wanted to do what he needed to get his money.

If he had known he was travelling to Egypt, Nick would have done more research, but all of this was arranged for him, and the trip itself did not allow time for touring. Once on the flight, he thought he would review the map of Cairo and Giza, but he still had no information on routes or modes of transport to the city itself. All he knew was that he was supposed to meet a man named Mr. Khalil at the transport concierge desk, who would then arrange transport for him to the Giza hotel.

Nick looked up at the driver's rear-view mirror and made eye contact with him, but the man quickly looked away. Nick tried to lock eyes with the driver again, but to no avail. He sat back and pulled his leather travel bag closer and carefully unzipped the brass zipper. Sitting on top of his pile of clothing, underneath a button-down shirt, was the valuable item wrapped in parchment. He unfolded the parchment and admired its contents. Nick felt a sudden force throw him to the side. He regained his bearings and realized the van had hit a pothole. He looked up at the driver's eyes in the rearview mirror. The man looked at him, offered a face of apology, then focused back on the road. *Communication breakthrough*, Nick thought. He re-covered the item in its parchment, zipped the bag closed, and looked back up at the mirror.

The driver was fully concentrated on the barren road. Nick relented and turned his focus on the road ahead as well. *My evening is in the hands of this stranger,* he thought. *Who is he? Does he know what I am carrying? Is he involved in this? And why is he not happy about this drive? Can he be trusted? This could be it. If something sinister was to happen to me now, no one would ever know.*

Nick surprised himself; he had never thought like that before. He was thinking foolishly. Someone did know where he was. Sure, that someone probably couldn't care less if Nick didn't return, but they knew where Nick was. Well, they knew he was in Cairo, headed toward a specific hotel in Giza, but they didn't know he was currently in the tiny, bouncy, white van driving away from the airport. Until Nick arrived at his destination, no one would know where he actually was.

His ridiculous thoughts were taking over his mind. *I could die right here and no one would know where the heck I am. I need to control this situation. I don't like this vulnerability. I'm in this driver's hands and he can do whatever he wants with me. Wait a minute, why am I assuming the man would pull into some dark alley, rob me, and leave me to die? How did I become so dramatic, so scared?*

Nick tried to focus on keeping a cool composure, but his thoughts continued to spook him. *If this driver wanted to mug me and throw me in a ditch, he could. If he wanted to drive me to some dark alley to beat me up, he could. If he was instructed to drive me to an abandoned warehouse and have me killed, he could. He is in control.*

Nick then reminded himself that he was sent here. But it was the damn warnings that raised red flags. "Don't trust anyone," were his contact's exact words. "Don't trust the concierge. Don't trust the receptionist at the hotel. Speak very little. Deliver this immediately to Mo, then leave. Don't dawdle. Don't take time to enjoy the sights. Don't even have a coffee. Just leave."

"What is all this?" Nick had asked.

"This is the best way to get rid of it and get your money," the man snapped back.

"Okay, Okay," Nick relented then switched to a gentler tone, hoping to calm him down and get more details. "Why so cautious and concerned?"

"I prefer not to tell you this but," the man replied. "There may or may not be word of a delivery." He looked like he had wanted to say more, but he had stopped and busied himself searching for a pen.

"What do you mean?" Nick had pushed.

"It's nothing." The man didn't add more, and Nick didn't get any other details, other than the address. The man's vague warning and his short tone had put Nick on guard.

Enough! Nick thought to himself. *Take control of the situation. What is wrong with you?* He looked up at the driver's eyes in the rear-view mirror again. This time, he held his glare until the man looked at him. Nick smiled, leaned forward through the divider—which was open—and spoke to him. "Do you speak English?" Nick said it loud enough to be heard over the man's radio.

The man hesitated before responding, then shook his head, and glanced again at Nick through the rear view.

Nick put his hand to his chest, nodded, and said his name.

"Ahh." The man relaxed, smiled, and patted his own chest. "Mehmet."

"Mehmet," Nick repeated. "Parli Italiano?" *It was worth a try.*

Mehmet adjusted his seat but again, shook his head no. He lowered the radio. Nick was relieved Mehmet began to show some interest. That his attempt at conversation had broken down the man's aloof and vaguely hostile attitude.

Nick looked at him again. Mehmet was smiling more and seemed to show his consent, like a game or mystery to be solved—

or that the two of them were going to solve together. Yes, it was like he and Nick had agreed to the mission of breaking down their language barrier.

Nick proceeded by pointing out the window. "Cairo?"

"Yes," Mehmet said.

He did know some English. Nick assumed, as a driver, he had experienced many travelers or visiting scholars, so he must have been exposed to simple or at least common English words. *Or was he not a driver and some henchman hired to rob and kill me?*

"See?" Nick continued to encourage him. "You do speak a little English."

Mehmet cocked his head, smiled, but then shook his head as if to say, "Thank you, but no. I don't know English."

Nick smiled again and sat back in his seat. Although the two of them couldn't really have a full conversation, he felt much more comfortable now that he was able to break the driver's wall and form some type of connection.

"Michael Jackson?" Mehmet suddenly asked, sitting up with excited eyes in the rear-view mirror.

"What? Oh, yes! Michael Jackson!" Nick laughed. "Yes, very good."

"Sott." Mehmet continued to use any English language word he knew or had previously heard. Or possibly, playing the act that he didn't speak the language.

Nick frowned, not familiar with what he was trying to say. He encouraged Mehmet to repeat it.

"Sott-a," the man repeated, making the drinking motion with his hand.

"Oh," Nick laughed. "Soda!"

"Yes," Mehmet exclaimed and laughed with him. "Sotta!"

"Soda." Nick repeated. He wanted to continue to keep the man talking.

"So-da," Mehmet confirmed. "Soda."

Again, Nick wasn't sure if the man was pretending not to know English. Was this his game to fool some foreigner into believing whatever he wanted? How was it possible that a man working in the travel industry was not familiar with any foreign words— even the basic hello? *He's a killer. No. He can't be. Why not?* Nick pushed away his suspicion. He decided to just let the man be as he wanted and ended the soda conversation.

"Yes, Soda."

Mehmet's van approached some buildings, which Nick assumed would be Cairo city. The heavy traffic merged onto a ramp leading to a major highway.

Mehmet slowed down as they approached a busy square. Nick turned his focus out the window and saw people crossing the street haphazardly; not respecting cross walks or cars not waiting for traffic signals. Similar to what he often saw in Naples.

A group of people approached the minivan, reaching into Mehmet's window and asking questions. Mehmet replied curtly, pushing their hands away from him and his vehicle. Nick was used to random people going up to cars at stoplights in Naples, but rarely ever did they reach inside so aggressively. Mehmet looked back at Nick and signaled for him to sit back behind the curtain. Nick followed his instructions, his fear had suddenly returned.

What was happening? Why was Mehmet, the driver/killer, telling me to hide? Where were they?

More people appeared to surround the van, trying to peek through the thick, yellow curtains. Mehmet continued to drive slowly, moving closer to the ramp that led to the highway. Or maybe toward the square?

Through the curtain on his right, Nick could make out a busy street market. The driver kept shouting at the pedestrians on the left, to what Nick assumed was a warning to get out of their way.

"Soda?" Mehmet turned back to Nick, pointing to the busy square.

Mehmet seemed to want Nick to buy him a drink. *Is this how he is going to lure me out and mug and kill me?* Nick remembered the concierge's words on repeat "...the driver is instructed not to make any other stops." He looked at Mehmet, shook his head, smiled, and said, "No."

"Yes, soda," Mehmet insisted and turned the vehicle into a dark alley behind the busy market.

Nick felt his nerves quake. He thought about how the concierge had warned him not to stop anywhere until his final destination. And tried to determine why Mehmet would go against the instructions by pulling the van into a dark alley.

Chapter 2

"NO, SODA," NICK repeated.

The van was turned off, the lights turning off soon after. Mehmet removed his seatbelt and reached for the glove compartment.

"Mehmet, no soda," Nick repeated with more assertion, adding, "Giza. Giza."

"Soda," Mehmet's reply was more of a whine; a tone that said, *Come on man. One drink.* He slid some documents into the glove compartment and locked it with the key. Nick watched as he opened his door, also locking it behind him. The man then walked around the van and slid the side door open for Nick.

Nick gestured to his bag. Mehmet offered his hand and pointed to the compartment under the back seat. As Nick moved aside, Mehmet use his key once again to unlock the compartment and nodded for Nick to put his bag inside.

"Giza?" Nick asked again.

Mehmet smiled and helped Nick slide his bag into the compartment. *This man is determined to get me out of the van. What is about to happen?* Nick relented. He was in Mehmet's hands. If the man insisted on a soda, Nick had no choice but to have a drink with him. He considered taking his bag along and maybe making a run for it, but he feared he would only be advertising the fact that he was a lost tourist.

Nick looked around and saw the bustling market at the end of the alley. *At least there will be people around.* He would let Mehmet lock his bag up and then would rush toward the end of that street—forcing the pair to be in a public setting. *But isn't it easier for a murderer to slip away after killing someone in a crowd?*

Nick looked at Mehmet, trying to scan for a weapon of some sort but didn't notice anything suspicious. *Maybe he is hiding a knife somewhere in his pants? Or maybe he really is just a driver.*

"No," Nick blurted. "I want my bag."

Mehmet looked back at him, confused.

Nick pointed to the bag. "I want my bag."

Mehmet gestured to the lock on the compartment.

Nick shook his head and said, "No."

Mehmet raised his hands in defeat and handed Nick back his bag. He then motioned for Nick to follow him out. Nick looked around, then forced himself to step out of the van. Mehmet signaled 'wait here' as he closed the curtains inside the van.

The end of the alley that led to the open market was to Nick's right. He glanced at Mehmet still shuffling inside the back of the van, before quietly sidestepping toward the front of the van—the side that faced the market. He looked back and saw Mehmet climbing out of the van. He again turned toward the market and evaluated the distance. He heard Mehmet close the door behind him. Nick took another step, then another, and continued in the direction of the end of the alley. *The closer to other people,* he thought, *the better.* He continued his steps as quietly as possible, as his mind worked on an escape plan.

This is it. This is how I'm going to die?

Nick quickened his pace and lost himself in the crowd. He heard Mehmet call out to him.

How did I get myself into this?

Chapter 3

THE SUMMER HEAT in Naples hits you like a strong bear hug. It makes its presence known as it pushes away the crisp morning air, reminding you that it will be accompanying you throughout the day, and through to the night—depending on where you happen to be.

Nick thought about the heavy heat while seated on a bench underneath a tree located at the west end of the park. The sun had now trickled over it, forcing him to get up and walk into the shade between the buildings of Viale Gramsci. He continued toward the rotary at Piazza Sannazaro, where sat the large fountain of a mermaid with her left arm in the air, as if in a pose of triumph.

The heat was still weighing on him, and the shade wasn't helping. Nick always hated summer in Southern Italy. He tried not to think about the torture to come in the coming months—when he would typically shift himself north near the lakes. It killed him to have not done it this year, but he had recently moved to a new apartment and couldn't justify the cost to also rent a summer home for the season. Instead, he saved his money and remained in the south longer than he had originally intended.

His new apartment was much larger than his last, but it didn't have air conditioning. If only it was located by the bay, he would at least get some sort of breeze. Although, he wasn't even sure if that would have been the case. In short, Naples in summer was hotter than hell.

He forced a stroll along the *lungomare*, hopeful that a breeze would cool him off, or at least pause the sweating. But the breeze did not seem to exist. He stood by the peninsula and stared at the boats docked at the main pier. Just as the shade hadn't helped, the walk wasn't working for him either. He had to get out of the scorching heat, even if it was only for a moment.

He walked up to a hotel, intending to take a little break in its air-conditioned lobby, and then would be on his way. He approached the revolving door and pushed as the doorman monitored his every move—analyzing his purpose for entry.

Nick didn't work at this hotel, but as a former hotel bartender, he was familiar with the doorman's purpose; to prevent any potential persons from committing crimes at the establishment. These men stood at the entrance with a welcoming smile, assessing everyone passing through. It usually took just a look, but sometimes, it required a bit of small talk to determine if the person was a purse-snatcher, drug dealer, or prostitute. The latter always seemed to find an easy way inside.

When Nick stepped into the lobby, his body immediately relaxed. He filled his lungs with the faux-fresh, cool air, as if breathing it in from a mountain top. He looked around and realized he was being watched again. Two clerks behind the reception desk appeared to be gauging him—waiting for a cue to approach and ask if he was in need of any service. More scrutinizing for crime. He looked away and surveyed the plush sofas and chairs laid out into several, mini-conversational settings for guests to make themselves comfortable in, as they waited for whomever was to come.

Nick took a seat on one of the woven cane chairs placed at a small, round, wooden table along a wall of books. Almost immediately, one of the reception clerks approached. "Are you enjoying your stay, sir?" said the young woman as she pretended to tidy the magazines on the coffee table not far from him.

Nick would do the same when he was assigned to front-desk duties back in the day. He knew this young woman was sent to deduce who he—the unknown man—may be. Was he a guest? Was he invited by a guest? Was he looking for potential customers or marks to swindle? Did he belong? The key, Nick recalled, was to talk to the patron and surmise their purpose.

"Oh, yes," Nick responded. "I'm just waiting on my wife." He lied, but it was a safe answer for the woman. That was all she really needed. She smiled and pretended to straighten the final magazine before heading back to her station.

Nick realized he now had to pretend to be a guest waiting for an imaginary spouse that would never show up. He had hoped the lobby would have more activity for him to easily blend in, but the quiet emptiness made him appear as if he was center stage, being watched by his audience: the two clerks who monitored him inconspicuously.

He shifted in the chair and shuffled through the one magazine on the table—some city-focused publication that showcased high-priced shopping and restaurants. Nick didn't really care about the topics; he just needed something to focus on as his audience continued to make him uncomfortable. They clearly didn't want him dawdling. He pretended to take a call on his phone.

"Oh, you're already outside?" He said it louder than he needed to, but that's how many tourists typically talked to each other, so he went with that. "Okay, I'll be right there!" He stood up from his chair, stretched his arms, and nodded to the clerks as he walked out the door.

He was out of the cool-conditioned air and back into the heavy and sticky heat of Naples. Parched and in want of a drink, he turned the corner and found a bar with a neon-red sign above a heavy, black door that read *il malocchio* (the evil eye). He pulled the door open and welcomed the embrace of more refreshing and artificially cooled air.

The soft blues music filled the small, dark space. A long, black lacquered bar was lit up by a neon-blue strip underneath the outer lip. Out of the eight red leather stools, the only seat that was available was being wiped down by a staffer. Rather than wait, Nick sat at one of the high-top cocktail tables scattered along the back wall. He wanted space, so he chose a table by the window that offered an unimpressive view of the back alley.

"Welcome," the server greeted him from another table. He pushed in its stools and wiped the tabletop as he spoke. "What can I get you?"

"Beer, please. *Bionda*," Nick replied. It was unlike him to order a beer, but he knew a light blonde beer would refresh him.

"Of course. *Certo*," replied the server.

Nick looked around the room and analyzed the patrons. It was a mix of people, and no one really appealed to him.

The server returned with a bottle of local beer, a chilled glass, and a dish of assorted nuts and crackers. "Anything else I can get for you, sir?"

"No, grazie," Nick responded and focused on carefully pouring the blonde pilsner into the chilled glass. The beer's cool touch reached his lips, into his mouth, and down his throat—managing to cool his insides, as the air conditioning was doing for his exterior. Immediately, he felt relaxed and refreshed. He licked his lips and glanced up, inadvertently locking eyes with a woman who had been watching him from the bar.

CHAPTER 4

NICK FELT ONLY a little guilty for sleeping with someone just to have a night in her air-conditioned place, but the Naples heat was unbearable, and he needed the escape. Why not have some pleasure while cooling off? Sure, she wasn't too happy when he skipped out early that morning, but he did try to linger by showering at her house.

He always found it odd showering in a stranger's bathroom, though. It wasn't like a hotel bathroom, where everything was kept at a minimum and perfectly placed—like a blank canvas for the occupant to fill its void. Instead, someone's home bathroom tells a story; their story. Even the way the towels are hung portray the type of person they are. Are they haphazard? Mis-matched? Or are they uniform in color and folded to perfection? What color? Boring beige or exciting yellow? So much can be said by the simple selection of a towel.

A lot could also be said by one's medicine cabinet or beauty products. Or, in this case, a fern hanging in one end of the shower. But Nick didn't really care. He just wanted to take his cold shower and leave. He reached for her face towel, then hesitated to use it. But then shrugged and ran it under the stream of cold water, covered it in soap, and scrubbed all his parts—especially the parts that had touched her over and over again. He wanted to clean her off of him. Of course, the soap smelled like her, but he could cover that scent up with a sample spritz of cologne from a shop nearby; the first thing he planned to do when he left.

When he emerged from the bathroom—already dressed—she was on the patio caressing her plants and drinking her coffee. He popped his head through the flowing curtains and watched her turn around. She looked different than what he had recalled from the night before. He remembered her being so easy. Just a rub of her leg and he was invited up to her place. Before he said yes, though, he first had to confirm it was worth the time. He slyly slipped a question about air conditioning into the conversation. Once she confirmed she had it, he agreed and followed her home.

He didn't step onto her patio that morning. He stayed within the curtains and looked her over. She stood by the railing with the tiny espresso cup in her hand. Her body was beautifully curved, but there was something about her face that didn't match it. Her nose hung high, giving the appearance of a creature sniffing for something awful in the air. Her eyes drooped like boredom, or as if she was angry at everything. She took the espresso cup away from her mouth, and he cringed at the sight of the lips that were all over him just moments ago.

"Thank you for a fun night," he recovered and offered a fake smile. "I have to get going."

She forced herself to smile back and nodded. Her dull eyes held a hint of hope, as if they were pleading him to stay, asking him not to reject her. He looked away and closed the curtain.

He turned back to the bedroom, feeling a slight regret for using her for her air conditioning. He brushed off the feeling and focused on leaving. After all, he did get what he wanted—a cool escape from a very hot summer night. He walked out the front door and left her apartment building, glad he would never see her again. Or so he thought.

Chapter 5

NICK ADJUSTED HIMSELF in his oversized bathtub. The cold water had become lukewarm. He had soaked longer than anticipated, but he loved his bathtub and would use any excuse to stay in it longer than needed. Washing away the heat was just as good as any.

He caressed the outer lip of the tub and breathed out in serenity. He remembered when he had found this apartment, he immediately fell in love with the oversized white basin, its claw feet, and classic shape. It sat under a window in a large bathroom, tiled in forest green with brass accents along the walls.

A cool bath on a warm day was one of his favorite ways to clean the sweat off of him. In addition to cleaning off any trace of a recent lover.

Nick released the drain plug and listened to the water begin to drain. He grabbed the showerhead, turned the nozzle, and let the stream run down. The water washed off the suds left behind.

He dried off, put on his loungewear, and went into the living room to grab his phone from the coffee table. He sat on the couch and scrolled through the daily news notifications that had appeared on the screen. When he swiped to clear the messages, the phone rang.

"Pronto?" Nick's voice was a bit hoarse. He cleared his throat and listened.

"Mr. Terenzi." The man's voice was unfamiliar. It was English with a hint of softness, or desperation.

"Yes," Nick replied. "Who's calling?"

"Oh, Mr. Terenzi," the man replied with relief. His voice had more energy. "I'm from San Gregorio—the art dealer. I have some news for you."

"San Gregorio?"

"Yes," the man replied. "I'm sorry it took us a while to get back to you, but…"

"The art dealer," Nick said it aloud when he remembered. San Gregorio was not any ordinary art dealer but an underground market dealer for art, jewelry, and other stolen items. It had been a while since he last talked to someone from the organization. *Art dealer.* Nick remembered. *The bracelet!* It was the last time he had spoken to anyone in that world. *Could this man be calling about that damn bracelet?*

The bracelet was sold to him by an antique shop in Rome. It was in a box made of tin with brass or gold etchings. It was particular to Nick because the images portrayed plants, flowers, and animals. He had lifted the lid and found the bracelet wrapped in purple velvet. It was made of brass or copper, with designs depicting the sea and maybe a few creatures. He had asked the shop owner for a price of the box and its contents, to which the shop-owner then foolishly revealed that he had forgotten about the box and the bracelet altogether. Nick took this as an advantage in negotiating a lower price, and after some haggling, the shop owner finally relented.

The shop owner had claimed the set—bracelet and box—was probably from the pre-war era and pointed out the Greco-Roman inspired images. He admitted the items had come to him separately and that he had never taken them to get analyzed by a professional. The bracelet was procured by unconventional means—one of his "suppliers" had taken it off a dead body at a train station in Rome a while back. So, he had stored it in the tin box matching its style and forgotten about it until Nick walked into the shop and showed interest.

"Mr. Terenzi? Are you still there?" the man on the phone implored. "Please, I will explain."

"Yes," Nick stammered back to the telephone conversation. He sat up and asked, "Sorry. I had some trouble hearing you, Mr....?"

"Oh, yes," the man replied. "I am Gaetano Pentolino. We've never properly met, but I was hoping we could speak in person. I have an offer that may be of interest to you."

"Offer?" Nick responded, trying to remember the men he had met years ago, but time had erased the certainty of any facial description.

"Yes," Gaetano replied. "Are you available to meet me today?"

Nick hesitated in his response. He didn't want to give Gaetano any impression that he was desperate to get rid of the bracelet. He had found it years ago and was unable to sell it. He couldn't find a buyer, which was why he had contacted these underground dealers.

"Mr. Terenzi?" Gaetano repeated.

"Yes," Nick stammered again. "Yes, I'm available. In an hour?"

"Great," Gaetano responded. "At Caffé dell'Ovo, just behind the castle."

"Okay," Nick agreed. "See you there."

CHAPTER 6

IT DIDN'T MATTER how hard Nick tried concentrating on the book he was staring at; his mind just didn't want to read. His eyes would follow the letters that formed the words on the page, but his brain would not compute the meaning. It took him three or four attempts before realizing he had been reading the same sentence over and over—as if not understanding the language that the words were expressing.

Is my mind going? he thought. *Here I go again; down a mental path of potential health issues that could be the reason for my not understanding the words on the pages. At what age does Alzheimer's kick in?*

He slammed the book shut and let it fall onto the small table in front of him. The landing made a sound louder than he had anticipated. He looked around in embarrassment and smiled at the one startled patron a few tables away.

Nick gently grabbed the ice-cold drink sweating in front of him. The hot Italian sun streamed onto the auburn vermouth, accentuating the bubbles of the soda and the glistening melt of the large cube of ice; which had melted enough to be able to now bobble and clink inside the thick glass.

He sat back and looked past Castel dell'Ovo, through the cracks between the buildings in front of him, at a view of the Bay of Naples and beyond. Through the warm haze, along the surface of the sea, a cargo ship was anchored. Its distance gave the false impression of appearing smaller than its actual size—resembling a child's toy floating in a bathtub.

Although he couldn't see it in full, he knew Mount Vesuvius stood ominously just past the ship, further to the right. While the buildings in the small piazza did not allow Nick a clear view of the mountain, he imagined the notorious mammoth now crowned by the dark clouds creeping in for the anticipated rain. Whatever the climate, Vesuvius' presence always loomed over one's shoulder in this region. He wondered if those who are born here have some sort of anxiety over the mountain. Whether in view or not, one doesn't have to see it to know that the volcano was there, waiting.

Waiting. Nick was tired of waiting. It seemed he was always waiting in life. Whether it be for the right time to act or for someone else to make a move. Today, he waited for the person he was supposed to meet, but this particular person was late.

Nick hated when a task was incomplete. If an agreement was made to meet at a specific time and location, both parties should show the other respect and get there at that set time. But sometimes, life likes to remind Nick that not everything goes as planned.

His beautiful, new watch confirmed he had been waiting longer than he had agreed. He monitored the gray clouds floating in from afar and contemplated the time it would take to walk back to his apartment. He paid the tab—two vermouth and sodas, with one espresso in between—and collected his book to free the table. As he was about to get up from his seat, he spotted a man walking toward him from the left.

The thin, lanky man was dressed in a brown linen suit, a fabric Nick detested because it naturally gave the appearance of a disheveled traveler. As the man got closer, Nick noticed the disheveled appearance was not just from the suit. The man was moist with sweat and wore an anxious look on his face. He carried a brown satchel and constantly looked around, as if he had lost something. Some people always appear to be worried or sad, but add the man's choice of linen on top of that, the total package could label this stranger as a worry wart.

Nick watched as a server approached the worried man, offering him an empty table. After asking the server to repeat his question, the man politely declined and looked around, clearly seeking someone. Amused by the spectacle, Nick sat back down, watched, and waited. If that was the man he was supposed to meet, Nick had little confidence that this meeting would have any outcome.

Annoyed with the delay, Nick decided to move things along by causing a bit of attention to make the man look toward him. If it was the man that had contacted him, then he would approach. If it wasn't, then Nick would leave.

So, Nick lifted his book and shuffled the pages, but they made no sound. He then picked up his empty glass and shook it, making what was left of the ice cube clink around like a little bell. It worked. The man looked over and immediately approached.

"Mr. Terenzi?" The words came out of him like a whisper, solidifying his overall weak demeanor.

"Yes," Nick gestured for the man to join him.

"Thank you," The man put out his sweaty hand. "I am Gaetano. We spoke on the telephone." He shook Nick's hand and sat down. "Thank you for meeting me today, Mr, Terenzi." He looked around again and finally gestured for the waiter to bring him a coffee.

"Are you looking for someone else?" Nick asked.

"I'm sorry?" Gaetano responded.

"You keep looking around. Is there someone else meeting us?"

"Oh, no," Gaetano responded in a quieter voice. "There was a young woman lingering around back there, and I didn't know if... well, for some reason, I thought I was being followed."

"Followed?"

"Yes, by the woman." Gaetano sat back. "But I don't see her anymore. I'm sure it was my imagination. Not to worry, Mr. Terenzi."

Gaetano's anxiousness was making the meeting uncomfortable. Nick had the urge to end the interaction and leave, but he continued. "Mr. Terenzi," the man repeated his name more than necessary. "As I mentioned on the telephone, I have an offer that may be of interest to you." He tapped his satchel as he said this.

"Yes," Nick replied. "I have to admit, I was a little surprised by your call. It's been a while since I last communicated with your people."

"Indeed," Gaetano responded and looked out at the sea. "I see the clouds coming in. The weather is going to change soon. Probably quickly." He turned back to Nick. "Allow me to be direct."

"Okay. So, tell me about this offer." Nick sat back in his chair. "Did you find any information on the bracelet?"

"I will explain." Gaetano took the espresso from the server and sat forward as he twirled his sugar with the little, silver spoon. "A while ago, you came to us with the item."

"The bracelet," Nick responded.

"Correct. Well, although the sale, at the time, was not a success, shall we say, I am here to make you another offer."

Nick was perplexed. A lot of time had gone by since he approached these men about finding more information on the damn bracelet, and a buyer. He had purchased it without knowing anything about it—its value or significance—he just thought it may have held some value to someone. But he had trouble finding anyone with information on it.

"You mean, you found a buyer?" Nick asked. "After all this time? I assumed when you guys passed on it, it was over. Why now? Who sent you here?"

"Well, Mr. Terenzi," Gaetano replied. "We had forgotten about the item, in fact. To us, it was a deal that failed, and we moved on. However, as you know, our line of work also involves us looking for items. Items that may or may not have crossed through the black market. And we remembered your bracelet."

"Someone hired you to find it?"

"Well, yes and no," Gaetano continued. "You see, we get a list of items that are in demand from different sources. And sometimes, we either have the items, stay on the lookout for the items, should they come our way, or as in this case with you—we've seen the items and go back to try and retrieve them."

"And one of these lists included my bracelet?"

"Yes. At first, we didn't realize we had seen the bracelet before. As I said, we had forgotten about it. But the list sat with us for quite some time, though it wasn't until we were approached by another one of our buyers that we remembered we had seen the bracelet."

"Wait. Someone else is looking for it?" Nick leaned in. "You mean, in addition to the list from your first buyer?"

"Well, the first is not a buyer, really. It's more of a—" Gaetano stopped himself, opened his satchel, and shuffled through his papers. "Let me talk to you about this buyer. You see, our buyer brought us more information about the bracelet. Details that were not included in one of those lists I had mentioned. Ah, here—a drawing and a photograph of the bracelet. That is what triggered our memory of seeing it."

Gaetano handed a copy of the drawing to Nick. It was a hand-drawn etching with notes written in German and some sort of Arabic letters of which Nick was not familiar with. H. Schliemann was written on the bottom right corner; a name Nick had also not recognized.

"The drawing you see there," Gaetano said. "That is believed to come from a notebook that once belonged to the German archeologist—long passed now. The photograph, though, was taken in Berlin, maybe thirty or forty years ago, by the last person known to have possessed the bracelet."

Nick looked at the photograph of the bracelet being displayed by an elderly woman. "Who is this woman?" Nick asked.

"We don't know that," Gaetano replied as he returned the papers to his satchel. "It's of no significance to us really. What matters here is that we eventually remembered the bracelet. We remembered you and that you wanted information on it and possibly, to sell it. We hoped you still had it in your possession and that we could broker this deal for you, on behalf of our Egyptian buyer."

"Egyptian?" Nick asked.

Gaetano opened his eyes wide and looked back down at his satchel. Apparently, he had said more than he had intended. He sat back and took a deep breath. "Our goal here, Mr. Terenzi, is to obtain the best possible deal for your bracelet for you, which allows us the best possible commission, of course."

"Of course," Nick replied. "Who is this buyer?"

"You know I cannot tell you that, Mr. Terenzi," Gaetano responded. "Not yet, that is. First, the important issue; do you still have the bracelet?"

"Yes," Nick replied. "I have it stored in a safe place."

"Wonderful," Gaetano exclaimed. He sat back with content. "Well, are you interested in a deal?"

"I suppose I would need to know the details first, of course," Nick replied. "And I am still in the middle of researching its origins and significance, so I may not be ready for a sale just yet."

"Well, we might have someone who can help you with that," Gaetano offered.

"No, thank you," Nick dismissed Gaetano's offer. The dealers would most likely recommend someone who would suggest a low value for the bracelet. "I appreciate the offer but I am close to my answers, really," he lied.

"We can respect that." Gaetano paused. He stared into Nick's eyes and reached inside his satchel. He pulled out a white paper and slid it across the table. He silently watched as Nick read the figure.

"I was expecting more here." Nick slid the paper back to Gaetano.

"I did not come here to negotiate, Mr. Terenzi." Gaetano slid the paper back to Nick. "This is the offer as configured by our analysts."

"I expect more," Nick retorted.

"And on what do you base your price increase?" Gaetano sat back in frustration.

"I told you I've been doing my research on the item," Nick continued the front. "And I now know where I can take it. Where it belongs." Nick knew that last phrase was a hidden threat. Typically, these underground dealers knew it meant Nick was intending to give it to a museum.

"You don't plan on just handing it over to UNESCO? Ha!" Gaetano scoffed. "You are not that foolish."

"They have expressed interest," Nick said.

"Yes, but they offered much less than the Egyptians." Gaetano stopped himself again. As before, he had let information slip that he meant to keep to himself.

"So, the other buyers are from UNESCO," Nick replied, as if he had guessed it prior to Gaetano spilling the intel.

"We always work with the United Nations," Gaetano admitted, but worked to minimize his words. "You know this. Everyone knows this. But you also know that they don't offer much—they have this belief that they are entitled to every artifact out there, so they should all be handed to them. But they also understood they were competing with buyers in this market—buyers with a lot of money and resources."

"Why this Egyptian then? Money?" Nick asked. "Who is he?"

"Of course, it's money," Gaetano replied. "But it's also more than that."

"What do you mean?"

"Well, you've been researching the item in question. You should know the Egyptians think they deserve it." Gaetano collected his documents and slid them into his satchel.

Nick had no idea what Gaetano was talking about, but he wouldn't let on. What was the bracelet, and why do Egyptians want it?

"To be honest, Mr. Terenzi," Gaetano continued. "The Greeks are also interested. However, they also believe the item belongs to them, not the Egyptians, and that they are the ones entitled to it. So, their offer was not even close to what the Egyptians put on the table." Gaetano closed his satchel and added, "Surprisingly, no interest from the Turks."

Nick was even more confused. This conversation with Gaetano had made it clear that Nick had been holding on to a very valuable artifact. Greece. Egypt. UNESCO. The bracelet had more importance than Nick had ever considered.

"Who have you been talking to about the item?" Gaetano asked.

"I have people," Nick lied again.

"Well, I'm sorry we couldn't finalize a deal today, Mr. Terenzi." Gaetano looked genuinely disappointed. "But I will advise you to be careful who you talk to about the bracelet. I say that because this is the reason why we are coming to you now."

"What do you mean?"

"Mr. Terenzi," Gaetano lowered his voice. "It is usually a warning when we see multiple interests in one particular item. It often means that discussion of the item has been happening in the market. That, most likely, someone who has the item has shown it to the wrong person."

"But I haven't shown it to anyone. Except you."

"Well, someone must know it exists and that it is out there." Gaetano stood up. "If you want my advice, take our offer. Relieve yourself of this piece. It will only lead you to danger."

"Are you threatening me?"

"No, no, Mr. Terenzi. The danger will not come from us. But, from my experience, when talk of something is out there, it leads to trouble." Gaetano looked up at the sky and pushed his seat back in. "Looks like the rain will start soon. Thank you for the coffee. We'll be in touch."

CHAPTER 7

NICK SAT AT his old wood desk clicking through information about UNESCO—the United Nations Educational, Scientific and Cultural Organization. As described on several websites, *UNESCO is an agency of the United Nations created after WWII... to promote world peace and security through international cooperation in education, arts, sciences and culture.*

Nick jumped at the sound of thunder. He exhaled, sat back, then rushed to close the nearby window. The rain splattered against the double doors of the room's small balcony overlooking the main street.

He sat back at the desk and fiddled with the mouse. He glanced at the green glass ashtray to his right. It must have been in the apartment for many years, as suggested by the faded gold etching of some sort of bird in the center. Probably taken from a local lounge, it was placed on the desk, available to be used by many of the apartment's previous tenants, and one that actually had the courage to pocket it and add it to the décor of the space.

The ashtray held an unlit cigarette. Nick was not a smoker, but he enjoyed the company of a cigarette close by when he worked. It made him feel like someone else was there with him. He knew it was a strange habit, but he supposed it was better than actually smoking the thing.

The lights flickered, as did the screen in front of him. Should the lights go out—as they usually did during a rain storm—he had a set of candles standing up in their holders placed in almost every room. He looked at the upper right corner of the laptop's monitor and saw that the battery level was low. He hunted for the charger when a loud splash of rain beat against the windows. Behind it, a burst of lightning briefly illuminated the dark sky and the rooms in the apartment.

Nick walked over to the window again. The rain had filled the streets, just like the weather report had suggested. The lights flickered again, and this time, actually gave in to darkness. The roaring thunder soon followed.

He turned to the marble-top side table by the leather armchair and flipped open a brass box. He pulled out a set of matches and lit the single candle held in a matching brass holder. This flame would be his second companion this evening. He always admired the soft glow of a flame against wood and leather. The one flame managed to even trickle light into the next room.

Nick turned off the light switch as he left the room and proceeded to light the four candles standing on a narrow table against the wide hallway. This candelabra was set in a strategic location, allowing light to flow into each room that was adjunct to it—a living room, a kitchen, a bathroom, and a bedroom.

He heard the steps of neighbors stammering up the stairs, shaking off the rain that they apparently had been caught in. Arguments followed between them; it was a couple each blaming the other for taking longer than needed at wherever place from which they had returned.

Nick monitored the light switch in the kitchen, even though he never turned lights on in a room he was not using. In fact, he rarely turned on the lights in his home at all. He liked darkness. There was enough natural light that came in from the windows; he didn't really find the need to fill the room with the unbearable brightness of artificial light. It always made him squint, and he didn't like to do it. If one had to squint, then the light was too bright. And besides, squeezing the eyes caused wrinkles at the edges. He had done enough irresponsible squinting while lying in the sun during his teenage years. Now that he was in his forties, he noticed the hint of those intruding wrinkles and refused to allow them an easy path to grow.

He looked in the mirror near the candelabra but couldn't clearly see the state of his aging eyes. The lightning brightened the room behind him again, followed by a crack of thunder that still managed to startle him. Or maybe it was the idea of his age that shocked him. He looked away from his reflection and decided he would research anti-aging face cream in the morning, just in case. He was not ready to let his looks fade. It was bad enough he was struggling to keep his weight and physique in decent form. Now this?

He shuffled to the kitchen, grabbed a glass from the dish rack, popped open the freezer, and added a couple cubes of ice. When he returned to the study, he poured himself a whiskey from his collection of liquor in the wood bar cabinet that stood promptly to the left of the doorway, facing the windows and the leather chair.

He took a sip of the whiskey, sat back down at the desk, and, with a shake of the mouse, he brought his laptop screen back to life. Continuing his research on UNESCO, he scrolled through the overly-written description to find any connection that would prompt the agency to want his bracelet. ...*looking for ways and means to rebuild their education systems.* He continued to scroll until he saw a phrase that he thought probably had some connection: *cultural heritage artifacts.* He read on. *The UNESCO Treaty of 1970...prohibiting and preventing the illicit import, export and transfer of ownership of cultural property—*

The screen shut down and would not allow itself to reboot. The battery had drained. Deflated, Nick took his glass of whiskey to the couch. With the little that he had read, he tried to piece together the connection between UNESCO, Egypt, Greece, and his bracelet.

The lamp in the corner flickered back to life. Nick sipped his whiskey and looked up at the bookcase to his left. He raised his eyes to the top shelf, and his gaze followed the leather-bound books. He stopped between Shakespeare and Umberto Eco and stared at the untouched, green tin box stuffed in between.

CHAPTER 8

IT HAD BECOME an acceptable irritation to find a coating of dust on areas touched infrequently. Particles fall on top of cabinets, under furniture, and onto items set on the highest bookshelf. They continued to collect, peacefully undisturbed, and ready to annoy anything that would carelessly move them with the slightest encounter. A short breeze from a window, disrupted air from a passerby, or a brush of the arm was all that was needed to cause a flurry of particles to float around and cause annoyance to anyone or anything that had come into contact. Of course, frequent use of a duster or a rag would help alleviate the cloud of disruption, but as people become comfortable in their space, the duster handled less and less. The particles gather again, a lot of times unseen, waiting for that one slight movement to displace them back to a floating mess falling on the closest empty surface.

Nick coughed and sneezed as he reached for the untouched green and brass-colored tin box squeezed between the classics. He blew at the layer of dust on top, causing another chaotic cloud to irritate his eyes. He stepped off the stool and placed the box on the coffee table, allowing time to gather himself from another sneezing fit. He was embarrassed to think that his space was not as clean as he led himself to believe.

He went into the kitchen, washed his hands, and returned to the living room with a cloth he had moistened under a slow trickle of water. Particles of dust filled the ray of light emanating from the large floor lamp arching from the corner. Nick almost wished the lights had not come back—he didn't want to see the dust. He broke through the cloud and reached for the tin box.

With each swipe, the layer of dull gray easily wiped away, revealing the shiny, bright luster of the brass flower petals pushed out from the tin. The art-deco design featured white flowers—maybe tulips—scattered around green and gold, reminding Nick that the box once contained a champagne bottle that was given to him for his birthday years back. He remembered lifting the lid on the long end and seeing a dark green bottle decorated with similar art-deco flowers laid flat inside the plastic black mold. The champagne was fresh and delicate, with hints of apple and peach. He had enjoyed it with a lovely woman he had been seeing at the time. That romantic evening had turned into another carnal night that entered his mind on occasion. Unfortunately, that relationship had fizzled away not long after.

Nick felt he was blushing. He shook away the returning memory and opened the lid. He unfolded the layers of silk scarves, and within the folds of an ugly purple one, he freed the bracelet that he had purchased a while ago.

It was clunky. The links were very thin, and the brass—or whatever material it was—had some tarnish. He grabbed his mobile phone and took several snapshots of the bracelet, making sure to catch every detail of each section. He zoomed in on the etchings along the side. They were rubbed down and unclear, depicting symbols that could be musical instruments, plants, or maybe flowers. Were they horns or roses? On one particular section, there appeared to be some sort of creature or animal—maybe a bird or a fish. Or was that a bear?

Nick had wanted to get the bracelet appraised by a professional, but he would heed Gaetano's warning—he didn't want to bring attention to it. He researched on his own, but still, he had not deduced what the images meant or even portrayed. He had no idea where to begin—he was not experienced in jewelry design. He would probably end up having to accept Gaetano's offer to help. Nick wanted to avoid using Gaetano's connections, but the art dealer would be able to find the right professional that would understand discretion was of highest importance. In any case, Nick knew he needed some sort of base to understand a value for the bracelet. It was time to get the bracelet professionally looked at and definitely cleaned.

He gently rewrapped the bracelet in the purple scarf and returned it to inside the tin. The landline phone rang in the hallway; shrill and consistent. Nick slid the tin back between Shakespeare and Eco, hopped off the stool, and went out to the hallway to answer the relentless call. He picked up the receiver on the entry table and coughed. "Pronto?" Nick's voice cracked.

There was nothing but silence on the other end.

"Pronto, pronto," Nick said it louder, but still no response.

The dial tone bubbled up in the receiver. Nick set the phone down, trying to guess who could have called his land line. Gaetano? But he hadn't given Gaetano that number.

Nick went back into the living room, scrolled through his cellphone, and tapped on Gaetano's name. He held the phone to his ear and listened to the ring answered by the art dealer's voicemail greeting. Nick tried again—still no answer. Finally, he sent a text message, asking for Gaetano to return his call.

Nick plugged his laptop to charge, bringing it back to life. He connected his phone and downloaded copies of the photographs he had just taken. An email notification popped up on the screen. It was a response from the art frame shop—the package he had been waiting for had arrived.

Nick closed the intruding pop-up window and opened the new photos. He zoomed in to examine the metal; was it gold plated? Maybe brass? He needed to figure that out. He focused on the designs. With the larger screen, he was convinced the etchings were flowers, or maybe leaves.

He opened the web browser and searched for types of flowers, hoping to find a match. He thought if he could start with identifying the metal and the plant, it would be a step closer to finding some sort of basis to value the bracelet. But within a minute of his search, Nick soon remembered he had tried this before—back when he first got the bracelet—and had failed at identifying anything.

Frustrated again, he closed the browser window, closed his laptop, and went to bed.

CHAPTER 9

THE MORNING AIR already felt heavy with heat, and the streets were dry—not even a puddle. It was as if the rain from last night hadn't ever fallen.

Nick stood at the bar and scrolled through the morning news as he waited for his coffee. He sipped the sparkling water—a palette cleanser—and thanked the old barista that placed the espresso cup on the saucer in front of him. Nick preferred his coffee without sugar, but the Neapolitan style was very bitter, strong, and dark. It always surprised him when he took his first sip. This time, though, he remembered to add a half spoon of sugar, stir it well, and then sip the shot.

The hot, spicy, bitter-yet-slightly-sweetened liquid embraced his tongue and throat; convincing Nick he had taken in a burst of charged energy, which was needed for another morning in Naples.

He skipped the pastry that morning—an effort to cut down on the fattening foods. However, he knew full well that a freshly baked sfogliatella would find its way into his mouth within the hour. All it would take to entice him is a slight sensation of the aroma wafting past his nostrils. His choice leaned more to the *frolla* style—made with a short-crust-type of crust, but wouldn't turn down the classic seashell shaped *riccia* style either. Both offered the same flavors, with same ricotta and candied orange filling; it was just a matter of texture really. But, for the moment, the slightly sweet—but not too sweet—flaky crust of the sfogliatella frolla was his favorite of the two. No, wait, he liked either, but never had he ordered more than one at a time.

Okay, fine. He wiped any lasting dust of powdered sugar from his face—a tell-tale sign of a man who had just enjoyed his morning pastry and was trying to convince himself it had never happened.

Nick continued up via Toledo, dodging the morning flurry of people filling the sidewalks for the shops along the street. He passed Piazza Caritá and turned down a narrow street to the right that housed small antique and artisan shops on both sides. He stopped at the window of a woodworker's shop that displayed an armchair in mid production. The owner was smart to show a passerby each step of his chair-making process, enticing a potential buyer to walk in and order a custom-made piece.

Among the twists and curves of the rattan and bamboo, Nick spotted his reflection. He was focusing on his hair when he noticed another reflection just past his shoulder. It was a woman looking at the same window, probably admiring the same chair. He inadvertently locked eyes with her; she smiled and opened her mouth as if to say something. Instead, she looked away with widened eyes and rushed toward Toledo. Her reaction was suspicious, but Nick brushed it off as her keeping him from approaching, or maybe she was just embarrassed. Nick would have approached her, introduced himself, and maybe invited her for a drink later, but she had turned so quickly, cutting the opportunity for him to do so. He accepted her reaction as a sign of no interest. *Too bad*, he shrugged and continued on toward the art frame shop in the historic center.

Nick was always told there was a criteria to selecting the proper frame for a painting. Was it painted on stretched canvas? Or maybe paper? What type of paint? Acrylic or oil? Glass or no glass? If glass, then UV protection would be a must. Correct? Do we add a matte? If so, what type? Maybe linen or paper? Nick preferred linen. He felt it added texture to an otherwise boring, flat, paper border. Aside from texture, though, the color was important. As the frame shop owner explained, "You don't want the matte to take away from the artwork."

To which Nick replied, "Do we even need a matte on this?"

The frame shop owner went on to explain that a matte would distance the artwork from the frame, allowing the piece to be centered. However, as the man had noted before, the color must be subtle. Choosing a color from within the painting itself would allow the frame to match the artwork, but still blend in like a piece of the background. Although it bordered the art, it must not take the focus from the work itself.

The painting was an original work of acrylic paint on paper. The gallery owner had explained to Nick that the artist, from somewhere in Southern France, was known for his modern style, which was described as a combination of abstract, street, and pop art. He was best known for his figurative subjects, but this particular painting was part of his new series focused on still life of wildflowers. Its dimensions were 50 centimeters by 60 centimeters and included an assortment of colorful flora that popped against the dark-green background, which represented the foreground of what would be a grassy meadow.

The frame maker latched on to that green, placing three shades of linen mattes on different corners of the painting.

"I like the darker one," Nick offered, and the man agreed.

"It allows the yellow, red, purple, blue, and white of the flowers to pop." The frame-shop owner voiced every color with passion, giving Nick the notion they were *simpatico* in taste.

"I was picturing a frame with a gold or brass color," Nick added, feeling more confident in his taste and pairing.

"Absolutely what I would suggest," the man replied, placing one of three gold frame samples down on the darker green matte. "I think this bright one will draw attention to the rest of the colors." He continued to explain that because the frame was away from the actual artwork, the bright gold border would draw the eye to it. As he spoke, he discarded the other two options without even bothering to place them down. The first, the brightest gold, was the clear winner. A perfect match.

A perfect match. This was a common phrase one hears when designing—interior design, especially. Nick used to know an interior designer, and she taught him a lot when they were together. She often used the phrase "a perfect match," except never with Nick. Eventually, that affair had fizzled out, just like many of his romantic escapades of the past. Nick just could never seem to get it right. Maybe it was because he always seemed to find himself running around with those who were already taken. Maybe.

Nick continued to admire the artwork and its soon-to-be matte and frame as the man before him punched numbers into his calculator. Nick had fallen in love with the painting when he first saw it at that small gallery in Cannes and had become attached to it since he purchased it. To dress it properly with a gold frame made it appear even more elegant.

"I'll order the pieces and see you in a about a week," the man said and handed the receipt order with a breakdown of the cost to Nick.

A floral scent had stopped Nick on his way back from the center. The aroma came from a boutique just across the street. The window was full of plants and flowers, with images of bottles and vases etched in copper surrounding the name *Botanica: Fiori, Profumi, Saponi, e Gin* (Flowers, Soaps, and Gin).

Immediately, Nick wondered if inside he would find a professional that could help him identify the plants on his bracelet inside.

Chapter 10

THE LUSH GREEN ferns caressed Nick's head and shoulders when he walked through the entrance. A small bell tinged from the door he had just closed behind him. Beyond the forest of fauna, he heard the voice of a woman welcome him with a soft *prego*.

Nick followed her voice through the maze of shelves made of dark wood and metal. Beyond the wall of plants, he came upon a wide clearing, exposing a much larger sized shop than appeared from the outside. The center showcased a round, art-deco style station designed in a pale-green and silver hue. On top of the white marble counter sat an antique brass cash register, adorned with floral elements. An array of bottles in a variety of shapes and colors were clustered to its left. Further left, was a large pile of floral paper and spools of different colored twine used for wrapping bouquets or maybe boxes.

"Arrivo," the woman's voice came from behind the back wall of flowers.

Nick spotted the top of her wavy, black locks of hair shake about as she worked on whatever she was working on. "No problem," Nick replied in English. His Italian was still rusty, so he naturally started his encounters in his native tongue.

"Ah, yes," she responded. "One moment, please." Her accent was thick and sexy, and her tone offered a more soft and higher pitch. Nick had noticed Italians tended to change to this softer tone when speaking English.

He continued perusing the shop. On the far-left wall was another station that was set up as a small bar. Behind it sat large bottles of gin infused with herbs and spices and an assortment of cocktail accessories. At the opposite wall was another counter, with glass cases that displayed beautifully colored, tiny bottles, which must have been the perfumes and scented oils.

He walked to a round table next to the cases and browsed the bars of soaps that came in several shapes, ranging from basic brick and oval to carved out flowers and seashells. The options of scents ran the gamut, including lavender, dandelion, rose, teakwood, and basil.

"Welcome," the woman walked out from behind the wall of flowers holding a large bouquet of peonies and some other flower he did not recognize. She set the flowers in an opaque, porcelain vase near the antique register and turned to Nick. "How can I help you?"

When she looked up at Nick, he recognized her immediately. She joined him in his look of shock. They had recognized each other. She was the woman with the air conditioner. After that night of "transactional" sex, he'd hoped he'd never see her again. He practically ran out on her that morning. What does one do when unexpectedly encountering the person one had spent the night with just recently?

He tried gauging her reaction, and she was probably trying to do the same. Finally, he smiled and acted as if they were polite acquaintances or former colleagues.

"Well, it's nice to see you again," he offered and waited for her reaction.

She exhaled and smiled. "Yes, yes," she replied. "Err…"

"Nick."

"Yes, Nick," she responded. "I am Lavinia."

"Lavinia, of course," Nick repeated.

"It's nice to see you again," Lavinia replied, blushing. She shook herself out of her thoughts and again asked, "How can I help you?"

"That is a beautiful bouquet," Nick replied.

"Thank you." Lavinia's response had a hint of nervousness. She breathed out and asked, "Are you looking for flowers?"

"Well, in a way." Nick relaxed. He was relieved Lavinia was keeping it cordial too. "I assume you are an expert in flowers and plants?"

"Yes," Lavinia laughed, gesturing to the shop. "Look around."

"Yes, of course," Nick blushed. "I was wondering if you could help me identify a plant or flower."

"Do you have a description or a photo?"

"Yes." Nick shuffled through his snapshots and showed Lavinia the close up of the etchings.

Lavinia's first response upon seeing the image was silent and positivity. She breathed in and, without moving her head, she shifted her eyes to Nick, then back at the screen. She leaned in to the image and squinted her eyes. She reached behind the counter for her violet glasses and asked, "May I?" before using her fingers to zoom in on the details.

Nick watched her staring at the image. He realized he was harsh in judgement about her looks. She was actually a beautiful woman. Her face structure gave her nose a larger appearance than it was. Her cheekbones were high and sharp. Her lips—now in a pout as she examined the etching—had quivered when she stretched out a smile.

"This is it," she mumbled finally.

"What's *it*?"

"Huh?" Lavinia looked up. "Oh, no. Nothing."

"Do you recognize something?" Nick asked.

"Yes, I think so," Lavinia replied and shook away a lock of curly black hair as she continued to zoom. "This looks like a flower, but it is a little difficult to determine the type. I didn't expect a flower."

"Didn't expect a flower?" Nick responded, confused.

"I mean," Lavinia stumbled. "I didn't…don't recognize this flower. Not yet."

"Ah," Nick accepted her response. "Well, do you think you can help me identify it?"

"Maybe," Lavinia replied and handed back his phone. "I might need a better look at the etching. Where is this?"

"It's on a piece of—" Nick stopped himself before adding, "an old family heirloom. I'd like to identify the flowers on it."

"Do you think you can bring it here, to me?" Lavinia asked. "It might help me with identifying the flower."

"No, unfortunately," Nick stammered. "I don't have it with me. It's not in my possession."

"Ah," Lavinia replied, deflated. "Well, can you leave a photo here with me? So, I may take some time to research."

"Do you have any guess, from what I showed you?"

"Well, maybe," Lavinia replied. "But I'd like some more time." She walked behind the counter and reached for an old, thick book. "Maybe we can meet again to discuss?"

"If you can give me some idea now, that would be helpful," Nick said.

Lavinia flipped to the back of the book and followed her finger down the page. Nick glanced around the shop and noticed people looking at the display in the window before moving on. But one passerby remained. She looked familiar. Was it the same woman he saw earlier when he stopped at the chair shop?

"From what I see," Lavinia interrupted his thought. "This flower resembles the trumpet." She flipped through the book again, stopped, and silently read the page.

"Trumpet?" Nick turned and leaned in. "You mean it's an instrument? Not a flower? And here I thought it was a rose or tulip."

"No, no," Lavinia responded without looking up. "Not a trumpet, as in the instrument. Trumpet is also a type of flower. From a plant. Like this one…" She turned the large book around and showed Nick. The page was an old sketch of a plant featuring large, green leaves and narrow, white flowers that hung from their branch and drooped down.

"You see here," Lavinia continued as she pointed to the page. "The flower of this plant hangs down like so. At night, in the moonlight, these flowers blossom, giving them a shape that resembles a trumpet."

Nick followed her finger. Next to the drawing of the flower were the words: *trombone d'angelo.*

"Trumpet of the angel," Lavinia translated it before he could ask.

Nick was silent. He examined the sketch while trying to make any connection to anything, but nothing came to mind. At least he had the flower—another thread to pull on. He could continue his search with that in mind.

"But if you look at the flower straight…" Lavinia gestured with both hands. "It looks like the image you showed me. Very similar."

"Do you know if this flower has any significance?" Nick asked. "Another meaning, maybe?"

"No," Lavinia replied. "I don't know. Maybe. It would require more research. I'm sure there must be some significance somewhere. A lot of plants and flowers have a connection to some saint, or God, or something. Maybe. But, please understand, maybe this is not the flower in your picture. This is just a guess for now. It could be datura—another plant, something similar—but I need to think on it."

"You have a good point there," Nick replied. "But this is a start. Thank you, Lavinia."

"Of course. No problem," Lavinia replied. "If you want, you can bring the item here and we can research some more on it together. It would help to see. Maybe there are more details. I don't know." She closed the book and returned it under the counter.

"Thank you. Let me think about it for a bit. I'll be by again, I'm sure," Nick responded automatically as she walked him back to the entrance. "You have a lovely shop," he added.

"Wait. Please." She plucked a flower from the bouquet she had set earlier. "Take a flower."

"Oh, you don't have to give me that."

"But you liked it, no?"

"Yes, it's very pretty, but..."

"May I?" Lavinia asked, and before he could respond, she placed the flower into his front breast pocket.

"It's very nice. Thank you." Nick looked in the mirror to his left and admired the purple petals hanging down. They gave the impression of a ruffled handkerchief hanging out of his pocket. "What is it?"

"It's called *digitale*," Lavinia responded, admiring the flower as well. "I don't remember what it is called in English, but it's pretty, right? Makes you look even more handsome." She caressed the flower and his chest, then added, "Just don't eat it."

"Eat it? Why?" Nick blushed, smirked, and turned to the door.

"Some flowers can be dangerous if you eat them." Lavinia's reply was soft, with a hint of flirtation. "We must always be vigilant when handling them." She turned away and took one of the lavender and green business cards stacked on a small table nearby. "Take my number. It's on the card," she said and handed the card to Nick. "Will I see you again?"

Nick stared into her dark eyes, lost in her deep-brown irises. He then looked down at her mouth painted in violet. He felt his face drawing closer to her. He didn't know why he wanted to kiss her, but he stopped himself.

Nick offered a half smile in reply. He opened the door, readying himself to step out onto the sidewalk, but then turned back to the shop and said, "Thank you for your help."

"I will research some more," Lavinia responded with a smile and kept her eyes on him as she closed the door.

CHAPTER 11

A GUNSHOT. THE feeling of confusion. Fear followed by a sudden sadness and remorse. Then, the typical sensation of desperation; like someone trying to reach out through her to the outside world.

It's happening again, Laura thought to herself. She couldn't stop these feelings. They just came at any time. It was another one connecting to her.

Someone in the café is being sought out by this desperate soul trying to communicate. Laura couldn't shake it off. *Not this time,* she kept thinking herself. *No, I will fight it.* She shifted in the tall wicker chair, turned to a blank page in her journal, and pretended not to feel the lost soul trying to squeeze out a message. A feeling of being lost. Or a wrong turn, maybe? She shook her head, grasped her black pen and doodled. Doodling always helped her control her thoughts. Although she knew she couldn't stop these feelings, she always tried.

Enough! she thought, screaming it loudly inside her head to the soul invading her thoughts. No matter how hard Laura tried to ignore it when it happened, she could not. Partly because she knew she could help the spirit or the person the spirit was trying to reach. In the end, it always turned out that way.

Who is it? she relented. *Who is this spirit trying to reach?* She looked around at the other patrons seated at the tables around her: an American couple examining a map; probably on their honeymoon. But no indication from the spirit bothering her that it was with them that it wanted to communicate. She kept scanning the tables: an older, sophisticated woman with a dog. *That must be her; it's probably her dead husband.*

The images popped in her head more vividly: running in a desert? No, a small village? Suddenly, darkness and a rush of cold ran up and down her body. Convinced it was the woman, Laura got up from her table and walked over to her with confidence mixed with trepidation. The images were now rushing through her with more energy. She tried to ignore the rush as she approached. She always remembered to be as gentle as possible when walking up to strangers with this kind of information; as not to frighten them. Some welcomed the information, but some would shut her down and walk away. When she reached the table, the woman looked up from her rose-colored reading glasses and welcomed her with a half-smile.

"Scusi, parla Inglese?" Laura asked with her rough Italian, the American accent ever so prominent. She was nervous. She didn't want to do this, but knew that when a spirit came to her, there was no shaking it off. She hoped the woman would be rude, say no, and look away; giving Laura the justification that she tried.

Instead, though, the woman smiled even bigger and replied, "Yes, I speak English." The woman was excited for conversation but full of wonder as to what this strange woman wanted. "How can I help you?"

"I'm sorry to disturb you," Laura blurted out the words but fought to remain calm. "I'm getting a really strong reading, and I think it's someone you may know."

"I'm sorry?" The woman clutched her over-sized purse and reached for her dog's leash.

"Did you know a man who was shot or running from someone shooting at him? In a desert, or a dry place? Wait! The coldness is coming back—a basement?"

"I'm sorry?" The woman repeated, this time picking up her little dog, readying herself to get away from the odd stranger talking to her.

"It's stronger now, I'm getting a name…" Laura closed her eyes and snapped her fingers. "May I hold your hands? It's stronger if I hold you."

"No, you may not," the woman replied sternly. "I don't know what you're going on about, but please leave me alone."

"I'm sorry, I should explain. You see, I'm a sort-of-like a medium. I speak to dead people…or rather, they come to me to communicate a message. And I'm getting such a strong feeling around you…at least, I think it's you. The vision keeps showing me a dark basement—does that have any meaning to you?"

"No, I'm sorry. It does not. I would prefer if you left my table, please."

"But this man wants me to give you a message!"

"A message," the woman replied sarcastically. "What man? What are you talking about? Should I call a policeman?"

"No, don't. I'm sorry. I'll leave you alone. I apologize," Laura stood stiff and squeezed her eyes shut. "Ow! I'm feeling a pinch. Cairo! Do you have any connection to Cairo? Wait! Turkey?

No…a younger man. Sports jacket. He's here. Getting into a taxi?" Laura looked around and winced again. "Piazza Plebiscito! He's here! Wait! It's not you…I'm sorry." Laura tripped over the chair behind her. "I'm sorry, madame. Forgive me. Wrong person." She looked around the tables again, then over the barrier into the large piazza. Her eyes widened in shock when they locked on to a man in a blue blazer stepping into a taxi. "Wait!" she called out, tripping over the barrier and watching the taxi drive away.

CHAPTER 12

THE ANGEL'S TRUMPET plant… Datura *is a species of flowering plants from the nightshade family…Nightshade…flowers grow or blossom at night…most not safe to eat…* Datura *…night symbolism: believed to be property of the Devil…*

Nick shuddered at the shrill ring of the hallway telephone. The tone of that bell traveled up his spine every time it rang. It was such an unappealing sound, he wondered why anyone would choose that particular pitch for a "new" piece of technology back in the day. He closed the browser window and shuffled into the hallway to answer the call and put a stop to the incessant ringing.

"Pronto."

"Mr. Terenzi," Gaetano responded. "I'm sorry I could not take your call earlier. I tried your other number, but I couldn't get through."

"Oh, really?" Nick looked back at the coffee table in the living room, but didn't see his cellphone in its usual spot. "That's very strange. I wonder if it needs a charging."

"Well, I'm glad I reached you," Gaetano continued. "I need to speak with you. We have reason to believe there may be another party asking questions about your piece."

"Another offer?"

"Well, not really. Not yet, at least. But I want to talk to you about the Egyptian buyer as well. Can you meet me for lunch, and we can talk about details?"

"Yes, of course."

"Great. There's a great little spot by the university. I'll text you the details. See you there in about an hour?"

"Sounds good," Nick said and continued to scan the living room from the hallway, finding his phone sitting by the small table near the armchair. "Ah, there's my phone…Okay, see you there."

"A presto," said Gaetano and ended the call.

The aroma of fried seafood wafted in the air around the small eatery located on a semi-busy street, just behind the university. Nick joined Gaetano seated at one of the several empty outdoor tables.

"Thank you for meeting me on short notice again." Gaetano shook Nick's hand and sat back in his seat. "I hope you like baccala."

"Not a problem. And who doesn't like a good fish fry?" Nick replied and opened the menu.

The eatery specialized in fried cod (baccala)—a staple in Napoletano cooking—served in a basket, cioppino style, in a paper cone, or with assorted small fishes, including smelts, and anchovies, and an abundance of calamari. Both men opted for the basic fry with a side of potato salad.

The server placed a bottle of sparkling water and breadsticks on the table, which were immediately followed by two baskets of five delicately fried pieces of baccala, and one shared dish of the cold potato salad, made of cubes of boiled potatoes, smothered in olive oil and sea salt, with fresh herbs on a bed of arugula.

The men placed their forks in the pale-gold pieces of fried baccala that broke apart easily. The delicate crunch of the batter accentuated the soft, fleshy taste of the Mediterranean Sea. Nick remembered a fish monger once told him that if a fish tasted too fishy, then it was not fresh. This baccala had a very light hint of fish, confirming to him the level of freshness this small eatery served.

"Is that…?" Gaetano stopped himself mid chew. He looked behind Nick, then shook his head. "Never mind."

"What is it?" Nick looked behind him and turned back to Gaetano.

"Nothing. I thought I saw that girl again."

"What girl?"

"The one I saw when I met you last time," Gaetano responded, still shaking his head. "But I doubt it. I'm probably getting paranoid. Let's eat."

"Paranoid?" Nick put down his fork and picked up his glass of water. "What are you talking about, Gaetano? Are you in some kind of danger?" Nick said this half-joking, but he felt something was a little off with Gaetano.

"I think I'm just reading too much into it all," Gaetano replied. "We were approached by someone about the bracelet, and it was just brushed off to no importance, at the time." He looked down and poked at the potato salad.

"But now you think it could be something more?" Nick prodded.

"Well, it was strange, that is all," Gaetano said and chewed the potatoes away.

"What do you mean?" Nick asked. "Should I be worried? Or do you have another buyer?"

Gaetano put down his fork and placed his elbows on the table. He looked around before speaking. "This person approached one of our men and asked about the bracelet."

"So, another buyer?"

"No," Gaetano responded and lowered his voice. "We don't know who this person is. But the strange part of the situation was that she knew it was here, in Naples. Have you spoken to anyone lately?"

"She?" Nick froze. "The only person I spoke to about it was a woman in a flower shop up the street."

"Mr. Terenzi—"

"Please, call me Nick."

"Nick, then," Gaetano shook his head.

"But I didn't tell her it was a bracelet," Nick responded.

"But you spoke to someone else, Nick." Gaetano sat back, exasperated. "I warned you not to speak to anyone about this."

"But I didn't really tell her anything much. I just mentioned that I had a family heirloom, and that I was trying to identify the etchings on it…"

"Who was this woman?" Gaetano took out his cellphone and tapped on the Notes application. "Give me a description and where she is located. Maybe there is a connection."

"Relax, Gaetano," Nick said. "She's just a shop owner. She sells flowers and perfumes. How can that hold any danger?"

"Nick, you never know who someone knows or is connected to," Gaetano scolded him. "I've warned you that this bracelet has been stirring up something that gives us reason to be concerned. People seem to know this item exists, and they want it. You never know who is after it and what they'll do to get it. You need to be careful. We all do. And we are doing our part to be discreet. We only ask you—doing business with us—to be discreet as well. Please."

"I understand," Nick relented. "I apologize. It was just a part of my research, that was all."

"We're happy to find a buyer for you," Gaetano continued. "But you have to work with us, not against us. You'll only make the transactions more difficult. For all involved."

"Okay, okay." Nick put his hands up. "I apologize. I'm sorry. I will be careful with whom I talk to."

"It's best you just keep all the work to us," Gaetano responded shortly. "It would be easier to have full control."

"I understand, Gaetano, but you have to accept that I am just trying to get my own knowledge of the item's value for myself. To help with negotiations."

"Mr. Terenzi," Gaetano switched to his formal address again. "That is what we do for our clients. That is our business. You just have to trust us with all of this. We would not steer you wrong. Why would we? How would that benefit us? We are not criminals."

Nick let out a small scoff. It made him laugh that these people thought selling on the black market would not make them criminals of any kind; that they were not doing anything illegal.

"I appreciate that, Gaetano," Nick leaned in. "I just need to do my part to educate myself on all this. I can't do business without knowing things for myself. I'm sure you can understand that."

"Of course, we do," Gaetano softened his tone. "But we ask you to please be more aware. Now, please give me any information you have on this flower shop and this woman, and we will do our part in research."

Nick gave Gaetano the details about Lavinia but left out the detail about his first encounter with her. Gaetano didn't need to know about his sexual escapades.

Gaetano took all the details and placed his phone back in his pocket. "I'll find information about this woman. In the meantime, let's plan to meet again tomorrow."

"Sounds good, and I'm sorry," Nick replied. "I really didn't mean to cause any problems with this whole transaction."

"I just hope you understand how important it is to be careful."

"Yes, I can respect that."

"Thank you." Gaetano smiled. "Because we are about to close this deal with the Egyptians. They seem to be offering the most, so far. I'll have more details for you next time we meet."

"Oh, great." Nick exhaled. "I just want money, Gaetano—a lot of it."

"We shall see, Nick. We're trying."

Chapter 13

THE WOMAN GLARED at the designs the make-up artist had placed on her face in a rush. Their time together had been cut short due to the horrid traffic she had endured getting to the theatre. And again, the staff had treated her as if she purposely walked in late—as if she was sending a message. Exactly to whom was she supposed to be sending this message to? And what message did they think she was sending? She had had enough of it. All of it.

She was tired of the gossip. The whispers were now careless—the staff no longer put any effort into disguising them. They hated her.

She continued staring at the blotches of white and violet he had applied haphazardly. When she wanted to address the horrific work, he had disappeared. Was he really done with her makeup? Did he really want to send her out on stage like this?

She removed the clips from her hair, careful not to disturb the feathered bonnet. She rose from the chair and walked over to the rack of costumes. She pulled the green feather boa off the hanger and wrapped it around one shoulder, leaving the other exposed. The violet sequined beads all over her body sparkled as she shuffled her feet into the slippers. She grabbed the cigarette holder and walked to stage left, ignoring all the glares. She kept her focus on the music and waited for her cue.

The whine of the violins led to a flurry of notes from the harpist. When she stepped onto the stage, she became the fairy Tatiana— dismissing the fact that the ridiculous production was a failing modernized version of Shakespeare's magical play.

The vision changed.

The woman was suddenly back at her dressing table. She stared at her reflection and thought about her situation. The only reason she had taken this role was money. She didn't want to resort to dealing with the pettiness of all these other actors, but she knew it was only temporary. She met someone from a travelling acting troupe that was in town for a month, and she decided she would join them to wherever they were headed next. She was done.

She didn't want to have to take these local jobs anymore, but she now needed to pay rent—something she didn't have to do when she was living at the villa. But she had been asked to leave. Well, forced out would be more accurate.

How could the rest of the women allow her to be released like that? Even the ones who supported her cause. It wasn't fair. They knew she deserved to take over, but when it came time to confront the newly appointed leader, they abandoned her. The role of leader was taken from her. Her place to stay was taken from her. She was left with nothing and no one.

Fortunately, through connections, she landed this acting job, but the money was not worth the treatment.

For a while, she had been determined to get her place back in that villa, but she wasn't certain of which route to take. Should she apologize and make amends with the new leader? Or should she try to take the job from her?

She continued to stare at her reflection as she wiped the makeup off her lips. Her eyes watered again. Every night; it was the same treatment. A feeling of sadness, loneliness, and disappointment swirled around her. She was done. Done accepting the half-done designs on her face. Done with the short whispers. Done with the glares. And done with the shoulder shrugs as she walked by. She was done.

She suddenly looked up and said, "Tell my son I love him. Tell him to be careful."

Laura awoke from her afternoon nap with a start. She inhaled as if she was out of air. The dream was more vivid than usual. She didn't understand who the actress in the dream was. The same woman had been appearing in her dreams occasionally for months now, but this was the first time she had actually spoke. It was a message. But for whom? The dream she just woke from was different this time; the emotions were stronger. Laura still felt that dark loneliness conveyed by the mystery actress backstage.

Laura tried to place the era—it wasn't too long ago, but the play was Shakespeare, so it could have taken place at any time in history. However, the woman in the dream did specify that she was about to walk on stage for a "modernized version" of Shakespeare. Was it the Eighties? Laura tried picturing anything else in the scene that would give her more of a hint of the time period or who that woman could be. She jumped out of bed and rummaged through her dream journal on the table.

…woman in a limousine. Headed to a party. Sadness…Loneliness… Was she a performer or a guest? On stage, singing a song…was it synth pop? What year was this?... Heartache…

Laura read through her previous notes and surmised this actress to be the same woman. The common factor in each dream was that loneliness. And it wasn't just any ordinary melancholy feeling. Laura didn't know how to explain it, but she knew it was the same. She flipped to an empty page and noted the details of this new dream.

Loneliness. The word affected her more after this particular dream. She wondered if the woman in the dream was once real. But if so, who was she? Laura needed more information. She didn't even know where these dreams took place. Her concentration was broken by the bright light reflected off her watch. She looked at the time.

"Shit," she said aloud, closing her dream notebook, and shoving it into her bag. She checked herself in the mirror, grabbed her keys, and bolted out the door.

CHAPTER 14

"IN THE SCENE, there are no flying penises." The lecturer pointed to the screen behind him. "Here, the penises are growing from this tree—which, of course, is surmised to be a tree of fertility."

The lecturer had a strong Spanish accent and a light lisp, pronouncing the word surmised as "thurmized." Laura cringed every time he said the word, but fluttered her eyes each time he looked in her direction. He was a handsome, young professor from the University of Madrid. His expertise was in relation to the legends and crimes against women and witchcraft in 1800s Europe. As a master of this brutal history, he was invited to discuss the discovery of a mural in Tuscany.

"Just below the tree, we see eight women appearing to be using sticks to fight off black birds above—I go into detail about that symbolism in my book, but, for now, I want to focus on what else the women are doing. You see here, using their sticks, they are also trying to force the penises to fall from the tree..."

He turned away from the image behind him and faced the small crowd of mostly young women. "Now, we all know, witches were typically depicted chasing or catching penises—sometimes, flying penises. And this mural was a perfect example of such a depiction. Such a scene tells us the common theme: these women were thought to be a threat against fertility." The professor walked the aisle of silent spectators and continued speaking, while looking each woman in the eye. "As you may recall, these women were accused of wanting to procreate and give birth to a spawn of the devil . And they would take whatever means necessary—from your husband, your son, your father, etcetera—to make a spawn happen…"

Laura focused on his light-brown eyes, imagining him hinting at procreating with her. Immediately, she felt like a failure to feminism, ogling the man instead of focusing on his assessment of the mural of Maremma and the history of trials and punishment of women as witches.

"Thank you all for joining us tonight," the owner of the bookshop suddenly took over. Laura didn't even hear the professor end his talk. "And thank you to Professor Millás for that wonderful preview of the study on the history of witchcraft." The crowd clapped, and the woman continued, "The professor will sign copies of his book at the back table. Please form a line and have your books ready."

Laura was still disheveled from arriving late to the event. She had rushed in and silently took the only seat left in the far back of the room. Fortunately, for her, it allowed her to be third in line to meet the handsome professor. She composed herself, adjusted her shirt, and smiled.

"Professor Millás, I am Laura. It is such an honor to meet you in person." She offered her hand and he shook it. His hand was soft, gentle, and cold.

"Nice to meet you, Laura," he responded with his warm, Spanish accent. "Are you a student of history here?"

"Err," Laura stumbled. "Yes. Well, no. I mean, yes."

"You don't know?" the professor smirked as he opened her book and wrote a note on the first page, before swooping a signature full of bold curves and swooshes.

"Well, I do, of course," she flustered her response. "I'm working on my thesis. So, no, I'm not a student here, per say. I'm just writing…"

"Your thesis," the man replied with a soft tone as he stared into her eyes. "What is your thesis about, may I ask?"

His eyes were hypnotic. He could say anything to her and she would oblige with no question. If he were to ask her to go out to dinner, grab a drink, maybe go dancing, or perform some disgustingly dirty deed, she would agree. She suddenly hated herself for even thinking any of that.

"Laura?" he called her name, waking her from her thoughts.

"Oh, I'm sorry," she stammered. "I should go." She grabbed her copy of his book. "It was nice meeting you, and good luck with the book." She shoved the book into her bag and walked out the door.

Laura wandered the streets back toward Via Toledo, hoping to clear her head from the embarrassment at the lecture hall. She walked down the street, looking for a spot to dine alone. When she reached Via Chiaia, she headed straight toward a pizza restaurant she had visited before.

She turned the corner and felt a sudden rush through her veins, accompanied by a headache and wooziness. She stopped, placed her hand on the building closest to her, and waited for the feeling to subside. She looked around, hoping no one noticed any of it.

She continued on to the restaurant and asked for a table for one. The waiter looked at her with pity and led her to a small, round table in the middle of the room. Laura couldn't help but feel all eyes on her as she followed the disappointed waiter and took her seat. She ignored her paranoid thoughts and ordered a beer and a Margherita pizza, prompting the server to respond with a raised eyebrow.

"Yes, a whole Margherita," she snapped at him and urged him to make it fast.

Laura pulled out her dream notebook as the server returned with a pint of blonde beer. She thanked him before he could speak and then looked away to shuffle through the notes of her dreams.

The server placed the hot pizza down on the table and scattered away in silence. Laura watched him with a smirk—happy to have shut him down for trying to shame her earlier. Her table for one had turned from a spectacle of a lonely woman to the throne of a resilient queen who would not take any bullshit from the man who sat her, or any patron who glared at her.

She let out a slight chuckle, closed her notebook, and sliced into the light and airy dough. The classic tart, smooth taste of tomato married with the sharp mozzarella and fresh basil, truly deserved its classic accreditation. While her mouth tasted the savory standard, her mind worked at piecing together some sort of connection with her random daytime visions and the woman in her sleep-induced dreams. Other than the feeling of loneliness, nothing in her notes showed any common thread, and she knew that was typical. Messages had always come to her at random, and they were not always connected, but she had a strong feeling these recent bursts of vision were connected in some way.

She never allowed herself the time to hone in on her skill. So, she only had herself to blame, really. When visions came, her first instinct was always to push them away. She didn't have the energy or time to take on other people's issues. She was struggling as it was, trying to make her way in the world, and the visions only made things more difficult for her. Not many people understood, nor could handle the distractions they caused. So, no, this was not the first table for one in her life.

She paid her bill and asked the server to bring her a takeaway container. She boxed up the other half of her pizza and walked back to her room.

CHAPTER 15

NICK SHOOK THE water off the razor that he had just run under the faucet. The occasional clean, close shave gave him the confidence boost that his looks were still effective. He still had pull, and he wanted to meet someone new.

He heard the ringtone of his phone, which sat on the coffee table in the living room. He placed the razor in a glass that he kept on the shelf by the bathroom mirror and went to answer the call. It was the art frame shop owner.

"Signore Terenzi?" the man on the other end was less calm than his normal self.

"Yes, this is Nick. How are you?"

"Ahh, hello sir," the man took a deep breath and continued. "Well, I could be better. I'm sure you may have heard about the news this morning."

"News? No, I have not," Nick replied as the anticipation of bad news grew within him.

"Our shop had a break-in overnight."

"Oh, I'm so sorry to hear that."

"Yes, but all is well, fortunately," the man's breath fluttered out of him. "None of the artwork seems to be missing. It's just an annoyance, really...You know, having to clean up and change locks and dealing with detectives, of course. But I shouldn't complain; all the artwork is fine."

"Well, that's a relief. Did they do much damage?"

"No, just to the back-door entrance. And some frames not yet finished. But again, all the art seems to be fine, including your piece. This is why I was calling."

"Oh?"

"Your painting is done, framed. I did find it out of my storage wall, but it's okay. It's all intact. Some damage to my frame, of course, but it is all fixed and ready for you."

"That's a relief."

"I may need a couple of days to fix up the shop, but you are welcome to pick it up after that. Should we say the end of this week?"

"Oh, no rush on that, sir. It's kind of you to call me. I'm sorry this happened to you and your shop. My painting can wait."

"Thank you, Terenzi."

"No problem," Nick replied.

"It is such a beautiful piece of work," the man continued. "Do you mind if I display it in my shop window? Once, the window has been fixed, of course."

"I don't mind at all. Focus on fixing your shop, and we'll be in touch."

"Great, thank you, Mr. Terenzi. Have a good day."

Nick stared at his phone screen and scrolled through the news until he found it.

Break-in at art frame shop on Vico San Domenico. ...assures that none of the pieces were harmed...money taken from the till totaled to €347. ...police believe it...a crime by local youngsters. ...anyone with any information is encouraged to contact local authorities...

Nick's favorite jacket was his navy-blue sports jacket he picked up at one of the menswear shops in Chiaia. It was a spur of the moment purchase, during a morning stroll through the upscale neighborhood. The jacket was displayed in the window on Via Filangieri. The deep blue was what first caught his eye. The thick weave of the light-wool material intrigued him more. He followed the contrasting black stitch accents to the yellow sign that listed the size—his size—and the discounted price. He convinced himself that it was fate, so he went inside and bought it.

The jacket looked great on him. He was always pleased seeing himself with it on in the mirror. He wore it often. It was his lucky jacket. With it on, he always succeeded to pick up a woman and go home with her. And tonight, he put on the jacket because he knew it would not fail him. He was on the prowl, and he didn't want to waste any time.

One last glance at himself, and he turned to the hallway, picked up his keys from the catch all, and closed the door behind him. He skipped down the three flights of stairs to the ground floor. He was in a good mood—confident he was going to have a great night.

On the sidewalk, the sun still setting, he heard a familiar voice calling him.

"Nick!" The voice shook him. It belonged to Lavinia.

He turned and saw her overly exaggerated smile staring back at him.

"Lavinia. Hello," Nick responded politely. He didn't want to give her too much attention. Was she stalking him?

"Nice to see you," Lavinia commented as she quickened her pace. "Is this where you live?" She looked up at the building and examined it in awe.

It was an ordinary building—nothing special—so her amazement was more about finding him in the wild. Coincidently or planned? Nick didn't want to confirm it for her.

"What brings you to this neighborhood?" he asked, avoiding her question.

"Oh, I had a delivery close by," Lavinia pointed to the street behind him. "I was just about to leave. Go home…"

"Oh, you're done for the day?" the words fell out of his mouth and he cringed inside.

"Yes," she responded with a softer tone. "I am free. Could I interest you in an aperitivo?"

And there it was. She asked him. There was no evading it. He looked at her as she stared at him up and down, waiting for his response. It was clear she was interested in him, and being that they had already met and had an intense night together, it would be easy to just go along with her. If he were to go out on the hunt, he'd have to find his target and put on the charm with hopes she would agree to have some fun. But the woman standing in front of him would probably welcome him without any work on his part. They were past the introductions and convincing stage. He could just easily go home with her and get his deed done. Lavinia was a guarantee, no fuss score, and a wild one at that.

"Sure, let's do it," he replied and slid his arm around her waist. It was familiar. It was easy. He was probably going to get some action again with her tonight. If so, he would try to make it just as extreme.

CHAPTER 16

NICK WAITED FOR Lavinia in her living room. He had meant to skip out earlier that morning, but when she initiated another round of passion, he didn't want her to stop. After a what-seemed-like-forever post-sex cuddle, he suggested he had to go.

"What time is it?" Lavinia groaned.

"I think about seven," Nick took the opportunity to end this encounter by reaching for his watch. He gently rolled away from her and pulled it off the nightstand. "Seven twenty-five to be exact."

"Oh, no!" Lavinia jumped up. "I need to open the shop. Do you mind if I jump in the shower first? Make yourself some coffee. We can walk out together."

Walk out together? Nick felt she was trying to turn their encounter into something more than a casual romp.

"That's okay," Nick replied. "I can shower at home."

"No, no. I'll drive you. Wait here."

He didn't want to linger in her place longer than he needed. He was fine just getting dressed and skipping out. He should have just done so earlier; he knew if he lingered it would have been more difficult to break away—and he was right. But he liked it when she reached down on him when they woke. It felt really good.

He put on his boxers and almost knocked over a potted fern when he put on his trousers. His clothes were piled on a tall, orange armchair in the corner of the bedroom. He quickly looped his belt and put on his socks. He fastened his watch and adjusted his hair in the vanity mirror. He remembered his shoes were by the door in the living room. He walked in there, latching his watch, he looked down at the desk by the window. It was covered in documents and several books, which had titles that varied in topics from plants to history. He stopped when he noticed a paper hanging out of a green, leather journal.

What prompted him to pause was the word *angelo* (*angel*) hand-written on what appeared to be a list. Above it was the word *tromba*—which was another word he remembered her telling him in her shop—it meant *horn*.

"Are these notes on my flower?" he called out to her. "Have you been researching?" But Lavinia didn't respond. She probably couldn't hear him from under the running water.

He opened the journal and read the list, which continued with the words *stramonio* (which he didn't know) and *Diavolo* (Devil), both having a question mark after them. The list was titled: *Datura*—again followed by a question mark. Underneath the title was written: *Nick = bracciale(?)*, which he knew translated to *bracelet*.

Nick paused to remember if he had ever mentioned to Lavinia that the photos were of a bracelet. He thought he had specifically *not* mentioned the bracelet to her. Gaetano had warned him not to talk about it with anyone, and he didn't. When Lavinia asked him what the photos were of, he remembered he was vague with his response, brushing it off as a random heirloom. *Why would she write bracelet on this list?*

He took out his phone and flattened the list on the open journal. He focused and took several snapshots. He heard the shower stop running. He shoved the list back in its place, grabbed her empty notepad, wrote *Sorry, had to go. Thank you.* and left it on the coffee table. He then put on his shoes and rushed out the door.

CHAPTER 17

LAURA SPENT THE morning reading and rereading the first few pages of Professor Millàs' book, but her mind was just not taking in any of the information. Was it his style of writing? Whomever translated it overused the thesaurus, so that every sentence included some ridiculous word, making the writing sound like a middle-school child trying to impress his teacher. She set the book down on her pile of unread books and brought her coffee cup to the kitchen sink. She'd wash it later. She wanted to get out, enjoy the morning air before the scorching heat enveloped the city for the day.

She turned the corner, onto via dei Tribunali and stopped at the bronze statue of Pulcinella mounted on a stone pillar. She remembered reading about it: a memorial to the patron masquerade character of Naples. The statue was only of his head adorned with his characteristic mask and floppy hood. His long nose was the only polished part – the spot one would touch for good luck. She caressed it in hope that her research would lead to write an interesting paper. She took out her mobile phone, snapped a photo, then continued her walk.

The sunlight was just about to take over the streets, leading Laura to turn down a narrow lane that appeared dark, covered from the bright, hot rays. She noticed large awnings stretched above the street, practically reaching the buildings opposite. She was impressed at the clever covering, shading the whole path for walkers to escape the heat and shop comfortably.

The narrow street of Via San Gregorio was tightened even more by the tables and displays along both sides. Buyers spoke with craftsmen about their handmade figurines, some bargaining for the relics, some ordering custom-made statuettes.

Although the figurines were made specifically for use in Christmas nativity scenes, these craftsmen popularized the art of making figurines depicting modern personalities. Some were popular figures like the Pope—yes, religious but current—to renowned soccer player Maradona. The figures that regained popularity were those that mocked news and current events, like Putin or pop star Madonna.

Laura shifted her way down the alley, inadvertently bumping into shoppers around her. As much as she tried to avoid it, she couldn't prevent herself from being bumped into by one or two shoppers along the way. No one apologized. There was no way one would not bump into another on that busy street. It was just accepted. It was Naples. Many streets in Naples were narrow. It was the way.

She stopped underneath an awning that belonged to a fried pizza vendor. She monitored her phone map to gauge where she was, with no intention of where she was going to go next. She just wanted to walk and explore.

She placed her phone back into her bag and stopped ignoring the fried delights sitting in the display behind her. She looked them over, unbothered by the vendor who was arguing with another customer trying to haggle a bulk price.

Sting! A pain on her temples forced her to crouch over, as she held her head and whispered to herself, "Stop. No. Not now." The pain throbbed and immediately disappeared. Laura looked up and saw the vendor staring at her with concern and a hand reaching toward her.

"Signorina," he said. "Are you okay? Do you want to sit down?" His English was perfectly spoken with his rough voice and deep accent.

"Oh, no. Thank you," Laura replied, standing up straight to hide any evidence of what she had just endured. *It rarely happens as often as it has since I stepped foot in Naples,* she thought. *Not this strong, anyways.* She looked up, "I'm fine. Thank you." She smiled, bowed and walked away. Why she bowed, she had no idea, and that thought followed her as she moved on.

She had to shake these bouts. Over the years, she had learned chocolate helped control or quell them. She stopped at a chocolate shop and bought herself three small, dark chocolates. She then asked the man to fill a bag of the knotted, round breadstick-like *taralli* that also sat in the display. She stepped back onto the bustling alley, unwrapped one of the chocolates, and popped it into her mouth. She felt another painful sting on her temples, closed her eyes, and bumped into another person. She apologized, but when she looked up, she saw a somewhat familiar man looking back at her.

"You," she said, when she placed his face. The pain hit her again. Weakness came over her. She stumbled back, dropped her bag of chocolate and tarralli, then fell forward into and out of the familiar stranger's arms.

Chapter 18

NICK WANDERED THROUGH the historic district, not caring that he had walked in the opposite direction from his apartment. His focus was on the photos he had just taken and trying to decipher Lavinia's list. Part of him wanted to stay and talk to her about the list, but his gut instinct to disappear had kicked in. He also didn't want to give Lavinia the impression that a romantic relationship was growing. He desired her, though. Something about her pulled him. He didn't want a relationship with her, but he'd be open to an occasional fling.

He swiped off the phone and looked at his surroundings. He got his bearings and changed direction, now heading south toward his neighborhood.

The heat was beginning to take over the city, and he did his best to remain in the fast-disappearing shade. He slipped down the first street that was too narrow to allow the sunlight to take it over.

The narrow street was filled with shoppers, as well as vendors who were loudly calling out to the crowd of mostly tourists and day trippers, encouraging them to collect some artisan trinkets to take home. Nick swerved out of the way to the nearest coffee bar and stepped off the bustling street. He ordered his espresso and stood by the window, watching the people shuffle up and down with shopping bags that rustled with each step.

His gaze passed the crowd and landed on a woman across the street. She stood by a window of a fried pizza vendor, staring at her phone. Something about her looked familiar. He continued to watch her. She placed her phone back in her bag and looked up and down the street. It was then that Nick realized where he had seen her before. It was the same face he had seen looking in the window at the flower shop a couple of days ago. Was she following him?

At their previous meeting, Gaetano had mentioned he thought he was being followed—specifically by a young woman. *Is this the same woman? Is she following Gaetano or is she following me?* He watched as she closed her eyes and reached for her temples. *It must be a really bad headache.* He watched the vendor ask if she was alright. She motioned that she was fine and bowed for some reason before stepping away.

Nick couldn't help but think it was all an act. That she had noticed he had seen her, so she had thought of a dramatic idea to slip away and lose herself in the crowd. He quickly drank the rest of his espresso and followed the woman down the street. He made it almost to the end but lost sight of her. *Where could she have gone?* He stopped and walked back up the street, looking into shop doorways left and right. He continued up when he felt someone bump into him. He looked down and saw that he had found her. She looked at him, opened her mouth to speak.

"You," she whispered, then looked at him quizzically, squeezed her eyes closed, and passed out in his arms and fall through onto the ground. Her bag of taralli opened and scattered the crunchy treats all around her.

CHAPTER 19

THE WOMAN RAN along a water basin in well-manicured gardens that continued for what seemed to be forever. It was almost sunrise. She stopped at the side of the large reflecting pool, rested her hands on the wall, and looked down at the water. The sunrise was growing brighter, but it was still too dark to gauge her distance from the palace. How far had she gone and where was the fountain? She looked down at the jewelry on her wrists and fingers. They sparkled in the soft sunlight by the reflecting pool.

The scene changed suddenly.

The woman was holding her head and glaring at a man. What had he done to her? She stumbled. Her face smacked the water—

Laura awoke with a strong gasp of air. She breathed heavily, catching her breath. The dreams were getting stronger and more vivid. She looked around to take in her surroundings. She had been laying on a couch surrounded by papier-mâché masks hanging on the walls – most were of that Pulcinella character. She sat up and fumbled to understand where she was.

"Well, well," the man appeared from behind a room divider with a glass of water in hand. "You had quite a fall. How are we feeling?" He offered her the glass.

She looked at him. It was the man she tried to speak to a few days ago in front of the fancy café. The man she had seen walk into the botanical shop. The man who she bumped into moments before passing out on the street. Did she fall into his arms?

"I'm Nick." He offered her the water again.

"Laura." She reached for the glass and slurped it down. "Ow! She felt a sharp pain on her elbow."

"Oh, sorry," Nick said. "I tried to catch you, Laura, but you slipped right between my arms and onto the ground. You must have fallen on your elbow." He handed her a white paper bag. "They're taralli. You dropped all of yours when you fell."

"Oh. Thank you," She adjusted her body and sat up on the couch. "Where am I?" She reached into the bag, pulled out one of the rounds of crispy breads, and popped it into her mouth.

"We're in the mask shop, on Via San Gregorio," Nick pulled a chair closer to her. "The owner offered the couch."

"Tutto bene?" The shop owner appeared from behind the divider.

"Si," Nick responded. "Tutto bene. Grazie."

"Di niente," the man replied and returned to the front of the shop.

Nick watched Laura stare at him. She looked straight into his eyes as if trying to read him. He shook his eyes away and adjusted his seat. "Laura," he said. "Are you feeling okay?"

"Yes," Laura replied. "I think so." She kept staring into his eyes, trying to provoke a vision. *Who is this man and why is he triggering my visions?*

"Good," Nick replied and continued to avoid eye contact. Her glare was making him uncomfortable. "So, tell me Laura, who are you, and why are you following me?"

Nick watched her face emote the different thoughts fluttering through her head, as if she was contemplating telling a lie. Or, maybe, telling him the truth? Eventually, her eyes relaxed and she relented.

"I didn't mean to follow you," Laura said it with a deep exhale. "You just happened to be where I happened to be." She decided to tell Nick the truth—that he sparked her recent visions. "But, in the end, yes, I suppose I was following you. Who are you?"

"I asked you first," Nick leaned forward with his elbow on his knee. "So, did someone hire you to follow me?"

"Huh? No." She rubbed her forehead, which was still groggy from the dream. "I just wasn't expecting to meet you. Not yet, at least."

"Not yet?"

"No, I mean," she stumbled on her words again. "It's silly, really. I don't know you. I don't know who you are. But I was drawn to you…"

Nick didn't respond. He found staying silent always coaxes people to say more.

"When I first saw you the other day," Laura continued. "The feeling came over me. You brushed past me way too fast, so I couldn't catch you." Laura stopped talking. She readjusted her legs and sat properly on the couch. She took another sip of water and closed her eyes.

Nick couldn't tell if she was playing him or if she was just some nut job. He pushed the conversation. "Why don't you tell me how long you've been following me? And why?"

"When did you first notice I was following you?" she replied.

"You first," Nick responded and sat back. "Tell me why you are on my tail. Who are you?"

"Fine." She placed the glass down on the side table and finished chewing another little tarallo. "I'm a PhD student here, working on my thesis—a study on the influence of Greek mythology in Italy. I'm focused on Naples right now. I'm researching the connection…"

"Please don't bore me with your academic topics," Nick interrupted. "Why are you following me?"

"I told you. I had a feeling when I first saw you."

"And when was that?"

"The other day. At Piazza Plebiscito. You stepped out of a taxi and walked past me. I was sitting at a café table, recovering from the embarrassment I caused with this older woman…anyway, as I was talking, all of a sudden, my head pounded and my body trembled. That's usually how it happens. But then you walked away, and the sensations stopped. That's how I knew it was you."

"What are you talking about?" Nick was confused. Laura did sound like a crazy person. He was beginning to regret staying by her side until she woke, but he wanted to know why she was following him. Was this his future murderer? Ever since he had met with a tarot card reader years ago, Nick had been convinced his life would end in murder. A stupid notion at the time, so of course, he brushed it off, but as he got older, he started to wonder if it could be a possibility. Someone he pissed off in the past or the future could possibly do it to him. Maybe a visit to a reader soon would be helpful.

"Could we go for a walk?" Laura asked as she got up from the couch. "I need some air. And I'll show you."

"Show me what?" Nick stood from his seat and pushed the divider aside. He thanked the shop owner and ushered Laura toward the door.

When they reached the end of the street, Laura stumbled and steadied herself against a building.

"Are you sure you're okay?" Nick put his arm out to help her stand again.

"Yes," Laura replied without looking at him. She was embarrassed. "I think I just need to eat."

"Do you want me to walk you home?" Nick asked.

"No, no." Laura reached in her purse and pulled out a little chocolate. She unwrapped the gold foil and popped one into her mouth. Then, she turned to Nick, gesturing for him to take one.

"No, thank you." Nick offered his arm again, and Laura took it. "Let's get something to eat."

"Yes, okay," Laura relented. "I suppose a proper meal will help. At least, I hope it does. I rarely get like this. I'm sorry."

"Don't apologize," Nick led her west, toward a street-food vendor. "We'll start with this." He pointed to the folded pizzas in the window. Each individual pizza was folded twice and wrapped in paper. They looked like flowers ready to be plucked. Nick ordered two, with two colas.

"Thank you." Laura took one of the pizzas and bit into the warm, comforting treat. Maybe it was in her mind, but immediately, she felt her body, her head, and her legs gain some strength. She sipped her cola, and it worked even more. Her body was convinced it was being nourished.

"And these particular visions have been more prominent since I arrived," Laura said and added another mouthful of the folded pizza into her mouth. She paused to chew the overly large piece, then continued. "Sorry, I'm really hungry."

"That's okay," Nick replied and bit into his own pizza. "So, what do these visions have to do with me? You mentioned you had a very strong premonition—the one about some man in a desert—and you realized it was for me. Why me? How can you be so sure?"

"I can't put into words how I knew." Laura sipped her soda and continued. "It's a feeling."

"A feeling?" Nick rolled his eyes and led her down to the wall overlooking the bay. They leaned back on the concrete barrier and finished their pizzas.

"I know it sounds ridiculous. I'm used to people not understanding, or believing."

"What makes you so certain it was for me, though?"

"At that first moment, I just knew it was for you. I felt it."

"Right."

"But I didn't know if I'd ever see you again, so I just pushed it aside and ignored it; like it never happened. Until, I felt the pain again."

"The pain? Like what you felt earlier?"

"Yes, exactly." Laura crumpled the empty wrapper and tossed into the nearest bin. "You see, I didn't realize it at first, but I started to get these sharp pains on the side of my head—similar to the pain I felt when I first saw you."

"Okay…"

"Then I realized *you* were there, in my vicinity. That's when I made the connection that these pains were caused by you—your presence."

"So, I am the reason you keeled over back there?"

"Yes, well, no." Laura closed her eyes and shook her head. The energy to explain how it worked took a lot out of her. It was always difficult to explain to someone who wouldn't accept her ability. It was rare that someone ever did.

"Whatever the case," Nick interrupted her thoughts. "Do you feel a vision now?"

"Now?"

"Yes, now," Nick asserted. "I'm sitting here, next to you. Why are you not getting a vision now?"

Laura looked at him in silence. She stared into his eyes and thought about her answer. Nick was right. She wasn't having a vision at that moment.

"Nothing then?" Nick prodded.

Laura put her hand up, politely silencing him. She closed her eyes and worked her mind to try and trigger anything, but nothing came. "No," she replied, defeated. She looked away at the sea. "But it doesn't happen like that. I can't force it."

Nick wanted to believe her, but her story had too many holes. Her trying to explain her visions to him only raised red flags.

He didn't want to believe she was crazy, though. He wanted to believe she was telling him the truth. She looked like someone who was honest and real. But one never knows. He began to strategize a way to end the conversation and separate from her. Would she follow him again? "Is that why you were following me?" he finally said.

"Huh?" Laura shook from her thoughts. "I wasn't following you. I mean, we happened to cross paths, and when I saw you, yes, I admit that *then* I followed you, but only to see if the visions would become clearer. I didn't mean to *follow* follow you. It wasn't like that."

"But you did follow me."

"Well, I was more struck by the fact that you and I happen to continuously be in the same place. Or maybe it was the energy that put me where you were—looking for you."

"Well, I hope you find the reasons for your visions," Nick replied and stood up straight. "Will you be okay?"

"That's it?" Laura was puzzled. "You're just going to leave?"

"Well, yeah." Nick put his hands up. "I mean, I don't know what you want to hear from me. I can't help you."

"But aren't you curious?"

"I mean, part of me is, but, quite frankly, I don't have time for this. It's all uncertainty and, to be honest, unbelievable. I'm sorry."

Laura grabbed his arm and squeezed it tightly. Nick watched her shudder, squint her eyes, and fall backward, almost hitting her head against the wall.

CHAPTER 20

THE OLD MAN *laid in bed. His body felt weak. Laura couldn't tell if it was an illness or just old age. The man was waiting for someone. Had he called out? He tried to stretch and reach for his leather journal, but his body wouldn't cooperate.*

A woman sat in a chair by the old man's bed. She had just delivered a tray of food. Her voice was inaudible—almost muffled. There was a notecard on the tray. It looked like a menu; the words Grand Hotel written at the bottom. The woman handed the brown journal to the old man. He struggled to untie the tassels wrapped around it. The woman smiled—she was actually a young woman. Was she a nurse? Maybe hotel staff?

The vision changed.

The young woman was in a small bedroom. She was removing her maid uniform. She pulled up her sleeve and revealed a bracelet— similar to the one in her previous vision. Then, she looked at her suitcase laying on her small bed behind her. She was ready to go home. But where was that?

Laura awoke gasping for air. She held onto whatever was close to her and breathed heavily until her body caught up with her and calmed her inhalations. She realized her fingers had been squeezing the leg of a coffee table.

She looked around the room, her heartbeat racing. *Where am I? Someone's living room? Who's?* Nick—the man she had just met. *What happened?* She sat up and rubbed her eyes. Her head spun only a little.

"Oh, you're up?" Nick's voice startled her. He had just walked in from another room with a glass of water. His smile calmed her.

She smiled back in relief. "Yes," she replied. Her voice cracked a bit.

"Water?" Nick set the glass down on the coffee table in front of her.

"Thank you," she responded and exhaled. She slurped the water faster than she had intended, then slowed her sips in embarrassment. She glanced at Nick who had turned back to his desk and looked down at his laptop. Laura sat quietly and thought about the dream she just had of the old man. *Who was he?*

"I didn't know what to do with you," Nick turned back to her. "I didn't want to leave you. You scared me, to be honest. I didn't know if I should call an ambulance or…"

"I'm so sorry," Laura rubbed her head. "This is all unlike me. I don't know what's happening. And these dreams are getting more and more vivid."

"What was the woman doing now?" Nick asked.

"It wasn't the woman. It was an old man."

"Old man?"

"Yes, but he looked familiar. I've seen him before. I think in a vision or dream…a while ago."

"Who is he?"

"I don't know," Laura replied, exasperated.

"Would it help to tell me any detail you remember?" Nick pushed, hoping to be of some use.

"These were small flashes of a scene," Laura began. "They seemed to be the same scene, but came to me in bits."

Nick walked over to the armchair by the couch and sat down, listening to her.

"He was in a bed," Laura remembered. "I think he was ill, or maybe dying. It was a hotel! Hotel Grand…Grand Hotel something…Naples! It was here, in Naples."

"Grand," Nick repeated as he ran the name through his mind. "I'm not familiar with it."

"It was typed on a menu," Laura explained. "A woman had brought him a tray of food."

"Did either of them say anything?" Nick prodded.

"I couldn't…I don't know," Laura sipped more water. "The room changed."

"Changed?"

"Yes, the woman was in another room. She had on a maid uniform—same uniform she had when she sat by his bed. She appeared to be packing her suitcase."

"And no name flashed in this either?"

"No." Laura exhaled and sat back. She stared at the coffee table trying to relax her mind—hoping it would spark another detail. She ran the images she could remember, but no name came to mind.

Nick's phone pinged from his desk. He ignored it and stayed sitting by Laura, waiting for more details. The phone pinged again, then again.

"Excuse me." He walked over to the desk, looked at his phone—messages from Gaetano. He swiped the screen and tapped on the messages.

Are you free to meet? I'm at the café where we first met—behind Castel dell'Ovo. Can you come?

Nick responded with *15 min* and a thumbs up emoticon.

"Are you reading Virgil?" Laura asked. Her question seemed out of place.

"Huh?" Nick replied as he tried to understand why she asked him that.

"The poet," Laura explained. "The Aeneid? The mystic, kooky, or legendary Virgil?"

"I…no…I don't understand. Why are you asking me that?"

"It's on your desktop screen," Laura blushed. "Sorry, I didn't mean to pry."

Nick looked at his screen that he had inadvertently awakened when he reached for his phone—just one swift movement of the mouse. The image was one of the photos he took from Lavinia's apartment. He had zoomed in to get details of the list, but the mouse moved the image down, revealing a closer look at the stack of books on the desk.

"The style of that font is beautiful," Laura explained. "Art deco, I think. Goldleaf…on green cloth. V-e-r-g-i-l. Virgil is spelled with an *e* or an *i*—depending where you look. Are you researching the city?"

"What?" Nick had no idea what she was going on about.

"Naples," Laura responded. "Virgil and Naples…? Sorry, my student research brain is sounding off."

Nick didn't respond—he didn't know how.

"Sorry," she apologized for a third time. "I see all your books here, and I assumed you, too, are fascinated by history." She gestured to the wall of books next to her. "I mean, you have Greek legends here and Naples' travel guides there—in English, Italian, and what's that? Arabic maybe?"

"Oh, no. Those were there when I moved in," Nick explained and turned to close the windows on his computer.

"And…up here." She stepped on the stool and reached up to the top shelf. "This is a beautiful edition of Umberto Eco. Wow. And Dante here."

Nick turned and panicked, seeing her standing on the stool. Her hands were caressing the books on the top shelf. Not far from the tin box he had shoved in between.

"Please get down from there," Nick pleaded, but Laura ignored him.

"I'm fine now, trust me," she said. "Oh! Shakespeare! That's a gorgeous bind. Goldleaf here, see?" She rubbed the spine of the volume. "What's this?" She reached for the tin box, just touching it to pull it out, before falling back off the stool.

Nick caught her in time. He held onto her and watched the box fall out of her hand, onto the floor, and open on contact.

Germany. 1940s? Maybe 50s? A cocktail party. An old, sophisticated woman greeting her guests. She looked familiar. Wait. Was this the maid? She appeared to be gathering the group for a photograph. Her arms waving about, trying to get everyone's attention. She wanted them all to see the bracelet dangling from her right wrist...

"Bracelet," Laura whispered from the couch. She opened her eyes and saw Nick frantically gathering the contents of the box that fell on the floor. She was not really looking at him; she was staring into the air in his direction.

"What?" Nick stumbled to rewrap the bracelet in the scarf and shoved it back into the tin.

"A bracelet," Laura repeated. "My dream. The maid. And, just now, my vision."

"Oh, you had another vision?" Nick hoped she had not seen what fell out of the box.

"I think it was the maid again," Laura sat down. "Or a performer? They might be the same woman. Maybe...she was older. An old woman. Where was she? Germany. Why would I think Germany?"

"Wait, what?" Nick was in a bit of a shock. He remembered one of the photos Gaetano had shown him: an elderly woman posing with the bracelet. The photo was taken in Germany. "Why are you saying that?" he asked Laura.

"I just had a vision," Laura replied. "It was Germany. A woman...Do either of those mean something to you? Who is she?"

Nick put the tin box back in its spot on the top shelf.

"I'm sorry about that," Laura said. "I didn't mean to..."

"It's fine," Nick interrupted her. "Tell me more about this vision—the elderly woman. Was she the same woman in your other visions?"

"No, No. She wasn't." Laura shook her head, wanting more details to come to her. "It could be a maid...I think...This woman was old, well dressed, and put together. I feel like it was the maid...grown old. Maybe? She was standing with a group and appeared to be showing off her jewelry. In particular, a bracelet."

"You saw the bracelet?" Nick had hoped she didn't notice it fall out of the box. *Damn! Did she see it? Does she know he had a bracelet hidden in his bookshelf?*

"Yes, the same one that the maid wore in the dream," Laura continued.

Nick was relieved she hadn't mentioned the contents of the box—his bracelet.

"I think the old man gave it to her?" Laura continued. "Or did she steal it?"

"Can you tell me more about this elderly woman?" Nick prodded. If Laura was talking about his bracelet, it was a crazy coincidence. But if she really was, she could give him a clue to figuring out the origin of the bracelet, and its value. He wished he had taken a copy of Gaetano's photo, to show her.

The door buzzer startled them both. Nick ignored it. He didn't want Laura to break her focus. The buzzer buzzed again. And again, but this time, longer.

"Whoever it is can go away," he said to Laura. "Focus on the woman. Can you tell me more?"

"I don't think so," Laura struggled. "She was wearing a black, beaded dress...a loud necklace with some oversized jewel—

costume. And it appeared to be a big deal to have a camera in her apartment. She forced the photos…and she made sure to display her jewelry."

"How about a name?" Nick asked. "Did you hear any names?"

"No." Laura concentrated. "No names."

Both jumped at a knock at the door.

"Who the hell is that?" Nick said, exasperated. "Excuse me a second."

"Sure." Laura sat back and focused on remembering details from this last vision and previous ones. They didn't seem to be connected. She needed her journal. She needed to write this one down. She walked over to the desk and looked around for a piece of paper and pen.

Nick peered through the peephole and let out a silent sigh. Standing on the other end of the door stood Lavinia with a bunch of mixed flowers in hand. He turned to Laura and gestured to remain silent before facing the peephole again. He watched Lavinia crouch down, as if looking into the keyhole. Then, she glanced down the hall and back, reaching into her bag. She stood stiff and smiled to whomever appeared on her right.

She pulled nothing out of her bag. Instead, she set the flowers down at the door and walked away, down the stairs. Nick went to the front window in the living room and waited. Lavinia eventually appeared to cross the street and walk down another, out of sight.

"Who was that?" Laura said as she folded up the paper and slipped it into her pocket.

"No one," Nick replied. "Listen, would you mind coming with me? I have to meet my friend Gaetano, and he has something I think you'd like to see."

"You mean, right now?"

"Yes," Nick rushed through the apartment, turned off the lights, and grabbed his keys. "Do you have the time?"

"Uh…sure," Laura responded. "I'm sorry, I'm still a bit frazzled. I kind of wanted to go back to my place and organize my thoughts, my visions."

"This shouldn't take long, I promise," Nick pushed. "I think you can help me with something—and it might help you too. If you could spare an hour or so. We shouldn't even be that long."

"Okay," Laura replied. "I suppose it's the least I can do. I mean, you did take care of me after all."

"It was nothing," Nick said. "And thank you." He opened the door and stepped on the flowers. "Oh, shit!" He kicked them out of the way, into the apartment. "Sorry about that. Come on."

CHAPTER 21

THE TAXI HAD dropped them in front of Castel dell'Ovo on the inlet that stretched out into the gulf.

"Nick, that's Castel dell'Ovo." Laura pointed at it from the taxi window. "Virgil?"

"Oh!" Nick responded as he paid the driver. They stepped out in front of the castle.

"So, you *are* researching Virgil," Laura said. "Is this what you wanted to show me?"

"Huh?" Nick led her toward the edifice. "No, no. We're meeting Gaetano. He has something I need you to see. Just beyond the castle. Come on."

Nick led Laura down a narrow street along the wall, toward a small piazza, then stopped short. He spotted Gaetano seated at a table, looking not as put-together as usual. The man seemed to be fidgeting and looking around him as if in fear. Something was not right.

"Listen," Nick turned to Laura. "I need to have a chat with my friend over there. Would you mind…?"

"Giving you some privacy?" Laura finished his question. She looked at the man Nick referred to and nodded. "Of course. I didn't have to come with you."

"I know, I know. But I need you to see something. Just give me a few minutes to see what's going on with him." Nick looked back at Gaetano, then back to Laura. "Something is off."

"Okay, I'll take a stroll around the area," Laura agreed.

"Just a few minutes," Nick replied. "He has what I want to show you. So, just give me a few. Thank you."

"No problem," Laura said and separated from him, losing herself in the small streets on the inlet.

Nick watched Gaetano squirm in his chair. He appeared uneasy and concerned. He watched the man open his attaché case and rifle through whatever he had in there.

"Gaetano," Nick announced his approach with exaggerated exhilaration. He felt it would help lighten the man's worrisome mood. It did, but only slightly.

"Nick," Gaetano responded with a crack of a smile. He stood up and gestured to the empty seat next to his. "Thank you for meeting me at such short notice…again. I feel like I keep saying that to you."

"It's alright." Nick took his seat and signaled for a coffee, thanking the nearby server. "Is everything okay? Did you find more information?"

"Yes, and I don't know." Gaetano looked down and waited.

When the server returned and placed an espresso in front of Nick, Gaetano requested another pitcher of water.

"Are you feeling okay?" Nick asked as he watched Gaetano slurp down two full glasses.

"Yes, I'm just very thirsty," Gaetano responded as he poured a third glass. "I don't know what it is, but today, I'm like a fish." He took out his handkerchief and wiped away the sweat that had beaded on his forehead and his neck. Gaetano smiled as if nothing was out of the ordinary.

Nick understood that the man clearly didn't want to discuss whatever he was going through. He didn't know if he should press Gaetano further or respect the man's attempt to ignore his awkward state.

"Gaetano," Nick decided to play along and ignore the uneasiness as well. "Do you have those photos you showed me last time? The one with the older woman in Germany?"

"Ahh, yes." Gaetano reached into his attaché. "I have it all here, in the folder. I put this together for you, actually."

"Put what together?"

"This is why I wanted to meet you." Gaetano pulled out a large envelope and showed it to Nick. "I compiled all of the information we were able to retrieve in regards to the origin of the bracelet. With the help of the Egyptian buyer, of course. That was what I wanted to discuss with you."

Nick reached for the envelope, but Gaetano slid it back into his case.

"But first, I need to tell you something." Gaetano leaned in. "I went to check on your florist friend earlier."

"Lavinia," Nick responded.

"Yes, Lavinia." Gaetano's eyes became dreamy when he said her name. "She is quite a woman, Nick. You really know how to pick them."

"Right," Nick responded and looked down at his coffee.

"Did you know she was the woman who I thought was following me the other day?"

"What?"

"Yes. Kooky gal," Gaetano replied. "Apparently, she's been wanting to approach me for quite some time. And was pleasantly surprised when I walked into her shop. "*It must be fate*," she said. What a lovely woman."

"She was following *you*?"

"Well, I wouldn't say following…I mean, that makes her sound crazy."

Nick couldn't help but think that that was exactly what she was. He wanted to tell Gaetano that Lavinia was at his apartment just moments ago, but he didn't.

"It turns out, she's just a kook," Gaetano continued. "I wouldn't worry too much about her. She's not working with anyone."

"I didn't worry about that, really," Nick replied. "You were the one who lost it. But I do…"

"She is a lovely woman, Nick," Gaetano interrupted with a dreamy gaze. "In fact, I should thank you."

"Thank me?"

"Yes, we erm…well," Gaetano said with a smile. "She's a very sexy woman; I couldn't resist."

Nick sat in silence and waited for Gaetano to finish his sentence.

"I didn't mean to mix romance in this, but she was persistent and…boy, she knew what she was doing."

"Gaetano," Nick said, shocked. "You mean you and Lavinia…?"

"I didn't intend to have sex with her," Gaetano repeated. "I went there, as you know, to see if she was someone to be concerned about. But she was so attractive, and she seemed to take a liking to me—which doesn't occur often, Nick—and so, things just happened."

Nick was still shocked. *Who is this Lavinia woman? And why is she bumping around with every man in town? First, me? Now, Gaetano?* Nick felt uncomfortable hearing Gaetano talk about his sex life. It was unlike him. At the same time, he felt a bit of relief to know that he did not have to fear Lavinia's advances. They were not a sign of obsession, after all. She was just as promiscuous as he. *And Even Gaetano?*

"She gave me this flower," Gaetano continued. He pointed to three white flowers perking up from his breast pocket. They had five white petals blooming from what appeared almost like a trumpet. *Trumpet!* Gaetano caressed the white petals and continued. "Do you like it? It smells like her."

"Yes, lovely," Nick squirmed. "Are they trumpets or something?"

"Trumpets?" Gaetano looked down and caressed the flowers again. "No, I believe she said Oleander, or something like that."

"Can we talk about the photograph? You mentioned the Egyptian buyer confirmed something about the bracelet?"

"Oh, yes," Gaetano replied, snapping back to his squirmy state. "We spoke to the buyer again—he has the most to offer—and asked him why the interest in this item? He explained that it had to do with craftsmanship and the theme of the designs."

"He knows what the designs are?"

"He only said that his buyer is an aficionado of Greek mythology," Gaetano responded. "We couldn't get more from him, but if it does have Greco/Roman ties, then I can understand why the people from UNESCO had it on their list."

"Did he say if it held any value?"

"No, just that the design reminded him of Greek mythology," Gaetano replied, going into a coughing fit. "Sorry, I don't know what is going on. I think I should go home and rest."

"Maybe it's your flower," Nick replied. "Isn't Oleander poisonous? You could be allergic." Nick thought back to his own flower and her warning not to eat it as *it could be dangerous.*

"Impossible." Gaetano looked at his flower and smiled. "This is a gift of romance."

"Right..." Nick commented and looked away. His eyes fell on a man sprinting around the corner. Then another followed. A woman rushed out of a little shop with a wet rag and also disappeared behind the building. Something was going on around the corner. *Laura!*

"Where's Laura?" Nick stood up.

"Who's Laura?" Gaetano held onto his chair, unsure of what was about to happen.

"I'll be right back," Nick responded and rushed around the corner.

The crowd of three were tending to Laura, who had been seated on a chair brought out to the sidewalk. A woman dabbed at Laura's forehead, just above her left eye. *Was she cut?*

"Laura," Nick called out and approached.

"Nick," Laura exhaled.

"Are you okay? What happened?"

"It happened again," Laura replied as Nick crouched down next to her. "I felt lightheaded…and my head started spinning…and I was looking at the map on my phone, and I saw it."

"Saw what?" Nick asked as he gestured to the others that Laura was alright. He helped her stand up. "Another vision? What did you see?"

"The name," Laura said. She adjusted herself and held onto Nick's arm. "It was right here. Where we are standing."

"What name?"

"Schliemann!"

"Shlee-Mun?" Nick repeated. "What does that mean?"

"Yes, Schliemann," Laura said. "Apparently, this little section of the street is called Via Heinrich Schliemann." Laura saw there was no recognition in Nick's eyes. "The archeologist? Schliemann's Treasure?" Still no reaction from Nick. "Troy?"

"Troy?" Nick had no clue what Laura was going on about. "Like, Helen of Troy?"

"Yes." Laura was exasperated. "He found what he believed was Helen's Treasure…or that's what they dubbed it at the time."

"Laura, what are you getting at?" Nick led her back to the café.

"That's the old man in my dreams!" Laura responded excitedly. "I finally have a connection. I finally know who that old man was at the hotel. I finally have a clue…I think."

"Forgive me, Laura," Nick said. "But I still have no idea what you're talking about. You had a different vision?"

"Huh? Oh, no. I mean, yes." Laura's reply was almost automatic. Her mind was clearly working at trying to put together whatever puzzle piece she just gathered. "I'm sorry, Nick. I know my visions are all over the place, but that's just how it happens. Do you know how difficult it is trying to figure out what the visions are about, who the people in them are, what the people are trying to say, and how or if any of these visions are connected? It's a lot." She put her hand up to her head. "My head is still spinning and pounding. I think I should go home and rest."

Nick didn't want Laura to go. He wanted to show her the photo of the woman that Gaetano had in his case.

"There's a taxi," Laura said and waved toward the vehicle. The man pulled his car around and stopped in front of her.

"Are you sure you're going to be okay?" Nick placed his hand on her upper back and helped her into the taxi.

"Yes, thank you," Laura said through the opened window. "I just need to sleep this off. Let's meet tomorrow, and we can go over all of this—and maybe make a connection?"

"Sounds good, Nick replied. "Let me give you my number." He put out his hand. "give me your phone." Laura handed him her mobile and watched him punch in his number. His phone buzzed. "There," Nick tapped the taxi. "Just reach out to me should you need anything. Okay?"

"I will. Thank you."

Nick returned to the café table and found two servers cleaning up where Gaetano had been seated. He was gone. One of the servers in the doorway waved to Nick, calling him over. He told Nick that the man he was sitting with had gotten very sick and left abruptly. "He left this case behind."

"Will he be back?" Nick asked, taking the case from the server.

"I don't think so. He just vomited in our plant over there and then ran off."

"Grazie." Nick paid the bill and walked away. He pulled out his phone and saw no texts or calls from Gaetano. He sent a message: *Hey. Are you okay? Where are you?*

No response.

He continued on toward the taxi stand by the bustling port area and waited for the next available car.

He looked down at the attaché and wondered if Gaetano had his address somewhere on it. There was no tag. He unzipped the top and searched for a business card or anything with an address. He pushed aside the large envelope Gaetano had shown him earlier, rifled through the loose documents, scanning them until he found a utility bill addressed to *Pentolino, Gaetano*. He was surprised to see that the address was only a few blocks from his own place. When the taxi pulled up, he got in, and asked the driver to take him to Vomero—the district just up the hill.

CHAPTER 22

THE COLD SINK water gave Laura a boost of energy. The day took a toll on her. She had had more visions in one day than ever before. She put on her sleepwear, brushed her teeth, and sat in her old armchair by the window. She picked up her vision journal and looked for her notes on the old man, adding her new revelations.

TO RESEARCH:

Heinrich Schliemann—archeologist

Naples—why?

Death

She then flipped to the notes about the elderly woman and compared them to the notes about the younger woman at the theater and by the reflecting pool. *Were they the same woman? What was their connection?* She skimmed the notes. *Jewelry.* She reviewed entries for all the visions; the woman's jewelry was prominent in each.

Laura flipped to an empty page and titled it *JEWELRY.* She went through each entry to find any detail she had noted about what the women (or woman) was wearing.

Actress, Backstage:

Putting earrings on at mirror.

Putting on necklace.
Reflecting Pool:
    Many bracelets on one arm.
Elderly woman:
    Showing off bracelet in vision (and photo).
    Photo! Who was this woman? Same time era?
BRACELET

She skimmed her notes again, looking for more about the jewelry, but that was all she had. She never could control her visions but would try to focus on a bracelet when the next one came to her. Whether it was the same woman or not, jewelry seemed to be a common theme.

She dialed Nick's number—no answer. She debated between leaving a voicemail or trying again in the morning. His voicemail picked up and she spoke:

"Hi, Nick. It's Laura. I just reviewed my notes, and the only theme I see is jewelry—I think maybe a bracelet. I was trying to figure out how all of this could be connected to you when I remembered; was that jewelry that fell out of the tin box on the bookshelf? Was it just my vision, or do I remember something falling out? Anyway, I'm going to bed—my head is still pounding. Talk tomorrow."

She ended the call, reached for her glass of water, and gulped it all down. She needed to rest. She set her journal aside and soon fell asleep.

CHAPTER 23

NICK DROPPED HIS keys into the leather catch all on the table by the door. He had gone to Gaetano's apartment, but the man wasn't home. *Where could he have gone? Maybe he was asleep.* Nick tried calling him but got no answer. He gave up and decided he would check on him in the morning.

He removed his shoes and noticed a vase full of fresh flowers in front of the mirror. Was it the same bouquet left by Lavinia? He didn't remember putting the flowers in the vase. He just remembered stepping on them and kicking them in the door, leaving himself to tend to them later.

"You're back," Lavinia's voice crawled up his spine. He saw her reflection in the mirror. She stood in the doorway to the living room with an open book in hand. The exaggerated slit in her deep-violet skirt exposed her upper thigh.

"Lavinia," Nick clutched the attaché and turned to face her. "What are you doing here? How did you get in my apartment?"

"Surprise," Lavinia replied without answering his questions. "I put them in water for you. I didn't like seeing them on the floor."

"I don't appreciate you showing up here unannounced," Nick continued. "And breaking into my place? That's not right. You need to leave."

She responded with a smirk, closed the book, and went back into the living room.

"Lavinia." Nick followed. "You can't stay. Please leave."

"Leave?" Lavinia sat on the couch and crossed her long legs. "But I've been waiting to talk with you."

Nick was in shock. The woman sat as if in control of the room—in a place that didn't even belong to her. He didn't know how to respond. She wasn't hearing him, or was choosing not to.

"You're wrong, by the way," Lavinia changed the topic. "What you're researching."

"What do you mean?"

"It's not a flower you're looking for," Lavinia continued.

"It's not?" Nick relented. He dropped the attaché on his desk and leaned on his chair as he spoke to her.

"No," Lavinia said. "It's an herb. You were focused on its blossom, and not the herb itself. I'm not surprised, really. Men never look deeper than what's on the surface."

"What are you talking about?"

"What you thought was an animal, was not an animal at all." Lavinia caressed the pillows.

Is she trying to seduce me? "Then what is it?" Nick stepped forward. "Lavinia, please get up. What are you doing?"

Lavinia looked at him, disappointed. She sat up. Nick offered his hand, hoping to lead her off the couch and out of the apartment. Instead, Lavinia looked away and said, "It's a thornapple."

"A thornapple?"

"A thornapple," Lavinia repeated and stood up, ignoring his offer of help. "One would think with all these books, someone like you would be intelligent enough to realize what you have. I'm not surprised, though, by a man like you not being able to see it."

"Lavinia." Nick tried to take her hand again, but she pushed away.

"Where is it?" she asked.

Nick didn't respond. Lavinia softened her stance and caressed his chest.

"Show it to me," she whispered and ran her thigh against his.

Nick began to feel the magnetism. Her movement, her voice, her touch was drawing him closer and closer. Her face nuzzled his neck and up to his ear.

"I want to see it," she seductively said. Her breath tickled his ear, giving him goosebumps.

He knew she was talking about his bracelet, but he heard something else. He didn't want to, but he wanted her. He reached his arm around her waist, turned his face to hers, and kissed her. She gave him a strong, heavy, forceful kiss in return. Her hand stretched up to his face, holding his head in place as she continued to wrestle his tongue. He led her out of the living room, through the hall, and into his bedroom.

CHAPTER 24

HE FOUGHT TO open his eyes. His pillow was missing from under his head. The top sheet wrapped around his waist. He looked behind him—no sign of Lavinia. *Had she gone? What time is it? When did she leave?*

He rubbed his eyes and his face, stretched his whole body, and reached for his phone on the nightstand. 9:30 a.m. One missed call; from Laura. He unwrapped himself from the sheet and rolled to the edge of bed.

He planted his feet on the floor and sat up. He ran his hands on his head, his hair, and then his face again. He looked down and found the missing pillow by his feet. He reached for it and flipped it behind him onto the bed. Flashes of rolling around naked with Lavinia ran through his mind. It was rough, energetic, and animalistic. *Man, she is fun,* he thought.

He looked at his phone again and saw the time: 9:30 a.m. *Laura!* He remembered he was going to meet her for breakfast *Shit!* He rushed to the bathroom and got himself cleaned up.

He picked up his phone again and scrolled through last calls. He paused when he saw that the call from Laura over an hour ago. No new voicemail. He called her back.

"Nick?" Laura answered.

"Laura. Hi! Sorry, I overslept. Are you still up for meeting today? I'd like to go over our findings…make a connection."

"Oh, yes! So, I was right then? Is that what was in the box?" Laura asked.

"Box?" Nick responded. *Is she asking about the tin box on his bookshelf? Did she see what was in it?* "Were you right about what?"

"My voicemail…" Laura responded. "I know it was a long message, but the least you could have done was listen to it."

"I didn't get a voicemail?" Nick looked at his phone. No new messages. He tapped the voicemail icon and sure enough, he saw a message from Laura. But already listened to?

"Oh," Laura replied, as Nick's thoughts swam in his head about this finding. "I left you a voicemail last night. It was about my notes. Schliemann? And a bracelet? I wanted to know—"

"Bracelet?"

"Yes, is that what you have in that box?" Laura asked again. "That must be why we are connected. Why my visions are connected to you."

"How did you…?"

"I wasn't sure when I saw it fall out yesterday, but as I was writing my notes and cross-referencing what occurred, I deduced it may be a bracelet…it was all in the voicemail."

"Laura, I didn't get a new voicemail from…" Nick didn't finish the sentence. His phone hadn't indicated any *new* messages, but a voicemail from Laura was there. Already listened to, but not by him. So, why wouldn't his phone indicate it as new? *Lavinia!*

Nick dropped his comb by the bathroom sink and went into the living room.

"Laura?" Nick said frantically. "What did you say in the voicemail?"

"I told you. I went over my notes, saying that I think the jewelry might be the connection. A bracelet. And I asked if you had a bracelet."

"Did you say where it was, in the voicemail?"

"I mean, I guess so. I wanted to know if that's what was in the tin box on the bookshelf."

Nick didn't respond. He stood at the bookshelf and stared, in shock, at the empty space between Shakespeare and Eco.

"Nick? Nick, are you there?"

"What the f—?"

"Nick?

"Lavinia," he said her name slowly, as if registering what Lavinia may have done. Glancing around, he found the box on the floor. The bracelet was gone. Lavinia was gone.

"What?" Laura repeated.

"Laura," Nick rushed to his desk and confirmed all his belongings were still there. Relieved Lavinia had not taken the attaché either. "Where are you?"

"I'm heading into the auditorium at the university. Professor Millás is taking us for an offsite lecture today."

"What? When will you be back?"

"Probably early this afternoon. Are you okay?"

"Yeah, I think so. I need to go." Nick grabbed the case and rushed into the hallway. "Call me when you're back. We need to talk."

"Alright…" Laura replied. "Are you sure you're okay?"

"Yeah, I'm fine." Nick threw on his shoes and grabbed his keys. "We'll talk later. Sorry, gotta go." He ended the call and ran out the door.

He tried Lavinia's phone again. No answer. The taxi dropped him as close as he could to the narrow streets of the historic district. Nick jumped out and hurried to her shop.

The door was locked. The sign on it announced that the shop was closed for "ferie". It's not even August yet, and she's already closed for the summer holiday? He rang her again, but still no response. Of course, she was not going to respond, she stole his bracelet.

He hustled his way toward the main road and jumped in a taxi standing by. The driver naturally sped his way along the waterfront into the Chiaia district. Nick wished he had tried her apartment first but suspected she might not even be there either.

When he arrived, he pressed the button next to her name on the call panel, but no one answered. However, a woman exited the building at that moment, allowing Nick the opportunity to enter anyways. He rushed up to her floor and knocked on the door.

No answer.

He knocked again.

Nothing.

"Are you locked out?" A woman from behind him had just come up the stairs.

"Oh, uh…" Nick stammered.

The woman stood at the last step and looked at him suspiciously, waiting for him to respond.

"No, I'm just visiting," Nick finally admitted.

"I don't think she's home," the woman said, curtly. She didn't seem to like Nick standing at the door and was probably wondering how he even got into the building. "I can tell her you came by. What is your name?"

"How odd…She told me to meet her here," Nick continued his story, hoping to gain the woman's trust. "I don't understand why she's not here. I guess I can come back later."

"Maybe that's best," the woman said and watched him until he turned and walked past her, going down the stairs.

Nick left the building wondering where else to look. *Gaetano. Would she be there?* He took out his phone and called the man. Voicemail. He was at a loss. He didn't know what else to do. His bracelet was gone, which meant so was his money.

Shit! Shit! Shit! Why would Lavinia take it? And where had she taken it?

CHAPTER 25

"...IF THE EGG was ever broken, disaster would overcome the city. Now, Virgil, in addition to being a writer and poet, was thought to be an actual sorcerer. So, the locals believed he truly did place an egg in a small container somewhere underneath this castle." Professor Millás concluded his description of Castel dell'Ovo. His accent ever so alluring, he asked the group if there were any questions, and the group obliged.

"Was there ever proof of an egg in the castle?"

"As a sorcerer, did Virgil conduct any spells? Or what the locals were believed to be spells or magic?"

"Great question." Professor Millás pointed to his left. "If you continue on this main road, past Chiaia and Margellina, you will see a Roman tunnel. Legend has it that Virgil built that tunnel using his mystical powers. In fact, the tunnel's entrance is known to be the location of Virgil's tomb. And as you continue down Via Margellina to Via Posillipo, along the water, you can see remains of what was once the sorcerer's house. Virgil, his sorcery, and, well, magic and witchcraft in general, is prominent in this city."

"Why was he associated with magic? What made the people connect him to sorcery?"

"Well, maybe it has to do with one of the most prominent legends of Naples—the siren Partenope." Professor Millás indicated for the group to return to the bus as he continued. "You see, in one of Virgil's poems, when he first came to this area, he mentioned the legendary siren of Naples. I'd like to point to that legend as we move on to our next stop, as it does have a connection to magic spells and is one of the most famous sorceresses in Greek mythology."

Laura heard the last words and perked up. Greek mythology was the focus of her thesis, and she had never heard of this siren of Naples. Finally, the handsome professor was giving her something useful for her research.

"Professor." She raised her hand. "Can you spell the name of the siren for us? I'd like to make sure I have it right. What Greek story is she part of?"

"Yes, the Greek spelling is P-A-R-T-H-E-N-O-P-E. Italians remove the *H*," Professor Millás said, speaking into the microphone connected to the tour bus speakers. "She was mentioned in Homer's famous Greek epic, the Odyssey, as one of the infamous sirens who tried to lure Odysseus to his death."

Everyone in the group gasped.

He continued, "In fact, one of the places where she was thought to be buried was underneath the Castel dell'Ovo." He looked at the group and asked, "Is everyone settled? Okay, let's move on to visit a fountain dedicated to the alluring and sad siren. As I was saying, the siren Partenope has long been associated with Naples. In fact, sometimes, you'll hear Napoletani also refer to themselves as Partenopenese; the two descriptions can be synonymous. But let me get back to the legend. Partenope was one of the three sirens that Odysseus was warned about on his travels. Can anyone tell me who gave him this warning?"

A young woman raised her hand with uncertainty. Professor Millás nodded to her and waited for her response.

"I think it was Circe. Could that be right?"

"You are correct!" Professor Millás gestured a silent hand clap and smiled. "And that's where sorcery comes to us again. When Odysseus outwitted the infamous sorceress Circe, she gave him a warning of what danger was to come as he continued his journey home."

"Are you saying that story took place here? I thought it was in Greece."

"Well, many Greek legends took place in Italy as well," Professor Millás responded. "For example, the story of Hades taking Persephone…some believe that occurred in Sicily. Don't forget, these people were sailors—travelling as far as Turkey or Spain."

"And Circe was here?"

"Well, close. It is believed that Circe's Island was what is now the island of Ponza—just off the coast between here and Rome. At least, according to Partenope's legend. But we are getting ahead of ourselves here…"

Laura rigorously wrote down all these mentions in her notes. She hadn't thought of Circe in her research. This story, and this siren, may change her whole paper. She stopped writing and stared at the words she had scribbled on the page. The blue ink that stretched across the pages, with the curves and swooshes of her penmanship, began to wiggle. She shook her head, her eyes fluttered, and her surroundings began to spin. *Oh no!* she thought. *Not here...*

CHAPTER 26

NICK POURED HIMSELF another double bourbon. He didn't bother to add more ice to his glass. He plopped down onto his couch, feeling a fool. He had finally gotten the opportunity to sell that damn bracelet, and he let it get snatched away. Why would Lavinia take it?

Nick had tried to convince himself that Lavinia had not taken it. After all, Lavinia didn't even know he had the bracelet. For all Nick knew, he only showed her the design details. Had she seen something of value in those details that he wasn't aware of? If so, why hadn't she shared it with him? Then again, why would she share that information if she could just steal the thing and turn it over for cash herself? *Damn bitch...no, I'm a damn fool!*

He took a big drink of his bourbon and slammed his glass back on the coffee table. He sat back and exhaled. He thought back to the clues he had gathered so far. *A bracelet. Floral etching designs on it. Lavinia mentioning it was an herb—devil...trumpet. Oh! And Laura's visions! The elderly woman in the photograph. And it was connected to her other vision: the old man. He was an archaeologist. Was it Shlee-man something?*

He looked around the room, trying to connect all the pieces. His eyes fell on Gaetano's attaché. *Maybe Gaetano has more information.* He reached for the case and pulled out the large envelope. He set aside the photograph he had seen before and focused on the drawing. At the bottom corner was written: H. Schliemann. Nick remembered now that Gaetano pointing that out to him at the first meeting.

A handwritten note with an address in Giza.

Contact name: Mo at hotel _____.

Drop the bracelet at the hotel and make the exchange.

Flight details enclosed.

Instructions for the sale. *Was Gaetano planning to go to Egypt himself?* The next paper was a drawing of the bracelet with new captions:

Armlet. Cassandra's Prophecy

Helen in Egypt?

Theory: Debunked

The next document was a folded note, paperclipped to a stack titled: *bracciale (bracelet).*

Object: Cuff of Aeaea

Origin: Ponza (date unknown)

Designs: Thornapple, Trumpet of the Devil, Jimsonweed

Theory: Still active. Requires analysis.

Trumpet of the Devil! There it was. Lavinia had suggested that was the design. Nick sat back in amazement. His bracelet actually was of value. And maybe of very high value too. He read on.

Purpose: Belonged to a high priestess or sister of the Order of witches. A tribute to the sorceress Circe.

Last Location: Maybe Berlin, Germany. Missing since 1980s.

Maybe found again in Naples.

Theory: Inconclusive. See: Nick Terenzi.

Nick tensed at the sight of his name. Why would Gaetano put his name on any document? Nick panicked at the thought of someone finding these documents and seeing his name. It was hard evidence he was connected to the black market and trying to make a sale. He swallowed the rest of his bourbon and exhaled. He thought about it. He was impressed that Gaetano had actually figured something out. But how could he be so irresponsible at the same time? And then Nick remembered again that the bracelet was no longer in his possession. *I've got to find Lavinia.*

He set the papers aside and reached for his phone, tapping Lavinia's number again. Unsurprisingly, all he heard was the shop voicemail message listing shop hours. Nick ended the call before the automated message finished and was about to set the phone back down, when he tried the number again—this time, listening to the full message in the hopes it would reveal anything new. Lavinia's voice thanked the caller for contacting Botanica.... Shop hours…Thanked the caller again. No back up number and no mention of closing for holiday. He made a mental note to go by the shop again.

He set the phone back down and picked up the papers again. He flipped to the other side of the page. All that was typed was:

Client: Redacted.

Below it, handwritten in black ink:

How does client know Terenzi?

Someone knew Nick had the bracelet. Someone had known his name. Gaetano hadn't mentioned this. Maybe he planned to, but where was he? Nick grabbed his phone and tried Gaetano again.

No answer. He dropped his phone on the table and slammed the couch arm in frustration. *Where the fuck is he?*

His ringtone startled him. He wasn't expecting a call back. Maybe it was Gaetano. The screen flashed UNKNOWN CALLER. The phone continued to ring. Nick hesitated. On the fifth ring, he answered the call. Static.

A knock at the door.

Nick stood up and listened in silence. The phone rang again. He answered the unknown caller by the second ring. Again, static. Another knock at the door. He stepped into the hallway and peeked through the peephole. It was Laura—and she looked a bit distraught. He unlocked and opened the door.

"Oh, Nick," Laura exhaled and followed him in. "It happened again. This time I think—"

His phone rang again. Nick apologized and led her into the living room.

"Sorry, I don't know who this is, but they keep calling me," he explained and gestured for her to take a seat in the armchair.

Laura nodded. She stared at all the documents on his couch and sat down where Nick had indicated.

"Hello," Nick called into his phone. "Hello?"

No response.

He ended the call. He turned to Laura. "Are you Okay? Would you like some water?"

"Yes, please," Laura replied. "I'm sorry for coming here..." she added as Nick went into the kitchen and poured her a glass. "I had another episode and I needed to talk to you."

Nick returned with the water and watched Laura gulp it down.

"Would you like another?"

"No, thank you," Laura breathed out. "Sorry, I was very thirsty."

"That's alright." Nick took the glass and set it on the table near him. "What's going on? What happened?"

"I had another episode," Laura repeated. "I was on a university group tour around the city, and when we were on the bus, I just had a dizzy spell. When I came to, the professor was hovering over me. I was so embarrassed."

"So, you had another vision?"

"Yes, and I'm almost certain there's a connection between all of them." Laura sat forward. "We were learning about legends of Naples—sorcery and such. In fact, we talked a bit about Virgil and went to visit the Castel dell'Ovo place."

"Oh, right, Virgil."

"Anyway, it wasn't Virgil that triggered it. You see, the professor told us about the legend of a siren." Laura pulled out her notebook and searched for the name. "Anyway, this siren—Partenope, that's her name. The legend says that she was one of the three sirens that attempted to lure Odysseus to his death. However, they failed. And in her failure, Partenope committed suicide on the rocks—over by where that castle now stands. Some legends say her body created what is now the coast of this city. Her head became Margellina, her tail is Megaride—the inlet where that castle sits. So, that was interesting."

"Okay...but I still don't understand." Nick sat on the coffee table across from her. "What does this have to do with anything?"

"Right," Laura continued. "Well, Odysseus had been warned about these sirens, whom, again, were believed to have tried to lure Odysseus somewhere near the Amalfi coast. You see, just before he encountered these sirens, Odysseus came from the island where he and his men were entrapped by Circe—the sorceress."

"Circe?" Nick held up his finger. "Hold on." He shuffled through the papers he had been reading and found the document. "According to Gaetano's papers here—"

"Yes," Laura said. "Is there a connection? The bracelet?"

Nick didn't respond. He looked up at her and contemplated.

"What?" Laura asked.

"How did you know about that, the bracelet, by the way?"

"I didn't," Laura replied. "I mean, I realized later—when I was looking over my vision journal—that a bracelet was the common thread. And I finally asked the question of what the connection with you could be. That's when I remembered something falling out of that box up there. I think it might be the same…"

Nick followed her eyes up to the tin box on his shelf. The tin box that was now empty of treasure he had possessed.

"So, is that what you have in there?" Laura asked. "Is that the connection to my visions?"

Nick didn't reply. A thought popped into his head suddenly. "Laura…"

"Yes?"

"Your visions. Would you be able to focus on something specifically if you tried—an item or a person? Like where it is now? Find it, for example?" He dropped the questions without thinking, but he had to open up and let her in. He realized she could be his way of finding Lavinia and getting the bracelet back.

"Do you mean the bracelet?" she asked, but Nick didn't respond. "I don't know what you're involved in, Nick. And I don't know if I want to get involved in it either. I'm just following my visions and want them to end. I think I have enough here to tell you and hopefully it ends here with me. That these damn things don't come back to me. In fact, it's all different."

"Different how?" Nick asked.

"They used to be messages," Laura explained. "From someone beyond, wanting to pass information along to someone living. I would get these messages and rarely ever knew who they were for. But, now…since I got here, it's been random visions. Like my ability is changing or morphed…I don't know. It's just different."

"Laura…" Nick tried to console her, but she brushed his hand away.

"I just can't handle this any longer," she said. "I can't function. I now have anxiety when these visions come to me, and who knows what danger that will put me in. Where will I faint, fall, drop?"

"Laura…Laura," Nick put his hands on her shoulders. "Look at me. Look at me."

Laura looked up.

"I won't let anything happen to you." He said the words but didn't believe them himself. "I need your help. I think you're the only one that can help me right now."

Laura looked away. Nick could see she was thinking about it. He could see that she really did want out. Her struggle was real. She wanted out, but the visions were out of her control.

"The vision?" Nick asked.

"What?"

"What was this last vision you had? The one that prompted you to come here. Maybe the contents of this vision will help."

"Oh, yes," Laura breathed out. "Right. It was—"

Nick's phone rang again. He tried to ignore it, but it continued to ring. He rolled his eyes.

"Sorry." He reached for the phone. Again, UNKNOWN CALLER.

"Nick!" The man's voice came through blotchy. "Nick, are you there?"

"Yes, this is Nick," he responded automatically.

"Nick, it's Gaetano."

CHAPTER 27

"GAETANO!" NICK LOOKED at Laura when he said it. "I've been trying to reach you since you left the café. Where are you?"

"I can't talk much now, Nick." Gaetano sounded weak, probably still ill from earlier. "I'm sorry, Nick. I really am."

"Sorry? About what?"

"Do you have my case?"

"Yes, I have it right here." Nick looked at Laura confused. "Gaetano, where are you?"

"Oh, good." Gaetano breathed out in relief. "Listen, I can't say much now. I'm in a lot of trouble. I told you this was getting dangerous. I'm glad you have the case. Please keep it safe."

"Trouble? What kind of trouble?"

"In the envelope." Gaetano ignored Nick's question and continued, "Look inside. You will see notes on the bracelet. There is one buyer that confused me."

"The Egyptians?"

"No, another buyer. They had your name and…" Gaetano's response was followed by a barrage of coughs. "Sorry, Nick. I'm still not doing well. I checked myself into the hospital."

"I hope you're okay, Gaetano."

"I think I should be fine. I wanted to call you to make you aware that, because your name and address was on their correspondence, that maybe they might come for you."

"What? Who?" Nick's voice was louder than he had intended. "Who is after me?"

"I don't know if they are after you, but they might come to you. In the meantime, I put in a request to track down who that buyer is." Gaetano lowered his voice. "Nick, I think you should get rid of it. I think we should sell to the Egyptians, and I think we should do it now."

"Gaetano, please slow down. What is happening?"

"Get rid of it, Nick," Gaetano continued. "Get your money and rid yourself of it. There are too many people after it, and they are coming out of nowhere. I don't like it."

"Gaetano, I would get rid of it but…"

"How do you feel about taking the bracelet to Giza?" Gaetano interrupted again. "If you feel comfortable, I left the contact instructions in my papers. Do you see them?"

"Gaetano," Nick insisted. "I don't know how to tell you this but, the bracelet…it's missing."

"Missing?" Gaetano gasped. "What do you mean? Where is it?"

"Well," Nick spoke but was interrupted by strange sounds from Gaetano. "Gaetano? Are you there?"

The phone crackled and eventually died out.

"Gaetano? Gaetano? Hello?" Nick looked at Laura with concerned eyes, full of many questions. He set his phone on the desk and turned to her.

"Are you in danger?" Laura asked and started to hyperventilate. "I should go. It's probably not a good idea for me to be here."

"What? No," Nick brushed her off. "Let me get you some water, and we can talk. Did something happen?" he asked as he poured her a glass of water in the kitchen. He returned to the living room, handed her the glass, and watched her gulp it down.

"So, what was that call? It sounded like there was some sort of danger."

"No, I mean…well…" Nick dropped onto the couch and said, "It's just that I'm supposed to deliver something, and I don't have it."

"Is it the bracelet?"

Nick didn't respond. He looked at Laura and thought about it. He figured he might as well tell her everything. After all, Laura could maybe help him find Lavinia and help him to retrieve the bracelet. But now that he has some stranger looking for him, he has to make sure he doesn't put Laura in danger. He turned to her and said, "Let me walk you home. We can talk on the way."

"Nick," Laura resisted. "All this information is all over the place; I just want to get it sorted and understand what is going on. Our connection, the old woman, Heinrich Schliemann…Is it all connected? And is your bracelet, or whatever the object, triggering all of it? Can we just sit and sort it out? Please?"

Nick looked into her eyes and thought again. Part of him wanted to talk to her, but the other part wanted to protect her. *Am I putting her in danger? Who is this person Gaetano had mentioned is looking for me? Could I be in danger? And in turn, be putting Laura in danger too?*

"Nick, please?"

"Laura..." Nick hesitated. "Just let me take you home—we can talk on the way."

"No," Laura resisted again. "We can talk here."

"Laura, we can't stay here right now."

"What? Why?" Laura stood up and glared at the telephone. "The phone call. Did someone threaten you? Are you in danger?" She sat down again and looked at Nick. "Am I in danger?"

"Come on," Nick replied ignoring her question. "Let's just get you home. And yes, we do have a lot to talk about." He walked over to the desk and picked up Gaetano's attaché. "Let's go to your place. And we'll figure it all out."

Chapter 28

"SO, YOU HAD this bracelet that you bought a while ago, and you were hoping to sell it for a lot more money," Laura reiterated Nick's situation. "Through the underground market."

"Yes," Nick replied. "And Gaetano was the man making the deal for me."

"But, all this time," Laura continued. "You had no idea where the bracelet comes from. Nor any idea of its potential value."

"Correct."

"Why did you wait to research it?" Laura asked the question as she jotted his answers in her notebook. "How did you not know its value? I mean, you've had it with you all this time, and you never thought to get that information?"

"Well, I did have it, and I did try," Nick replied with a hint of embarrassment. He didn't like it that Laura called him out on his procrastination and foolishness—not following through on all of it way back when he first got the bracelet. "I just didn't know where to turn. I'm no jeweler, nor historian. To be honest, I had no idea it would have any significance. I still don't, if we're being truly honest. I just thought it was a bracelet that would get me some sort of cash. In the end, I'm glad I never sold it. I would have let it go for much less than what Gaetano is offering me now."

"So, the bracelet does have some value then?"

"Apparently," Nick continued. "Gaetano had multiple parties interested; one of them being the United Nations."

"United Nations?" Laura repeated in shock. "What would they want with the bracelet?"

"That, I still don't know. It was their art division or something. But the other parties include someone in Greece—I think the government or some museum—and someone in Egypt."

"Government? Nick, what sort of trouble are you in? Governments are involved?"

"Well, I don't know, really," Nick stood up and paced the room. "Gaetano was never clear on who the people actually were." He picked up Gaetano's case. "I even looked through his documents in here, but there's no detail on who the people actually are."

"And what information does he have in there that indicates what the buyers believed they were getting?" Laura asked the question with the assumption that that information was actually in the case.

"Well, that's what I wanted to show you," Nick reached into the attaché, rifled through the documents, and pulled out the photograph and the drawing. "This was the woman you saw in your vision." He pointed to the photograph.

Laura's eyes opened wide, her lips trembled while her gasps fluttered in and out.

"And this," Nick continued and pointed to the drawing. His finger slid down to the name in the lower right corner. "Schliemann. The man in your other vision. The archeologist."

Laura remained silent. She stared at the drawing, lifted the paper, and examined it in detail. She was astonished to see a document that may have once belonged to the man in her visions. Realizing she was touching the document, she feared a vision would ensue, but nothing came to her.

"I was hoping," Nick said, as if reading her mind. "That, with your touch, maybe a vision would come to you. I don't know what, but something."

Laura's eyes remained on the drawing, following the lines and the curves of the botanical designs. There were no notes, really, to describe the drawing; just his signature: Schliemann. She continued to caress the paper. Eventually, a blast of images fluttered her mind. She winced and tried to focus on any of the flashes. *The desert. Turkey? Greece? Where was this desert? Egypt. Cairo. A sale. The bracelet! A boat. Italy. Train. Germany.*

"Laura? Laura?" Nick's voice infiltrated her thoughts.

Laura shook her head and looked at him.

"Are you okay?" Nick was holding her back. "You fell off the bed. I didn't want to break your focus, but I couldn't let you hurt yourself. Are you okay? Did you see something? What did you see?"

Nick held her hand, and she winced once again. *The hotel. The hotel bed. The busy street of Naples. The old man's hand caressing the knee of the young maid. The bracelet! The maid staring at the bracelet in a small box. Did she steal it? A vision of the man's body laying weak in bed. Was he dying? The maid rushing toward a train. Germany. Berlin. The maid meets a man. Marries him. Children. The maid was an old woman, wearing expensive clothes and heavy jewelry. Her right arm adorned with the bracelet. A flash of the camera. Fade to black.*

"She stole it," Laura's voice was almost hypnotic.

"What?" Nick rubbed her arm. He had propped her back up on a chair by her small table.

"The maid," Laura said to him. "She stole it. She stole the bracelet." Laura stood up. Her energy came back to her in a burst. "She was helping the old man—Schliemann. Feeding him, almost like a nurse. Then, when he got close to death, or really weak, she took the bracelet."

"Is that what you saw?" Nick poured her some water.

"No." Laura sat down again. "I mean, yes…well, I felt it." She reached for her candy dish and pulled out a chocolate. "Schliemann."

"What about Schliemann?"

"He purchased the bracelet. That's how he had it." She unwrapped the chocolate and popped it into her mouth. "That's how he got it. But why? Why would Schliemann want it? And to whom did it belong?"

"Laura." Nick sat on the edge of the bed and faced her. "Are you saying the bracelet is an actual artifact of some sort?"

"I'm not exactly sure about that." Laura ate another chocolate.

"Troy," Nick blurted out. "Didn't you say Schliemann was obsessed with Troy—Helen of Troy? Does the bracelet have some connection to his obsession?" Nick opened the attaché again and pulled out the envelope with all of Gaetano's documents. "There was something here about Helen…let's see here…Ah! Here it is. *Armlet. Cassandra's Prophecy. Helen in Egypt (question mark).* That is all that is written here that mentions any Helen, really. But it says that this theory is debunked."

"Cassandra's prophecy?" Laura asked, more to herself than to Nick, as she scoured her memory of Greek mythology.

"Who is Cassandra, and what was her prophecy?"

"Cassandra predicted the fall of Troy," Laura remembered. "She was one of Paris' sisters. She had the gift to predict the future, however, she was also cursed—that no one would ever believe her predictions. Anyway, she had warned the people that if Paris brings Helen back to Troy, it would be the fall and destruction of their city. But, again, no one listened or believed her. Brushed her off as a crazy woman, a drama queen—I can sympathize with her."

Laura stiffened again. Her eyes winced. She was receiving another message or vision.

"Wait," she said. "Yes...yes...it's coming in clearly now. Schliemann feels defeated again. Was the bracelet was passed over? Considered another false relic?"

"False relic?"

"Schliemann..." Laura explained. "He was famous for finding the Treasure of Troy—which included Helen's headdress and more. But he was not taken seriously as before."

"Don't lose your focus," Nick pleaded. "Stay with it."

"Ugh, I lost it." Laura shook her head. "It's gone. The last thing I felt was that the bracelet was found to have had no connection to Helen..."

"What?"

"The bracelet was not an artifact," Laura explained. "It seemed that it was made for some other purpose..."

"What purpose?"

"I don't know." Laura reached for her glass of water. "But in my visions…again, I saw a tree."

"A tree?"

"Yes, I didn't really pay attention to it before. I think it was overshadowed by other things in my visions, but there was always a tree. This time, though, the tree was larger. Stronger. What is it?"

Nick watched as she rummaged through her journal again. Her finger ran down each page, her eyes skimming her notes.

"I didn't write anything here about a tree." Laura continued to flip the pages. "How could I be so careless? There must be something…Nothing."

"What are you going on about?"

"I don't know," Laura dropped her book on the small table.

"How are you feeling?" Nick put his hand on her shoulder. "You want some rest?"

"Yes, I think that's best." Laura walked Nick to the door.

"See you tomorrow?" Nick asked.

"I'm not sure," Laura replied. "I need to get back to my research."

"Okay, well, maybe later this week or something?" Nick suggested.

"The program at the university is taking us on another excursion," Laura responded. "To some town outside of the city. I don't remember where, but I'm starting to wonder why I'm bothering with this program at all."

Nick was receiving her message. She wanted to walk away from his situation. She wanted out.

"Okay," Nick said. "Rest up, kiddo," he said that last part and immediately wanted to take it back. He didn't mean it to sound condescending but knew it probably did. "I'm going to see what else I can find out. Maybe reconnect tomorrow?"

"I don't know," Her reply was accompanied with a yawn. "Sorry. See you soon." Then added, "Hey..."

"What?" Nick stopped at the door.

"Are you going to be okay?" Laura asked. "I mean, that call you got earlier...it sounded like there was some trouble."

"Oh, right. I'll be fine. You're safe, and that's what matters." Nick turned away, then turned back again. You know what..." Nick sighed, clearly not happy with whatever he was thinking about. "Maybe it's actually best you don't contact me. Just in case...I would love to see you tomorrow, or any time this week for that matter, but I promised you wouldn't get hurt in any of this, and I intend to keep that promise."

"What do you mean?" Laura held on to her door.

"I just don't want you to get involved in something you shouldn't be involved in. This is all my problem, and I appreciate the insights you've given me. I just don't want you to get hurt on my account. I just want to look into Gaetano, and then I'll know." He help onto the doorknob then and added, "I'll contact you when the time is right."

He left Laura's apartment feeling at ease that she was back in her place, away from him, away from any potential danger. He hoped that whatever Gaetano had been trying to warn him about would not involve Laura. Hoped whomever may be looking for him, would not make any connection to her.

What was Gaetano's warning? He had to find him and find out. *What was it about the bracelet? Lavinia. Why did she take it?* He had to find her and get his bracelet back.

Chapter 29

IT TOOK ALL morning, but it wasn't until Nick branched out toward the outer rim of the city that he found the hospital where Gaetano had checked into. When Nick asked the front desk nurse if they had a patient by the name of Gaetano Pentolino, that he was there to take him home. The nurse had punched in the name on his computer and was confused by whatever had appeared on the screen.

"Yes...we *did* have a patient of that name," the man started. "Room 1567...but, here, it indicates he has already been released."

"Released?" Nick asked. "So, he should be home?"

"Let me confirm. One moment," the man picked up the black telephone, hit a button on the console, and waited.

Another nurse soon appeared behind the desk, and Nick could see she was holding several files. The man hung up the phone and asked her about patient 1567. "This man has come to pick him up," he told her as he indicated to Nick.

The woman smiled at Nick. "You've come here for Gaetano Pentolino?" she asked.

"Yes, is he still here?"

"No, I'm sorry, sir," the woman replied. "He was released last night. His wife picked him up."

"His wife?"

"Oh, yes," the man added. "A lovely woman. She brought us this incredible bouquet." He walked over to a flourishing assortment of tropical flowers, set in a white porcelain vase.

"Mr. Pentolino was feeling a lot better. Are you a relative?" the woman interjected.

"No…" Nick stammered. *Did Gaetano have a wife? The flowers. Was it Lavinia? Why would Lavinia pick up Gaetano? Even saying she was his wife? Were they really that deep in a relationship? They hardly knew each other. But why would she come pick him up if not?* Both nurses were looking at him in confusion, so he smiled at them and said, "Oh, yes! His wife…How stupid of me. I forgot she was picking him up. She's the one with the curly, black hair… right?"

"Ehh, yes…" the woman responded with hesitation, appearing to have some sort of growing suspicion over Nick.

"Oh, great," Nick said, keeping his smile plastered on his face. "I'm glad she was able to make it, then. She was worried she wouldn't be here in time and had asked me to pick up Mr. Pentolino. Well, I'm glad that is sorted. Thank you both for your help."

The back of the taxi was hot, but the warm breeze that blew through the window did offer some comfort. Nick rested his elbow on the window, directing the air to his face as he was driven across town, through the mid-day bustle.

Was Lavinia one of Gaetano's buyers? Why would Gaetano keep that information from him? The man didn't hesitate to share his affection for Lavinia and their intimate interaction. Why had he been so secretive about Lavinia being one of his buyers? And that is only if she is one of his buyers.

Nick continued to wonder; *Does Gaetano know that she stole the bracelet? Had she done it for him? Were Gaetano and Lavinia working together? Did they plan to steal the bracelet and get the money for themselves? No. Why would Gaetano bother to go through all the details about the buyers with Nick? Why would he push Nick to pursue the Egyptian buyer? And why did Gaetano not know Nick didn't have the bracelet? Was Lavinia working on her own? Who is she? But if she had the bracelet already…why would she need Gaetano? To sell it for her! That must be it. Who is she?*

The cab pulled up to Gaetano's apartment building. Nick paid his fare and asked the driver to wait, but the man refused and drove away without listening for Nick's response.

After about twenty minutes of watching the front door from across the street, Nick found his opportunity to get in. He saw a couple approach the door and open it with their key, so he rushed up behind them as if he, too, belonged in the building.

"It's a great day, is it not?" he asked them as he followed them into the lobby. The couple smiled back and pushed the button to the elevator. Nick nodded a goodbye to them and took the stairs up to Gaetano's floor.

He approached Gaetano's apartment door and listened. No noise came from inside. He leaned his head on the door, pushing his ear against it. Nothing. He reached for the doorknob and chanced a turn. To his surprise, the door was unlocked.

To be safe, he knocked gently again, but still, no response. He opened the door slowly and quietly—to not startle Gaetano. The door opened into a small hallway that led to a large living room.

At first glance, Nick was surprised to see the place disheveled. Gaetano appeared to be a put-together, organized man. Nick assumed his living space would reflect the same.

He let himself in and closed the door behind him. As he walked into the living room, he saw piles of papers stacked haphazardly on a dining table, a desk, and around the floor. Drawers to the desk were partially opened—one was actually pulled out and placed, empty, onto the coffee table to the left. The space was not just disorganized, it was ransacked. *Had Gaetano done this himself? What was he looking for?* Nick looked down at the attaché he was carrying. *Maybe it was someone else. Someone had rummaged through all of Gaetano's things and maybe didn't find what they were searching for. Maybe whoever had done this was searching for this case.*

The ring of the apartment phone startled him. Nick stepped back in reflex and exhaled in relief. He walked over to a pile of papers, held in place by a stone paperweight shaped like an elephant. He perused each one, looking for any clue to anything. The documents were mostly articles and notes on sculptures and art; which accompanied all the art books on the back wall. No indication of any sales or purchases, nor client lists. Nothing of the sort in this room.

Nick snooped around the corner, passed a bathroom and a kitchen, and into one of the bedrooms—all of them with doors wide open and all clean as a whistle. The door to the final room was closed; its large pane of frosted glass revealing a brightness that indicated that the blinds to the windows within the room were open, and the sound of cars from outside made Nick believe the windows were probably open as well. Nick stopped at the sight of a dark shadow moving within the bright light. He waited and listened—nothing but the traffic outside. The dark object moved again. It was a periodic, gentle flow—probably a curtain. Nick knocked on the glass to no response. He pulled the handle and slowly opened the door.

Directly across from him was an open balcony. The two floor-to-ceiling windows were wide open, its gray curtains flowing in the occasional breeze. Other than the bedcovers being a bit tousled, the bedroom was immaculate. Nick held onto the doorhandle as he glanced around the room. Suddenly, a man appeared from the left side of the outer balcony. Nick froze. The man came into view. Nick was overcome with relief when he saw it was Gaetano.

A sudden coughing fit took him over. When it subsided, he looked up and locked eyes with Nick—they both looked at each other in silence. Gaetano's eyes opened wide, as if in fear or maybe sadness. He turned away, held onto the railing and threw himself over.

"No!" Nick felt his scream echo along the walls, out the window, and bounce along the buildings outside. He rushed to the balcony, but it had happened so fast. He didn't hear anything. His head was spinning. *What just happened?!*

A woman's scream outside pierced the air, shaking him to his core. He heard a bustle of people in panic soon gather below.

Nick had to get out of Gaetano's apartment—no one knew he was there. No one had seen him; he didn't think, anyways. He rushed through the hallway and listened through the front door. Not hearing anyone, he opened it and rushed out. He ran down the stairwell, hearing the people outside get louder and louder. Sirens soon accompanied the chaos. Nick joined the bustle of neighbors in the building that rushed outside. When he got to the street, he looked past the people and saw Gaetano's body lying still in a pool of blood. He wanted to vomit. One neighbor grabbed his shoulder and wailed in horror. Nick shook and joined in on her state of shock.

After a moment, he composed himself and stepped backwards. When he distanced himself enough from the crowd, he turned around the corner, hoping no one had really taken notice of him. Once out of view, he ran.

CHAPTER 30

A TURN OF a page, a drop of a pen, an occasional burst of whispers—nothing compares to the serenity of a library. Add to that, the beauty of stained-glass windows and tall, oak shelves, Laura felt fortunate to have access to the library at the University of Naples.

It was early morning. She made sure to get to the library as soon as it opened to guarantee herself full access to an empty table. She took over a smaller one in the far corner of the main room and scattered her notes around a pile of books she had retrieved with the help of the front desk clerk.

The library was an escape for her. Not only from the overstimulating noise of the Naples' streets, but from the chaos within her head. She was a student, a thinker, and her mind worked overtime in almost every situation. Sometimes, even over how to take her coffee in the morning.

The past few days had thrown many random facts and theories at her, but they came to her chaotically. Her mind—already overwhelmed with her thesis—was unable to catch up and organize all the new, irrelevant information. She wanted to ignore it all—phase Nick and his problems out of her life—but she was interested in the topic. She was too intrigued, curious, and couldn't resist her nature to figure it all out.

Afterall, Nick—or whatever he had—was connected to her visions. Visions which, she just realized, had not come to her in a while, and she hoped they would subside for even longer, like she was used to.

She fiddled with her pen as she read excerpts from the book opened in front of her. She put her pen to an empty page of her notebook and added to her notes.

<u>Who Was Parthenope?</u>

· Name: derived from the Greek word <u>Parthenos</u>, meaning virgin.

<u>LEGENDS</u>

<u>Mythology: Parthenope was a Siren:</u>

· The siren of music and poetry.

· Originally one of the three winged sirens, sent by Demeter to search the area for her daughter Persephone — who had been taken by Hades. When they failed to find her, they were plucked of their wings and banished to live on the rocks off the Amalfi Coast. How did they get the fish tail?

· Li Galli Islotte (Location: <u>POSITANO</u>) — a small set of islands where it is believed the sirens had lived and attempted to seduce Ulysses/ Odysseus.

· Parthenope was one of these sirens who attempted to seduce Ulysses on his voyage home from the war in Troy (Odyssey).

· Note: Confirm with Odyssey. And was Ulysses/Odysseus able to escape the sirens because of Circe's warning? [Confirm this. And is it relevant? — See separate notes on Circe. Nick's bracelet.]

<u>Connection to Naples</u>

· When Parthenope failed to seduce Ulysses, she was so distraught, she killed herself — on the rocks where they typically ensnared lonely *sailors. Parthenope's body was later found on what is now the coast of Naples. [Or it created the coast of Naples? What?]*

- *CASTEL DELL'OVO! The siren's body was believed to have been found on the island of Megaride — which is now the peninsula where the castle is located. [Virgil connection?] ...believed to be buried underneath castle.*

[Note: How does a siren kill herself in water? Ridiculous... — Correction: Found later: Sirens are also depicted with wings. Were they birds? See notes on Persephone and the sirens sent to look for her. Is this relevant?]

POTENTIAL BURIAL GROUNDS FOR THE SIREN?!

- *Caste; Dell'Ovo (Prof. Millás mentioned this one).*

- *Corso Sirena: Going from piazza Procelle to Barra.*

- *Santa Lucia Maggiore (church built on a former temple to the siren).*

- *San Giovanni Maggiore (via Mezzacannone): plaque to the siren, claiming body is buried under foundations of the church.*

- *Hill: Sant'Aniello a CapoNaples (near piazza Cavour).*

Legend: Parthenope was a Human (Greek):

Parthenope was a young Greek virgin who eloped with her mate. They sailed and reached the coast of Campania, and with a group of other settlers, founded the future Neapolis, later Naples.

[Romantic legend. Who are the people from Greece that founded Naples?]

Laura dropped her pen, closed the book, and sat back. Although Parthenope's was an interesting story, its only connection to Laura's thesis would be Circe—the sorceress that warned Odysseus of the sirens. She then remembered Nick had mentioned a potential theory that connected Circe to his bracelet.

She blew away the hair in front of her face, leaned forward, and reached for the other books. She scanned the binds of the pile and pulled out a book on Greek mythology.

"What are you about, Circe?" she said to herself, but realized she had said it aloud. She looked up and blushed at the sight of the desk clerk glaring at her. She mouthed an apology and focused back on the books.

CHAPTER 31

NICK SAT IN his bathtub. The damp washcloth on his face blocked the sunlight. His body was still shaking from the shock of Gaetano's jump. *Why did he do it? What is happening? Did anyone see me?*

He sat up abruptly. *The nurses!* Water splashed onto the tiled floor. His washcloth fell from his eyes and into the water. *What if the police question them? What if they mention I was there to pick up Gaetano?* Nick didn't remember giving them his name, but surely, they would be able to describe him.

His phone buzzed. He looked over at it vibrating on the stool next to him. He did not recognize the number displayed. He waffled on ignoring or answering it, but thought, or rather hoped, it would be Lavinia. He reached for it, swiped, and answered.

"Hello, Mr. Terenzi," the woman's voice was unrecognizable. "I am Silvia Camporizzo from the UNESCO offices in Naples. We recently got your contact from Mr. Gaetano Pentolino. We were hoping to set up a meeting with you. Do you have some time today?"

Nick was skeptical. He remembered Gaetano specifically telling him he didn't share contact information. *Why would Gaetano give*

UNESCO my contact information? Did this woman know Gaetano was dead? Maybe it isn't UNESCO. Maybe it wasn't Gaetano. The police. Is she working with the police? Did someone see me at Gaetano's apartment?

"Mr. Terenzi?" the woman's voice continued. "We have a lot to discuss—concerning your item you have for sale. And well, concerning Mr. Pentolino."

"What about Mr. Pentolino?"

"To put it delicately, we heard the news," the woman continued. "And we think we can help you."

"Help me?" Nick's response revealed his fear. He composed himself and asked, "Help me with what?"

"Your situation, of course. I think it would be best to discuss this in person. Can you meet me?"

Situation? Nick thought. *Did this woman know something about Gaetano's death? Did she have information that I was there? How? No. Impossible. Why?*

"What situation?" Nick asked, hoping to confirm it was none of what he was thinking.

"I think it best we discuss all this in person," she repeated. "There is, apparently, some sort of danger involved, and we all need to be careful now."

"Careful?" Nick responded, as if repeating words from her sentence was all his mind could manage.

"Mr. Terenzi," her voice had lost some of its politeness. "Please come meet me. It is safe here. Do you know where our office is located? Meet me at the café on the roof of Castel Sant'Elmo. The security guards will guide you."

Safety. Careful. Danger. Castel Sant' Elmo. Security Guards. Maybe she really was from UNESCO.

"Mr. Terenzi?" she asked again.

"Yes," Nick responded. "Yes. I can meet today. See you soon." He didn't know why he agreed to meet with the UNESCO office. He didn't have the bracelet to sell them. But the woman mentioned caution, and maybe she knew something about Gaetano, and the danger he had apparently been in.

CHAPTER 32

"**HELLO, LAURA,**" **THE** sound of the professor's whisper made her insides flutter like a warm breeze caressing her body.

Before responding, her mind ran through what she was wearing, how her makeup looked, and if her hair was behaving. *Am I presentable? Do I look cute? What do I look like when in deep concentration? What is he seeing as he looks at me? How long has he been here, watching me? Did I do anything embarrassing? In other words, do I look attractive?!*

"Professor Millás." Laura felt the heat rush to her face. Was she red? Could he see it? *Relax, you idiot!*

"May I join you?" the professor asked as he was already pulling out a chair and taking a seat.

"Yes, of course," Laura responded as she watched him settle his leather bag on the table and unzip the top. *What is that delicious scent he is wearing?* It was like a mix of wood, pine and sage with a dash of pepper. *I could just eat him up.* She stared at the top of his chestnut hair, combed to the side, as he rummaged through the bag. She examined his rounded shoulders as he worked his manly hands. They were thin but veiny enough to give the appearance of offering a strong grasp. She imagined them clenching her thighs. She shook her head and focused back at the book in front of her.

"I hope to see you joining our excursion tomorrow," Professor Millás remarked.

Laura looked up and saw him watching her. *Why does he make me so nervous?!* He held out a pamphlet and offered it to her.

"Benevento?" Laura read the top of the pamphlet. "What's this?"

"We are taking a group to discuss the legends of witchcraft," the professor replied. "I thought it would be of interest to you. Isn't that what you're writing about?" He gestured to the chapter title she held open in front of her: *Sorcery in Greco-Roman Mythology.*

"Oh, this?" Laura blushed again. "No, no. I'm reading this for a friend. My focus is on—"

"I really was hoping you'd join us," the professor pushed. He didn't seem at all interested in her thesis.

"Me?" The word fell out of her mouth like a teenage girl, shuddering with excitement. *Damn it! Did he notice?*

"Yes, you," he replied. "What would it take to convince you? What do I have to do?" The questions were delivered in an even softer whisper. He leaned in and reached for her hand. His touch was gentle with just the right amount of roughness. She imagined the library empty; he would pin her down on the table and close in on her lips. A romantic score would roar in the background as they would connect in a passionate–

"…it's only going to be for a day," the professor's words broke her fantasy. "We would be back by dinner."

Was she panting? Did he notice her blushing? Was she touching herself?! *No. thank, God!* Laura sat up and composed herself. She didn't like the power this—very handsome—man was having over her. It was unlike her to act this way. It bothered her, in fact. She was more than that.

But she was also human. She was a woman. And she wanted him. Just one look at his face, his eyes, his shoulders and she was ready to give him everything. She would let him ravage her in a way that—

Laura, again, shook away her thoughts. He was like a drug. She had to get away.

"Are you hungry?" he asked her.

His question was unexpected. *Yes, hungry for you,* she wanted to say, but responded with a simple, "Yes." She packed her notebooks and followed him out of the library.

The walls of large sand-colored rocks gave the appearance that the osteria was located underground. An oversized, beige logo was placed against a wide, modern art-piece made of white plates that hung flat against the back wall—creating an art piece that juxtaposed with the pale stones behind it. The white tables and chairs were adorned with beige linens, matching the main art piece that commanded the space.

The professor greeted the owner—who appeared to be an old friend—sitting them at a small table in the corner. The owner proceeded to tell them about the specialties of the day, offering a small tasting. The professor thanked him for the generosity as Laura took the seat offered to her. She sat with her back to the rock wall, facing the small dining room.

After helping Laura push her seat in, the professor took the seat to her right; which also allowed him a view of the room and to be closer to Laura. It was not what she expected, but she was charmed. She watched him pull the setting that was at the seat opposite from hers, unfold the napkin, and place it on his lap. *Was this going to be a romantic lunch?* she wondered as she smiled at him.

"I hope you don't mind that I agreed to the tasting menu," the professor remarked. "He's a friend of mine and always likes me to taste his latest offerings.

"Oh, no, that's fine," Laura replied. "I totally understand. I mean, if the chef is excited about his food, then how can anyone refuse?"

"Indeed," Professor Millás replied. "He's a great man. Always lets me taste anything he's working on. Do you prefer red or white?" Then added, "We're having seafood. I hope you like seafood."

"I love seafood," Laura replied. "So, white, I suppose? I like the local wine I have been drinking recently...I think it was called Greco? It's local to the region...I think that's the type."

"Ah, yes," the professor signaled to the server. "*Una bottiglia di Greco di Tufo, per favore. Grazie, señor.*"

Hearing him mix that last word both in Spanish *señor* with Italian *signore* made Laura blush. She found it adorable. She also noticed that this time his *s* was not a Castilian lisp. It was more like a snake's hiss.

"What part of Spain are you from, Professor?" Laura asked him. If this was going to be a date, she thought she might as well get to know him.

"Please, call me Alfonso," he replied.

"Okay, Alfonso," Laura said his name, and it felt like warm, soft velvet flowing out of her mouth.

"I'm originally from Cordoba, in Andalucia," Alfonso answered her question and turned to the server who appeared with the bottle.

He gestured for Laura to taste the wine, and she obliged. She swirled the light and crisp wine in her mouth and swallowed. It was good, clean, and just right. Once she gave him the nod, the server poured each glass with elegance and placed the bottle on the table.

"But," Alfonso continued. "I live in Madrid and spend a lot of time up north in Navarre."

"I don't know Navarre," Laura replied and took another sip of the wine.

"It's located in Basque country. I inherited a family home in the Xareta Valley years ago. My mother's family. It's not far from Pamplona. Do you know it?"

"Oh, Pamplona," Laura responded. "Well, I've heard of it... Hemingway..."

"Ah, yes," Alfonso smiled. "*The Sun Also Rises*, was it?"

"Yes! That was it."

A server placed the first two of the tastings onto the table and proceeded to explain the dishes. The first was a small portion of their *parmigiana di melanzane*, cooked in a little, clay dish the Napoletani call *pignatiello*. It was accompanied by fried anchovies, that filled a paper cone they call a *cuoppo*.

Alfonso gestured for Laura to take the first bite, and she did as she was told with a coy smile. She noticed it was coy and she hated herself for it. Why was she acting "cute"? She forced the smile away and grabbed her fork and knife.

The eggplant parmigiana was made of thin, delicate layers of eggplant, placed so elegantly on top of one another and cut into one large and perfect cube. Laura sliced the cube in half and placed one onto her appetizer plate. Alfonso proceeded to take the other.

Laura broke away a small portion with her fork and lifted it to her mouth. The soft, umami eggplant flavor, mixed with the slightly tart mozzarella and bitter tomato sauce, was pure heaven on her tongue. A hint of smokiness surprised her and augmented the pleasure of the dish.

"I believe he said the tomatoes were grown on Vesuvius, over there," Alfonso said in between bites and pointed in the direction of the volcano. "Absolutely delicious. It might be an illusion, but it's almost as if you can taste volcanic ash."

Laura chewed her last piece and wondered if it was true. Was that smokiness truly from volcanic ash? *No. Impossible.*

"I was going to ask you more about your thesis," Alfonso continued. "But I think I'm more intrigued by you." He dropped the words with an air of nonchalance, as if they were expected to be said. Then, he proceeded to grab one anchovy, pop it whole into his mouth, and smile at Laura as he chewed.

Laura didn't know how to respond. Was he coming on to her? She busied herself with raising her glass of wine to her lips and contemplated a neutral response. But did she have to be neutral? Why not just be open? She watched his mouth and jaw work at the anchovy inside and silently sipped her wine. Was the top button of his shirt always unfastened?

The server removed the empty plates and replaced them with one individual steel balti dish. In it was a small serving of a modernized pasta and potatoes—a classic peasant dish of Naples.

The server went on to explain that it was only to be a taste of it, as the main dish was about to be presented. Immediately, another server approached with a plate of *baccala alla Napoletana*—cod braised with capers, black olives, and tomatoes—and a dish of simple mixed greens. More wine was poured before the two men slipped away, back to the kitchen.

Laura barely remembered tasting the entrée when the dessert arrived. The wine was stronger than she had anticipated and the professor's seat was closer than she remembered.

"Nothing like a classic Napoletan babà," his voice was deep and raspy. Was that his hand caressing her shoulder?

Laura smoothly shifted away, prompting the professor to remove his hand. "This is adorable." She indicated to the mini baba on her plate. "I've had these in coffee shops around town, but they were much bigger than this one."

"Well, sometimes quality and skill matter over size," the professor responded.

Laura ignored his possible innuendo and picked up her fork. She pushed it into the pillowy, rum-soaked cake and lifted a morsel to her mouth. As she chewed, she felt the professor staring at her. She turned to him and confirmed that he was doing just that.

"Delicious, isn't it?" he said through his smile. "Do you like the taste of it? It's so rich and warm…and not too sweet."

Laura froze inside. The man had begun to switch to vulgar mode. She was used to this. Men testing the situation with a pinch of vulgarity, a dash of inappropriateness to see how the other would respond. If she was game, she'd give a coy look, a small giggle, and a subtle smile. If she was not, she would be cold, ignore the comments, and if he persisted, respond with a curt *no*.

She felt that she blushed again and hated herself for it as she did the other times. There was no doubt she was attracted to the professor, but didn't know why she hesitated. He clearly was interested in her, and she knew all she had to do was let him know she was too. She swallowed, lifted her glass of wine, and turned to him with a coy, shy smile.

Chapter 33

"**I FIND THE** topic of your thesis interesting," Alfonso said in between sips. "May I offer a suggestion?"

Laura tried to chew her full fork of the cakey babá to respond, but she couldn't get through it. Instead, she silently nodded for Alfonso to continue.

"You've got a great topic—Greek influence in Italy. And I assume that will include the legends? Homer? Odysseus?"

"Yes, well, that is my new focus, I think," Laura was able to reply between her teeth. She finally completed the chewing and swallowed, embarrassed to have put so much in at once. She sipped her water and asked, "I was particularly interested in that siren story you told me. Parthenope?"

"Yes. Good." Alfonso sat forward. "Did you notice this on the menu?" He lifted the menu that his friend had left behind and pointed to the words *Gastronia Partenopea*.

"*Partenopea*," Laura read the word aloud. "Partenope?"

"Partenopese," Alfonso corrected her. "As in *of Partenope*. The word is synonymous to *Napoletano,* as in someone or something from Naples. Let me explain; this area, where Naples stands today, was founded by the Greeks as part of the Greek expansion of eighth and seventh centuries BC—Magna Grecia. At first, it was a small settlement, then came the military and commercial ports. And they erected an acropolis and such on the hill behind us." Alfonso paused before adding, "You know that Naples is pretty much a large hill by the bay, right? The hill today is sometimes referred to by its ancient name Pizzofalcone. You might see that name thrown around now and then. But to get back to the Greeks, they named this settlement Parthenope—in honor of the siren. And we spoke about that legend already."

"Yes, Odysseus and Circe," Laura responded like a student at lecture. She picked up her wine glass and sipped.

"Precisely," Alfonso said it like a proud professor. He then readjusted his posture and relaxed his eyes, as if he just remembered he was not at a lecture. "Sorry, I seem to put on my professor hat without realizing it."

"No, that's fine," Laura replied and brushed his shoulder. His hard, round shoulder. She felt a spark, then let go immediately, embarrassed she had gotten physical. She sipped her drink again and added, "This is all very interesting to me, as you know. You're right; it fits right in with my theme."

"I know," Alfonso remarked. "I was curious about your theme when you first told me about it—when we first met at the signing. But you ran off so quickly and didn't give me a moment to ask you."

"Sorry," Laura blushed. "I had a lot happening that day." She didn't know how to respond, so she brought the topic back. "You mentioned the settlers had named the city Parthenope. When did it become Naples? How did the name change? War?"

"Well, not really," Alfonso took the bait and continued. "The city of Parthenope was flourishing; its ports thriving, allowing the city to grow. Over time, though, maybe centuries, the Greeks built a new city, which eventually swallowed up Parthenope. And the new city, they called it simply *new city*—Neapolis…which eventually became Naples. So, this is why, to this day, you see the description of things from here as *Napoletano* or sometimes *Partenopese.*"

"I appreciate you sharing the realist perspective on this city with me," Laura replied. "I mean, the siren story is a romantic one, but, of course, it never gives us a true answer to history."

"Well, if you want romance," Alfonso leaned in. "There is another romantic story that is connected to this city."

Laura wasn't certain if Alfonso said it to come on to her, or if there really was an additional story. She gave him another coy look and said, "And what story is that?" *What am I doing?* she thought to herself, shaking her head.

"Well, apart from the tragic story of the siren," Alfonso replied. "There's the romance of a beautiful, young Greek woman, who was promised to a man but was in love with another. She ran from Greece with her love and they sailed here—with those settlers I had mentioned. They settled and spent their life together here. They had children and so on…some refer to her as the mother of Naples. Well, that was a story told in literature, so again— legends," Alfonso ended with a shrug.

"Legends are inspiring," Laura said but didn't know why she said it. The comment added absolutely nothing to the discussion. She cringed at the thought of her sounding juvenile. In the end, she blamed it on the wine. "Thank you for that insight, Pr—"

"Alfonso," he reminded her.

"Alfonso," she repeated. Calling him by his first name didn't feel right, but she reminded herself that he wasn't her professor, and she wasn't his student. To her, Alfonso was the author of a book he had signed. He was a lecturer for a research excursion. She was *not* his student, she reminded herself again. She was *not* his student.

CHAPTER 34

THE VIEW FROM the Castel Sant'Elmo fortress reminded Nick why tourists made the effort to come up to Vomero. Set high up on the hill, the space allowed one to look down at the whole city of Naples, the gulf, and the eminent sleeping giant, known as Vesuvius.

The sight of the volcano always gave Nick the illusion of a god-like presence looming over Naples and its people. But should the sleeping giant awake, was it guarding the city or threatening it?

Vesuvius was almost like a controlling abuser that fed on the fear of its people's imaginations. It was evident by its historically destructive past. Similar to the popular ruined city of Pompeii, its other trophied city of Herculaneum lay at the volcano's massive base.

Herculaneum—clearly a name derived from the famed demi-god Hercules, the same demi-god of which Vesuvius was itself named. Nick remembered his lessons from childhood. A teacher explained that the word *Ves* was another name for *Zeus*. *Vesuvius* translated to *son of Zeus*. He then tried to remember which of Hercules's labors took place in the area, but was soon ashamed he couldn't remember any of the tasks, nor much of the legend.

Or was the region just his resting area? Nick soon regretted not being a better student back then—and abandoned his thinking.

He continued around the fortress' rooftop to the café, located in one of the white buildings. He opened the glass door and found a woman seated alone at a table by one of the panoramic windows overlooking the city and bay below. She placed her sparkling drink on the table and was too busy reading documents to even notice Nick approach.

"Ms. Camporizzo?" Nick said it softly, hoping he had found her.

"Yes?" She looked up at him, removed her oversized glasses, and smiled. "Mr. Terenzi." She stood up and shook his hand. True to her people, she wore a green pantsuit with that Italian skill that makes anything look expensive. "Thank you for meeting me on such short notice. And please, call me Silvia." Her thick locks of brown and gray hair flowed just past her shoulders and bounced as she indicated for Nick to join her.

"Is it safe to talk here?" Nick responded.

"Oh, yes, yes," she replied and gestured for him to sit.

Nick looked around and noticed no one paying attention to them.

"It's fine, really," Silvia assured him.

"I was surprised you called me, actually," he said and finally sat down. "Gaetano…"

"Yes, tragic." Silvia looked down solemnly, then out at the bay through the window. "Are you okay?"

"Me?" Nick wasn't expecting that question. "I'm fine, thank you. I just didn't know why he did it. What happened to him? Why did this happen?"

"These are all questions we ask when someone passes," her response was sprinkled with a moment of indifference. "But, we all know, these are questions very difficult to, and sometimes never, answered." She shuffled through her papers and continued, "I was asked to contact you directly. I work here, at the Ministry, for the Environmental and Cultural Heritage. The department I work for focuses on Greco-Roman antiquities. Mr. Pentolino had mentioned that he may have come across an item we were seeking, and it turns out you may have had that item?"

"I'm sorry," Nick was confused. "But I thought you asked me here to talk about Gaetano's situation. You mentioned he had been in danger? What kind of danger? And does that mean I'm in danger too?"

"Mr. Pentolino was involved with a lot of unsavory people, as you know," she replied. "When we heard of his tragedy last night, we knew he was on to something big. Immediately, we assumed it had to do with some items that he may have been involved in. So, we are making calls to anyone he may have been dealing with recently."

"Are you investigating his death?"

"No," she chuckled. "The police handle all that. We are involved in a different manner. His business affairs, really."

"How did you get my name?" Nick asked.

"From Mr. Pentolino, of course," her response came at him with such a confidence that it demanded acceptance.

"When was the last time you spoke with him?" Nick pushed.

"A few days ago, I believe." Silvia adjusted her position and leaned in. "You see, we suspected another buyer was affecting our dealings. And again, who knows? That other buyer could be the danger. But, again, that's a matter for the police." She gestured to her papers and continued, "We had reached out to Mr. Pentolino and asked him to solidify or confirm our agreements."

"But he didn't do that, did he?" Nick asked the question in a tone that forced the woman to stop beating around the bush. Silvia sat back stunned. "Why did you call me today?"

"Well, to work out an agreement with you, of course."

"Because you weren't successful in sealing the deal with him."

"Yes, I admit that, now that he's passed, God rest his soul, we are concerned that the deal will not be completed."

"I have to tell you." Nick sat back. "I'm surprised you called me here. I thought you had information for me about Gaetano's passing. About the danger he was in. I thought you wanted to help me."

"Of course, we want to help you, Mr. Terenzi." Her tone revealed concern that she was losing whatever mission she had set for herself. "Being that there is some danger around, it would be best for you to rid yourself of whatever dealings you had going on with Mr. Pentolino. And as we understand, one of those dealings was set with us."

Nick was disappointed with her response—her only concern was the bracelet. Her office didn't care about Gaetano, nor did they care about the danger that could come to him. He looked away, then turned to her and said, "There was no set deal with your office."

"Yes, there was." Silvia searched through her papers. "We have a contract here…"

"Whatever contract you may have had with Mr. Pentolino, and I know you never had one, it's obviously invalid now. You do realize that, don't you?" Nick said the words as if he had some power over the situation—forgetting he didn't have the bracelet in possession anymore. However, it was clear this woman had no idea about that.

"Mr. Pentolino's passing does cause a bit of delay, of course…" Silvia squirmed and pulled out a document she was looking for. "I have, here, the agreement we had with him. If you would just take a look, and if it suits you, we'd be happy to pay the fee in full to you directly. We just want to end this pursuit."

Nick looked at the number on the document and fought to keep his jaw from dropping, to keep from showing any emotion. He looked at her and said, "Well, it's good to know the amount we're dealing with here."

"So, would you accept this offer?" her question showed enthusiasm.

"I will tell you," Nick had no idea how to respond, but tried to make it appear as if he was in control of the situation. "I'm sure you are aware that there are other buyers interested in this item. And besides…."

"Yes, we are aware," she replied. "But this is why I reached out to you. We wanted to make sure you understand the complications and danger, and the right thing to do here. That bracelet belongs in this region. Although, it may not be a true artifact, its legend is connected to this region. We'd be happy to help you locate it, but it would only be honorable to hand it over to us."

Nick was surprised by her last comment. He hadn't mentioned that he didn't have the bracelet.

"We can help," She added.

"The problem I'm having here is," Nick continued his first point. "I wasn't aware that Gaetano, Mr. Pentolino, shared any of this information with you. As I understood, his office doesn't share any information with buyers or sellers, nor buyers with buyers. So, again, my question is, how do you have this information?"

"I don't understand the confusion here, Mr. Terenzi. But it's standard practice to make dealings—"

"Without the agent that was making the deals?" Nick interrupted her.

"I'm only trying to do my job, Mr. Terenzi."

Nick contemplated her defense. He had a feeling she was not being upfront with it all. Something was throwing him off, but he couldn't put his finger on it.

"I understand your concern, of course," Silvia continued. "Rest assured. Your bracelet is in good hands with us. It belongs here, to the people, the region, its history, its legends. This is its home." Frustration began to enter her words. "You can't just hand it off to some random nobodies in Egypt or..." She transitioned direction, "You need to stop looking for it."

"Stop looking for it?" Nick looked at her, puzzled. He leaned in and asked, "Do you have information on other buyers?"

"I'm only following standard procedures." She adjusted her documents and slid them into her case. "While I do admire your protection of this sacred item, there is no reason to be this skeptical with us, Mr. Terenzi. We are the United Nations."

"How did you get this information from Gaetano?"

"I told you." She crossed her legs. "It's standard procedure. My office had the information. I thought I'd contact you directly and finalize the sale. I'm only following my duties."

"Your duties?" Nick asked. "Were you working with Gaetano directly?"

"Sometimes." She looked out the window. "It depends on the material."

"For this item—my item—did Gaetano work with you specifically?" Nick asked with growing suspicion the woman was not Gaetano's contact.

"No," she admitted. "But that doesn't mean we cannot make the exchange now. End the search."

"Why don't we go talk in your office?" Nick posed the question.

"There's no reason to bring you inside if you have no intention of making an exchange."

"Do you even work here, Silvia?"

"What kind of question is that? Of course, I work here!"

"I have a feeling you are not being upfront with me. Something is not right. I can't figure it out, but I will tell you: Gaetano was adamant in not sharing details with anyone on any exchange. I don't know how you got my information, but it makes me uncomfortable that you do." Nick stood up. "Ms. Camporizzo, while I appreciate you contacting me, I cannot make the exchange with you."

"Why not?" she replied with surprise.

"To be honest, I don't believe anything you're saying," Nick replied and walked toward the exit. "And it seems you know something no one else knew of—that I don't have the bracelet."

"Mr. Terenzi, you can't just leave," Ms. Camporizzo said, following him.

Nick ignored her and walked out the door.

CHAPTER 35

THE FUNICULAR DOWN to Chiaia was crowded, but Nick squeezed himself in anyway. He stood by the center door and took hold of a free handle swinging from above. To his left, sat two elderly ladies discussing some upsetting political situation that occurred recently in Rome. Nick wasn't certain what the situation was, nor what they were upset about, but their voices were loud and annoyed him. Theirs were the only voices that filled the space.

Nick knew that, although the people sounded combative, they really weren't; Italians are just passionate people, and the Napoletani were even more so. Nick reached for his phone to distract himself from the noise. The funicular continued to screech and rattle throughout its descent from Vomero. He searched for a number and upon finding it, called Lavinia's flower shop again, but the service was spotty, almost nonexistent. He waited for the funicular to pop out of a tunnel and tried the call once more. Still, no answer.

The funicular jostled to a complete stop. Passengers began to rumble, but the driver managed to get the vehicle moving almost immediately. At the final stop, the sudden rush of passengers talked over each other as they squeezed themselves out of the doors. Nick also pushed his way out, frustrated that these situations were never as organized as they could be.

He made his way through the shopping streets and looked for a place to grab a bite to eat. The aroma from the eateries around him made him hungry, his stomach burning with anticipation. All he needed was just a little something. He stopped at a kiosk selling toasted grilled sandwiches. He ordered one with prosciutto, fior di latte and lettuce, and continued down to the park and made his way back toward the old center.

He called Lavinia's shop again—determined someone was bound to answer. A car horn broke his concentration, and a driver shouted at him for walking across the street without looking. Nick gave the man a gesture and picked up his pace along the park.

He looked down at his phone and hadn't realized it was still calling the shop, but noticed the call had been picked up. He put the phone back to his ear and spoke, "Hello? Hello?" but heard an automatic voice talking. The message was said in Italian. It was Lavinia's voice, soft, raspy and welcoming: "…we will not be in the shop this week as we are working on an incredible installation for exhibition at Palazzo Fondi. The installation will be open to the public starting…"

Another car horn—not directed at him this time—drowned out the rest of the message. Fed up, Nick ended the call and pulled up the map. Palazzo Fondi was located not far from the main university. The closest metro stop was back at the funicular stop. Rather than backtrack, he chose to continue forward, toward the center. He didn't typically use a rideshare app, but he checked it anyway. No car was immediately available in the area.

He continued walking while keeping an eye out for a taxi along the way.

Just as he reached the end of the park, he felt tight grasps on both of his arms. Before he was able to acknowledge what had happened, he was forced into a doorway.

CHAPTER 36

HE CAME TO, restrained and foggy. The last thing he remembered was feeling three blows to his abs, face, and back before being pinned to the ground.

"Let me go," he shouted at the men who held him against a wall and attempted to escape from their hold. "What's going on?"

The men said nothing. Nick continued to struggle, but with every move, their grips tightened. He looked past them and noticed he was being held in a dark space with overly high ceilings and orange-yellow lights shining through archways. The air was cool. It was too deep to be a basement. Nick realized he was taken down to the tunnels underneath the city. In the distance, he heard the sound of a metal door unlocking.

"Help!" he shouted, his voice echoing throughout the space. "I'm being mugged. Help me! I'm over here!"

A painful blow to his abdomen shut him up. He keeled over, the men allowing him to fall to the ground.

The sound of footsteps entered the space. Nick heard them walk closer and closer. The men that held him stepped back. Nick lifted himself to his knees and worked at catching his breath.

"Mr. Terenzi," the man's voice was deep; English with a mixed Mediterranean accent. "Please stand up."

Nick looked at him and locked eyes with a distinguished-looking man with white furrowed brows, and a scar that ran across one of them, staring back at him. "Who are you?" Nick coughed as he spoke. "Why..."

"No, no, no," the man interrupted. "I ask the questions here." He then nodded to one of the men standing behind Nick.

The man brought over a chair and placed it behind his boss.

"I won't bore you with details, Mr. Terenzi," he said when he took his seat. Nick noticed a scar across his left cheek. The man continued, "And please, believe me when I say, I'm sorry for the dramatic surroundings, but to be quite frank, I've lost my patience and now that we have you, this can all be over."

Nick had no idea who the man was, nor what he was going on about, but he knew it had to do with the bracelet.

"Am I supposed to know who you are and what you want from me?" Nick's words fell out of his mouth before he could stop himself. He added, "Forgive me, but there's been a lot going on lately..."

The man smiled at him and nodded to his men again. The punch hit Nick on the side of his ribs, causing a slight loss of breath.

"What the fuck?" Nick breathed out his words. "Who the hell are you?"

"We had business with your friend, Mr. Pentolino," the elegant man responded, stood up, and paced around Nick. "I'm sorry for what happened to him. Very tragic."

"Was that you?" Nick replied.

His question was answered with another punch.

"Now, now, Mr. Terenzi." The man turned to face Nick. "As I think I understood, you were the one that was with him at the time of his death."

Nick's anxiety began to grow within him. Was this man an investigator? Was he accusing Nick of murder? Was he working with the police? Nick stood up straight, breathed out, and composed himself. The man stopped pacing and looked at him.

Nick asked, "Who are you?"

"We don't like playing games," the man continued. "In fact, I have absolutely no patience for them. I'd suggest you start the talking, Mr. Terenzi…" The man signaled to another man, who then showed Nick a photo. It was of Gaetano leaning over his balcony, behind him was a faint view of Nick's face, visible within the frame. Nick looked at the image in horror. His heart sank. .

"You see," the man continued. "Apparently, you have been noticed at the scene of the crime. And that could cost you." The man leaned in closer and added, "Now, tell me, Mr. Terenzi, are you a man who wants to play games?"

The lights in the room switched on and startled them both. The area had brightened as if by daylight. They all looked around, but saw no one new in the space around them. The distinguished scar-faced man sent one of the men to investigate.

Nick assessed the space and confirmed he was in the tunnels. To the far left were the pathways he had once taken on a tour. Further away, he saw the decrepit vehicles and motorcycles covered in dust.

Nick was still heaving from pain. The man grabbed his face and examined it under the light. He then turned to his men. "Didn't

I specifically tell you guys not to make any obvious marks?! Who did this?"

His two remaining henchmen looked at each other, then looked back at him. The elegant man shook his head in disappointment and turned back to Nick. "Now, Mr. Terenzi," the man continued. "I will tell you that we visited your apartment, but you weren't there. So, I'm sure you'll understand that we decided to look for what we came for. However, it wasn't to be found. Why don't you just tell us where it is, and we can let this go? No, wait…I'll even burn the photograph. No one will know you were with Gaetano when he…well, died."

"I…" Nick struggled in his response. *Who is this man? Would he really frame me?* "You had a deal with Gaetano?"

"Yes," the man replied. "He had found what we were looking for, and we learned you had it."

Nick didn't respond.

The one man returned and reported that the lights were on an automatic timer. That tour groups were probably about to begin the afternoon shifts. The man nodded and turned back to Nick.

"Terenzi," He continued, "When we were informed that the item in question—and I think you know the item of which I am speaking—was possibly stolen from us, we had to take other measures."

The man paused. Nick watched him collect his thoughts, or was he just trying to create some dramatic effect? The man continued. "Yes, Gaetano eventually shared the details with me; that you were his seller. And so, we have been looking for you ever since," he said, sitting in his seat again. "But when we heard you were going to sell it to Egypt, we, sadly, had to take matters into our own hands. Of course, the police have no inclination that Mr.

Pentolino was *helped* to his sad end, and no one, of course, knew who was there." The man tapped his chin and reached for the photograph again. "But this photo, here, could give them a nice story—if we were to share it with them."

"So, you're going to frame me for Gaetano's death?" Nick asked the obvious. Anger had begun to grow inside of him. This man had just admitted to causing Gaetano's death, and now he was threatening to frame Nick for it. Just who the hell was he?

"Well, I don't like getting involved, really," the man replied.

"Did you ever think that maybe you shouldn't get involved?" the words dropped out of Nick's mouth as if it were automatic. He wished he could just hit the backspace button and delete the phrase.

The man flared his nostrils, nodded to one of his men, whom landed a perfect punch onto Nick's back. Nick keeled onto the floor, feeling the sting all over him. He was propped up again, back to standing.

"Shall we keep going?" the deep voice cut through Nick like a bullet. "Let's make sure you and I understand each other."

Nick continued to catch his breath and let out a final cough. After some silence, he felt a thick hand squeeze his shoulder, prompting the soreness from the punches to rise up. "Ahh… Stop. Stop! Okay! Yes! Okay!" he cried out and fell over as soon as the grip had loosened. He winced. His left ribs throbbed with pain. He straightened himself again. His mind began to think about ways he could escape the situation. But he was trapped— surrounded by three men, including the scarred elegant man. His ribs were sore but he was fine. He adjusted his shoulders and gestured for the man to continue.

"Tell me, Mr. Terenzi," the man commanded. "Do you have it? Tell me, now."

Nick didn't want to respond. He didn't want to confirm to this man that he had the item in question. That he was actually involved. On the other hand, if he were to deny it all, the man would know he was lying. Either way, Nick believed there was no coming out of the situation easily. This man wanted that bracelet, and Nick now wanted to find a safe way out.

"Yes," Nick whispered it, then repeated it louder. "Yes. The bracelet. I had it."

"*Had* it?" the man asked in surprise. "What do you mean had it? Do you no longer have it? Did you actually sell it to the Egyptians?"

"No, I mean..." Nick stammered. "I don't know. Gaetano led the transaction. He finally paid me, but I don't know who bought it," he offered as a potential ending.

"No..." the man replied. "That is incorrect. Why do you lie to me?"

"I'm not lying," Nick said it with conviction. "That was it. End of story."

"You just let Geatano sell it? And you took his money? And then he jumped?" the man prodded.

"No," Nick stammered. "I mean, yes. Well, I left," Nick maintained his confidence. "And I want to get away from all this."

"Hmm..." The man sat on the edge of his seat, pondering the response. "You just left." His tone indicated disbelief.

"I took my money," Nick added. "I counted it, then argued with him about the amount..."

"Yes?"

"And I had had enough of him and the whole thing, so I left. I didn't want to be involved with any more of the bullshit."

"You just gave him the bracelet and you left," The man kept repeating, then added, "Why did he jump?"

Nick looked into his eyes. He didn't know what to say. The image of Gaetano looking at him, with a worried expression, silently. He just looked at Nick and jumped. Nick was still in shock.

"What did you do?" The man asked.

"Nothing!" Nick blurted. "I did nothing. I went for my money. I don't know why he jumped. I don't know…"

"He was helped wasn't he?"

"What?"

"Mr, Terenzi," The man leaned in. "As I said. We have photos of you on that balcony peering over just after he fell."

Nick's body shook. This man was threatening him and he didn't know how to respond.

"Then you left," the man continued. "And what did you do? You decide to visit with UNESCO. That doesn't sound like very innocent now, does it?"

"Were you following me?" Nick asked, trying to change the focus, but the man didn't bite.

"So." The man crossed his legs, rested his elbow on the arm of the chair, and held his chin as he pondered before asking his next question. "Where is the money?"

Concern creeped back into Nick's head. The man seemed to have known more than he was letting on. Nick maintained his look of innocence. "I left with an envelope of money. That's all," he repeated.

"So, when did you and how did you manage to take the bracelet back?" the man asked again.

"What?"

"Yes," the man encouraged him with a smile, as if he was playing a game. Clearly, he wasn't going to let Nick get away with that ending. "And where is it now? As I told you, we searched your place, and we couldn't find it. It doesn't seem to be there. So, where is it?"

"I…" Nick dragged out that first letter as he read the face of the man before him. Was the man going to flip in a rage if he continued to delude him? "I think that was a question for Gaetano, but…" The man knew, and Nick had been played. Nick frantically thought about ways to get out of the situation alive. "Listen," Nick finally said. "How am I supposed to know what Gaetano did with it? He mentioned a buyer here and a buyer there, I just asked him to get me the biggest bid." Nick kept pushing it back to Gaetano—the now dead connection. He hoped by repeating it, the man would eventually accept it. *Isn't that how gaslighting works?*

The man flared his nostrils and breathed out heavily. He did not like the response. He clearly had had enough. He stood up and said, "Mr. Terenzi, I know you still have the bracelet. Why do you insist on this pain?"

That was it: Nick was caught. He knew he was in danger. He had to get away. "Yes," he finally relented. "Okay. Fine. Yes. I have the bracelet. Well, had it…And feel terrible about it now. I didn't think Gaetano would be killed over it."

"Well," the man opened his arms, satisfied with Nick's admittance. "There you go. You remembered." He sat down again and continued, "Wait…what did you do with it?"

"Listen," Nick defended himself. "I didn't know what it was, really. To be honest, I didn't really like it—it's ugly. But Gaetano made me understand it had some value, although I never thought it would cause his death. I feel really terrible about that." Nick let out a deep breath after he spoke. He let it all out. He was done with it. He wanted it to end—the situation he was in at the moment, all of it. He was done with the life. He should never have taken the bracelet to Gaetano, and then never should have delayed Gaetano's deal after he did. He looked up at the man who sat in silence, taking in all he had spurted out.

"It is a shame, Mr. Terenzi," the man finally responded. "Gaetano is dead because of your petty greed. That is a true shame. But where is it now? You don't have it?"

"I feel horrible," Nick replied. He didn't know what to tell the man. He didn't want to put Lavinia in danger. He needed to get to her first and get the bracelet back.

"Where is it?" the man asked again.

"Somewhere safe," Nick replied. "I'll have to get it."

"We have been looking for that bracelet for years, you know," the man responded. "My radar was on that thing for a long, long time. When we finally had it, and it disappeared again, I was devastated—truly. It was right in our fingers, after all these years—and then, *poof*, gone."

"How did you find me?"

"Oh, Mr. Terenzi, that is irrelevant. The main question here is, where is the bracelet?"

"It's not here," Nick replied. "But, it's close by. I have it stored in a safe place."

"Well, go get it."

"I can't get it right now."

"Mr. Terenzi," the man's nostrils flared again.

"I mean, I can get it, but not at this very moment." Nick thought about it before asking, "If I bring it to you, will you burn that photograph?"

"Ha!" the man's laugh was genuine. "You are a very funny man. If you were to bring it to me, I would destroy the image, yes, *and* I would pay you. But why would I trust you to bring it to me?"

"Because I'm done with this. I didn't realize how much danger it would bring me. I want it out of my possession. I'll bring it to you, and we'll be done with the whole thing. Sound good?"

The man contemplated Nick's offer. When he reached into his front inside pocket, Nick shuddered. He was convinced the man would pull out a gun and end it. Instead, the man's hand resurfaced with nothing.

"We will come for you again," the man stood up. "I expect you to have the bracelet when we do. And when you retrieve the item, please keep it discreet. I don't want anyone to know." He then turned and walked out of view, into the darkness and through the metal door.

Nick looked at the two men who indicated for him to follow them up the stairs, through another door, and onto the street.

His eyes took some time to adjust to the bright sunlight. When he looked again, the men were gone. Nick stood still, shaken and frightened. He gathered his bearings and picked up his pace toward Palazzo Fondi to find Lavinia.

CHAPTER 37

NICK RUBBED HIS left torso, as he sat in the back of a taxi he had barely been able to lift his arm to hail. The pain from the beatings was now coming, and he hoped the marks on his face weren't too obvious. He almost forgot how roughly the men had handled him. They dragged him down the Bourbon tunnels with such force. He wondered why there were no visitors in those tunnels. It was midday, and, usually, those tunnels were filled with at least one tour group.

The entrance to the Palazzo Fondi was unmanned. Nick walked through the archway and straight into the courtyard filled with walls of greenery, flowers, and other live botanical décor. According to the sign at the entryway, the space was hosting a themed exhibit on the effect climate change has on art. A group of staff members were building a cocktail kiosk, while others were securing green hanging moss, giving it the appearance of a curtain.

And there she was, standing by the curtain, directing the women who were then making the adjustments. He walked over to Lavinia and discreetly grabbed her arm.

"We need to talk," Nick said to her in a low voice.

"Nick," she replied with a somewhat relieved tone, but her look offered a hint of shock. "What are you doing here? You missed me already?"

Nick held onto her arm and pulled her away. She excused herself to the staff and followed, or rather led him to a nook in the far back of the courtyard.

"You took my bracelet," Nick seethed. "Where is it?"

"What happened to you?" Lavinia asked. She looked into his eyes and then at his face. She reached her hand to his left cheek and touched what must have been a bruise. Nick flinched at her contact and brushed her hand away.

"Just tell me where it is," he said. "I don't even want to know why you took it. I just need it. Where is it?"

"Nick, what happened to you?"

"Tell me, Lavinia," Nick insisted. "Just give it back to me, and I won't ask questions. Please, just give it back."

"What are you talking about?"

"Don't play stupid," he responded with an angrier tone. "I don't have patience for that right now. Just give it to me. Now."

"No," Lavinia dropped the word with a final conviction.

"No? What do you mean *no?*"

"It doesn't belong to you," she responded and turned back to the installation. "Now, leave. I must get back to work."

"Are you serious right now?" Nick's fury forced the words out louder than he had anticipated.

"Please, keep your voice down," Lavinia said. "You're making a scene."

"Give me back my bracelet," Nick demanded.

Lavinia looked at him and cocked her head with disappointment.

"Where is it?" he asked again.

Lavinia looked past Nick and signaled to the security guards standing behind him. Nick's body stung as the men grabbed hold of him. Lavinia looked Nick in the eyes, said nothing, and turned back to her installation.

"Lavinia!" Nick shouted toward her. "Come back here!" The guards pulled Nick away from the art installation and out of the courtyard.

"You can't do this!" Nick continued to shout. The men only forced him out through the archway. "You can't just take it! It's mine! I need it!" Nick was finally pushed onto the sidewalk, almost falling over into Via Medina.

"She stole from me, you know," he said to the guards and straightened himself up. "You're not even real policemen."

"Do you want us to contact the carabinieri?" One of the security guards retorted and called out to the man in the entry booth. "Pasqua'!"

"No, no," Nick replied. "No carabinieri. I'll leave."

"Very good," the man replied, watching Nick walk away in defeat.

Chapter 38

LAURA FELT THE professor slide his arm closer to hers as he took her hand. At first touch, a shock ran through her body. She stiffened. Another vision was about to take control.

Flash of naked flesh. Man and woman. The man pressing his lips on the woman's inner thigh, her torso, and her arm.

Flash of the naked woman standing with her back to the man. Her wavy, black hair hanging down her back. Her arms stretched in the air as she chanted.

Flash back to the coupling. The woman reaches down to caress the man's face—it was the professor!

Laura flinched and pulled her hand away. She looked at the professor who had been watching her in confusion.

"Are you feeling alright?" he asked.

The effect his voice had on her had changed from seduction to suspicion. The vision made no sense to her. Why would she be shown him making love to some woman? Was she of significance? Who was the woman with the long, black hair? Was this woman supposed to represent her? Were her fantasies mixing in with her visions? Or was it real? Was it a warning? She stared into his eyes, looking for more, but no other image came to her.

"Laura?" his voice offered genuine concern. "Is something wrong?"

"Uhh," she didn't know how to respond. She wanted to stall while remaining focused on him. She wanted more of that vision, but she didn't know if she could even force another image. "I'm fine. Sorry. My head sometimes...headache."

"Headache? Too much wine?" he asked with a chuckle and took the final sip from his glass. "Should we go then? Do you need to lay down?"

He was saying words that had normally sounded seductive to her. She liked him wanting her. She liked imagining that every word from his mouth was an attempt to seduce her. *Do you want to lay down?* She would have thought to herself, *With you? Yes!* But, she didn't now. For the moment, that fantasy was turned off.

She nodded in response and gathered her bag. She followed him to thank his chef friend and then out the door.

"Thank you for lunch, Professor."

"Alfonso, please," he replied. "And it was my pleasure." He opened his arms and leaned in for a kiss.

Laura turned his attempt into a platonic embrace. As she caressed his toned forearm, another flash of her vision shook her. *Naked flesh. Candlelight. Intense passion.*

"So, what do you think?" The professor asked. Had he said something prior to this? If he did, she didn't hear it. She pulled away, and the professor continued. "Would you be interested? I'm only going for the day, and we would be back in time to join the excursion to Benevento tomorrow."

"Are you asking me to join you?" She didn't know what he was talking about. She blocked him out as she tried focusing on her vision. "Where?"

"The coast," he replied. "It's a beautiful drive along the coast. Then, we'll stop for dinner at this amazing place I know. The most delicious seafood."

Laura stiffened. The man was asking her to spend more time with him. This could mean he was interested in her romantically. She hoped she wasn't blushing.

"I don't want to take you from your research, of course," Alfonso continued. "But you are working on Greek influence in the area, no?"

"Yes."

"Well, the coast was important to the Greek myths. And, further south, there's even ruins of a temple." Alfonso dangled the sights that Laura was clearly enticed to want to see.

Laura didn't know why she had to contemplate his offer. Why not spend more time with Alfonso? He was handsome. He was available—or so she hoped. He wanted to spend time with her, and she wanted to spend time with him. So, why not? She had no real reason not to go with him.

"We'll probably be back really late," she remarked.

"Yes, but who cares?" The professor replied with excitement. "Let's just go. Life's short."

"Okay," Laura replied with a smile. "Yes. Thank you."

"Great! I'll go get my car."

"I'll have to go back and drop my books off. Where should I meet you?"

"I can take you," the professor offered. "We just have to go get the car." He looked around for a taxi, but none were in sight.

"Let's just take the metro," Laura suggested.

"Alright," Alfonso agreed and followed her down the metro entrance. "I'm at Toledo."

Laura liked the metro station at the Toledo stop. In her opinion, it was one of the most beautiful in the city. She looked up at the ceiling of violet hues made from mosaic tiles meticulously placed by the contemporary artists involved in its design. As part of three stations, in what was called the Art Stations project, but the Toledo stop was the most alluring. It was probably because it is an unexpected treasure buried underneath the chaos of the bustling street above. Laura never got enough of looking up at that dome-shaped crevice in the ceiling above the escalators that took riders up to the surface on Via Toledo.

She followed Alfonso down a wide street off Via Toledo to the doorway of a large office building.

"I keep my car here when I'm in town," Alfonso explained as he waved a key and punched a code in the elevator descending to a parking garage. "It's just over here." He led her to a gray Mercedes Coupe, parked in a spot close to the elevator. With a touch of the button on his fob, the car flashed alive. He opened the passenger door and gestured for her to sit inside.

"Thank you," Laura slid into the mocha-leather seat. She waited as Alfonso climbed into the driver's side and remarked, "What a nice car. An AMG?"

"Yes! Thank you," he smiled and turned on the purring engine.

"I love the color," Laura said. "And the leather is lovely." She caressed the car seats and continued to gaze at the vehicle's interior.

"The exterior is called *Selenite Gray*," he replied. "I fell in love with it the second I saw it. I bought it a few years ago but only use it once in a while. This time, I had it brought here because I plan to go on a little road trip after my work here in Naples."

"Where are you going?"

"Up north," Alfonso replied as he pulled the car out of the garage and onto the street. "To the lakes."

"I love the lakes," Laura added.

"Have you been to the Amalfi Coast yet?"

"No."

"Well then, you're going to enjoy this." Alfonso revved the engine and drove along the water, south, out of the city.

CHAPTER 39

NICK'S DOOR WAS open a crack; the men in the tunnel really had broken in. Nick wondered if any of them were left behind to 'take care of him'. He contemplated turning around and running from his apartment building, but his anger won him over. The idea of someone rummaging through his stuff, mixed with his anger from being thrown out of the museum, gave him the blind courage to investigate.

He approached the door, paused, and listened. There was only the sound of the cars from the street below. A window must have been open. Immediately, he was reminded of Gaetano's apartment and Gaetano's fall to his death. He cringed; overcome with the desire to turn away and run back to him, but his anger, again, washed the fear away.

He looked through the crack and saw no movement. He put his hand on the door and gently pushed it open. To his surprise, the entry hall seemed to be in order. He stepped in and peeked into the open doors of the kitchen, bathroom, and bedroom. Nothing out of sorts.

He looked in the living room, acknowledging his desk, the book cases, and coffee table. Nothing appeared to have been handled. He went back, locked the front door, and exhaled with relief. He placed Gaetano's attaché back in its hiding place inside the armoire, then contemplated leaving it unattended. He picked it up and brought it into the bedroom, where he saw the window was slightly open. He closed it shut and latched it.

He was confused. Nothing appeared to be missing. *Why would someone break into his place and take nothing? Those men!* Nick felt a shudder with the thought of the men going through his stuff. They really did come for the bracelet. But would they have left with nothing? His laptop! He rushed back into the living room. The computer was where he had left it. The papers next to it were placed neatly beside it—not the messy piles he normally kept.

He flipped through the papers, seeing they were all notes on the bracelet, including some words related to Gaetano's mention of potential buyers. The notes of Laura's visions were still there too. Whomever had come in must have read the papers and placed them all back in the neat pile. Did they find the information they were looking for? And if so, what exactly was that information?

Wait! Laura! Nick looked through the papers again, searching for any hint of where Laura could be. If the person broke in to find information on the bracelet, and they found notes on Laura instead—another person potentially involved—then she could be in danger.

Nick flipped through more pages and saw his notes on Lavinia. Could Lavinia be in trouble too? If this perpetrator is after the bracelet, they could be looking for her. *Wait. Lavinia had broken in before. Maybe she was back again.*

Nick walked over to the windows. He continued to lock them all, including all the doors to the apartment. As he did, the pain in his shoulder and torso spiked. He needed to take some time to recover, to soothe his pain. He lowered himself onto the couch and paused, eventually falling asleep.

He woke, taking in his surroundings. He composed himself, realizing he was on his couch. The room was still filled with sunlight; how long had he slept? He struggled getting up from the couch and shuffled into the bathroom. He splashed water on his face, then turned to the bathtub. He ran warm water to fill it and went back into the living room.

He picked the attaché up from the floor and brought it into his bedroom. He opened the oversized oak armoire, pulled the bottom drawer, lifted his underwear, and slid the attaché underneath. The movements caused pain in his torso again. He winced, breathed, and put everything back into the drawer. He closed the armoire doors and sat on his bed to rest. He proceeded to undress, with gentle movements, so as to not bother the bruises. He shuffled back into the bathroom, stopped at the mirror, and caught a glimpse of himself. He noticed a small cut above his right eye—probably what Lavinia had referred to when she reached for him. Lavinia. He needed to get to her again. He looked more intently at his reflection; the cut was bordered by a bruise that made him flinch at the slightest touch.

The bathtub had filled, so he turned off the water and slid into the basin, testing the temperature first. He struggled to lower himself into the warm water. The muscles on his left side stung. He forced himself to sit still, allowing his body to acclimate. The warm water embraced his body, soothed every muscle, and relaxed him. He sat back and closed his eyes, letting himself escape reality—even if just for a moment.

He suddenly sat up. He couldn't wrap his head around why nothing else had been disturbed. The thought broke his relaxation. The men who broke in were not frantically searching for anything valuable. If they had come in for the bracelet, there was no desperate search for it. But what did they find? It couldn't be buyer information—Nick had the attaché with him. But still, the notes on Laura were there on his desk. Was Laura in danger? He needed to get to Lavinia again. He needed to get that bracelet. But first, he needed to make sure Laura was safe.

He slipped as he rushed out of the bathtub, water splashing all over the bathroom floor. He grabbed a towel and dabbed at his body as he ran into his bedroom for his phone. He made the call and continued to dry himself. Although less, the pain on his side hurt, but he ignored it either way.

The door buzzer broke his concentration. Nick continued to listen as his phone attempted to reach Laura, but ultimately, there was no answer. The door buzzed again. He went into the hallway and looked at the monitor. It was Lavinia. She looked upset, almost annoyed. Immediately, he buzzed her in.

"Who do you think you are, showing up at my work like that? You looked like a madman about to attack me! You need to stop. Leave me alone. It's over. Stop with all of this…this…pursuit! Or whatever you're trying to do. It's done."

"Done? Lavinia, you took my—"

"It was not yours! Stop saying it was yours. It was never yours. It doesn't belong to you. It doesn't belong to the government. It doesn't belong in Egypt. It belongs with us. Not you. Not anyone else."

"Us who?" Nick responded. "And if you really wanted it, all you had to do was pay Gaetano—"

"Pay Gaetano? Are you mad? Why would I pay for something that was ours? This belonged to us. It was taken many years ago, and we finally have it back. No one is going to take it again. Do you hear me? You need to stop."

"Lavinia, what are you going on about? I didn't take it from anyone..."

"Oh, really? Then how did you have it?"

"I bought it. A while ago, up in Rome."

"From whom?"

"Some merchant...it wasn't a big deal..."

"Now you insult me even further. This had absolutely no meaning to you. Of course, it didn't—you are a stupid man. Why would it?"

"Hey!"

"Why are you determined to stalk me and take it from me? It doesn't belong to you. You've just admitted it has no meaning to you. Why do you trouble me?"

"Lavinia, you stole it from *me!* Who do you think you are to come in and just take it? It does belong to me. I bought it!"

"It doesn't belong to you, and you, nor I, no longer have it. It's gone."

"You sold it?! You owe me money!"

"Money? Is that all you fools think about? Money? Ridiculous. Move on."

"Move on? Are you crazy? I can't just let you steal that from me then forget it. I was selling it."

"I know that. That is why I took it. I wasn't going to lose sight of it again."

"You mean you've seen it before? Why is it so important to you?"

"I'm very sorry, Nick. It doesn't matter to you, anyways. It belongs with us."

"Who's *us?* And, of course, it matters to me. It's *mine!* I found it!"

"Well, we thank you for finding it. And fine—we would be willing to compensate you with *money* if that's what will shut you up and keep you away. I'm just glad I was able to get it before you let it get lost again."

"What is it about this bracelet?"

"You don't even know? That infuriates me even more."

"Lavinia," he said, trying to calm his voice. "Please, let's just talk this out. Let me understand why you are doing this. I'll be fine with selling it to you if you can just explain to me why you did this."

"Why would I bother to waste my time with you any longer? I don't have to give you anything."

"But you do."

"Or what? You'll go to the police? Ha! We both know you won't be doing that."

"Oh, really? And why not?"

"How is your friend, Gaetano, by the way? I haven't seen him around...He was steering you in the wrong direction, you know. So, I had to get involved."

"Did you kill him?"

"Me? Ha! I wasn't on that balcony with him."

"What?"

"As I understand, *you* were there when he took his little fall…"

"I didn't do anything! That's false. Where did you hear—?"

"Listen to me," Lavinia softened her tone. "This will all go away if you just back off, turn away, and move on. It's over."

"It's not over. The bracelet was mine, and I was going to sell it."

"I understand. You want money. We'll get it to you. But I promise you, we will not be giving you what Gaetano was asking. So, how much will it take?

"Tell me first."

"Tell you what?"

"What is it? Why do you want it?"

"You don't need those details. How much?"

"Lavinia, you can't just take the bracelet and tell me to move on. I was selling that bracelet and for a lot of money."

"Yes, I said I understand that, but I couldn't take the chance that Gaetano was not going to sell it to me. So, I had to take matters into my own hands. I discovered you were the seller, then I tracked you down. I followed you. Eventually, I made my approach."

"Did you know who I was when we first met at the bar?" Nick asked.

Lavinia didn't respond.

"Lavinia," Nick continued. "if you want the bracelet, I'm fine with that. But you need to pay me, matching the highest bidder."

"Why would I do that? As I told you before, this was taken from us—"

"I don't care. I didn't take it. I found it. I bought it."

"Yes. After some consideration, I realize a finder's fee is only fair."

"Finder's fee? You're *buying* this from me—full price."

"It will not be your full price. It was never yours to sell. You will get your money next week."

"Lavinia, this isn't some *oggi a otto* situation. You don't get to take the bracelet then pay later. There's no credit situation here. You pay me now. Or you give me back what's mine—what I found. And when you have the money, maybe then you can have it. But believe me when I say that the sooner I get rid of it, the better it is for me. As you can see, that thing is already getting me into situations I'm not happy with. Gaetano had warned me too."

"What happened to you?" Lavinia asked, her tone offering a genuine concern. She caressed his arm. "What warning?"

"You're not the only one interested in this bracelet, you know."

"Who else approached you?"

"Well, the people at UNESCO for one. At least, I hope she was from UNESCO."

"What? Who?"

"And then there's this." Nick pointed to his face.

"Who did that?"

"I don't know who he was," Nick replied. "Some man with a group of other men—I have no idea who the hell any of them are. His accent was unrecognizable."

"Well, was he English, American, Italian…Spanish, Greek?"

"I honestly couldn't place it…maybe it was…"

"Oh, forget it," Lavinia brushed him off. "Gaetano shared enough information with me. This was why I had to take it. I was afraid you would get rid of it, and we would lose it again. Who were these men?"

"I told you," Nick replied. "I don't know."

"And you think these men that did this to you have an idea of where it is?"

"No. Maybe. I don't think so."

"So, you are in danger again?"

"Yes. I need to bring that bracelet to the right place. Get it off my back."

"Well, it is in its right place. It's with us. You work out your own problems. And yes, I will get you the money."

"When you say *us*, who do you mean? Are you working for someone?"

"I'm sure we can agree on a price…"

"No, Lavinia," Nick leaned into her. "Did you hear what I said? Those men attacked me today. They know where I live. They have been watching me, following me. They know who I've been talking to. They want that bracelet."

Lavinia flinched. Nick watched as she processed what he was telling her. Did she realize that she, too, was probably in danger?

"Lavinia, these men expect me to bring the bracelet to them."

"Do they know I have it?"

"No, I don't think they do. I didn't tell them you do, anyways."

"Good," she replied. "And I'm sorry…"

"For what?" Nick asked just as the needle poked into his neck.

CHAPTER 40

THE ROAD WAS a narrow two-way route along the coastal mountains that hugged the Mediterranean coast. It curved along the edge of the natural formations, and if it wasn't for the incredible view, Laura would think it dangerous. Alfonso commanded his Mercedes as he swerved away from vespas and little trucks that appeared out of nowhere. At times, Laura closed her eyes but then reminded herself to look at the incredible view.

The Mediterranean glistened in the early summer sun. Its deep, teal water hosted a scattering of boats belonging to fishermen and tourists alike. On its horizon, she spotted a group of islands. She knew one to be Capri—she had planned to visit there after her time in Naples.

"See that small group of islands there?" Alfonso broke her focus. "That's where it's believed Odysseus encountered the sirens."

"Oh! I read about those," Laura sat up. "Li Galli Islands or something, right? I had that on my list of places—"

"Exactly," Alfonso interrupted. "One of them is shaped like a mermaid... or dolphin, depending on what you see, really." He motored down the curving road and slowed as they entered another one of the coastal towns, pulling over before they got to it. He spoke to an attendant who instructed him where to park his car. "Come with me."

Laura followed him to a gate that led them to a set of stairs down to the water. "Where are we going?"

"You'll love this," Alfonso replied as he continued to descend. "I see there are no cars. We're so lucky there's no one here. Look!"

Laura followed his finger and saw the islands he spoke of before.

"Imagine the sirens singing their songs of treachery," Alfonso added, then continued to lead her down.

Laura looked to where they were headed and saw a handful of small boats drifting on a tiny dock at the end of the stairs. When they reached the bottom, she finally saw a sign: *Grotta dello Smeraldo.*

"Emerald Grotto?" Laura said aloud.

"Yes, and no one is here," Alfonso replied with excitement. "It's a rare occasion." He turned to the boatman and paid for the two of them. "Steady now," he said as he took Laura's hand and helped her gently step into one of the rocking, wooden boats. They were instructed to sit across from each other in the middle of the boat. The boatman nodded, winked, and roared them into the entrance of a cave.

"Down, Laura," Alfonso gestured for her to duck. Laura lowered herself as the boat passed through the narrow entrance. When they cleared the entrance, Alfonso nudged for her to sit up and look. The sight was beyond her belief.

The cave was enormous. Laura looked around in awe and disbelief. The sunlight entered from small inlets, forcing the water underneath them to glow in a bright, emerald hue. The rocks surrounding the cave reflected the light and appeared to be dancing as the water moved with each row. Laura couldn't help but think the whole experience was absolutely magical.

"Laura," Alfonso's whisper echoed around them. "Imagine the siren Partenope singing her song." Then, he sang the words, "*Tu sei Bellissima. Sei come l'acqua limpida...*" his voice was beautiful and, again, echoed around them.

Laura smiled at him. She deduced the man was a romantic, and that he was definitely trying to seduce her. "This is absolutely beautiful," she said. "Thank you."

"I'm glad you enjoy it," Alfonso replied and signaled for the boatman to take them back.

They climbed the stairs back up to the car and continued on the route.

Alfonso turned the Mercedes into a parking lot by the water and led Laura into the small town. They walked to an open piazza, to an elegant café bar. They sat at a table out front.

"You've got to try one of these," he said, then turned to the server and placed an order. "Laura," he looked back to her. "Espresso?"

"Just water for me. Thank you," Laura replied.

"So, I do want to show you the temple, but it's a bit further south," Alfonso said. "If you don't mind prolonging our adventure, I'd like to show it to you."

"I'd love to see it."

"Good, but first, let's get some dinner...there's a great spot..."

"Well, I don't want to stay out too late," Laura responded, not knowing why she said that. She was spending time with a nice, attractive man and didn't know why she was in a rush to head back to her lonely apartment.

"Oh, come on, now." Alfonso waved the thought away. "This is Italy. You have to enjoy life here. Just go with it."

She loved his devil-may-care response, just as much as she was loving getting to know the man. More and more, he was fulfilling her fantasy. But she couldn't help but feel it was too good to be true.

The server returned with a silver tray. He placed a bottle of water in front of Laura and the espresso in front of Alfonso. Then proceeded to place napkins and two dessert forks, followed by one lemon-yellow domed treat between them.

"This is called *delizia a limone*," Alfonso explained. "Lemon delight. It's made with the famous lemons of the coast. No one should leave Amalfi without trying one."

Laura's fork easily sliced into the mousse-like coating and sponge-cake interior. She lifted a morsel to her mouth and groaned with euphoria when it hit her tongue. The tang of the lemon matched perfectly with the fluffy, cream coating. The sponge cake was perfectly soft and soaked in lemon liquor.

She didn't realize they had finished when Alfonso broke her bliss. "We should get going," he said. "I really want to get out to the temple. Maybe grab some dinner on the way?"

Chapter 41

THE SERVER DELIVERED a bottle of *Fiano*—a white wine made with grapes grown in the region. Laura and Alfonso sipped while admiring the view of the sun just about to set on the Mediterranean.

"This is going to be a special meal tonight, Laura," Alfonso quipped. "You're going to taste a specialty from this little town that gastronomes delight."

The server returned to the table with ceviche of the day's catch, accompanied by a dish of fresh cut celery, and another dish, tiny and empty. He then displayed a little bottle of brown liquid. He poured a small amount into the tiny dish, nodded to Alfonso, and walked away.

"This is the gold of the coast," Alfonso explained. "Made in Cetara—one of these small towns. It's typically not served like this, but I asked the server to bring this with some celery for you to taste."

"What is it?" Laura reached for a celery stick and, following Alfonso's lead, gave it a gentle touch of the liquid. She put the celery to her tongue and tasted. A rush of salty seafood encompassed her mouth, filling her senses. It was like an essence of anchovy and oil. She flinched at the strong taste and looked at Alfonso, who was laughing.

"It's a strong one, isn't it?" he said. "Sorry, I should have warned you. It's used as a flavoring in pastas and such. So, a little goes a long way—as you can taste."

"I'm sorry," Laura said in between sips. "I wasn't expecting such a strong flavor. What is it?"

"No, that's my fault," Alfonso replied. "It's called *Colatura de Alici*. It's a fish sauce made from anchovies. Cetara is renowned for this. There will be some in our pasta…"

"Oh boy, that is way too strong," Laura replied while gently placing her celery on her plate.

"Don't worry," Alfonso assured. "It will only be a drop or so, just to round out the flavor. You won't taste it like that. It just adds this other level to the dish. You'll see. I just wanted you to taste it like that so you know what it is…maybe I should have had you try it after the dish."

"No, no," Laura insisted. "That's fine. I'm curious to taste the pasta. Thank you."

Alfonso offered a half smile of uncertainty. Laura smiled back in an effort to assure him she was not turned off by the gesture— she was still interested. She realized at that moment she was letting him know she was interested in him. He smiled fully in response to her and sipped his wine.

The spaghetti was served on an elegant, white plate with light touches of tiny, dark-blue fish painted along one side. Laura admired the dish itself, along with the fresh aromatic pasta in it. Laura took a mental note to best describe the scent later in her journal: *a warm, rich seafood broth without the broth*. She spun her fork into the spaghetti and took her first bite…her description fit the flavor almost exactly.

"Wow," she exclaimed.

"You like?" Alfonso asked.

"Very much." She shook her head slowly as if in disbelief. "What a difference. I'm actually glad you had me taste the sauce first. It may have enhanced this pasta experience. What a difference. The flavor is just beautiful. It's only a hint, but as you said, it rounds it out; a whole other level. Wow."

"I'm so glad to hear that," Alfonso replied with excitement. "I was worried I ruined the experience for you."

"Not at all," Laura assured him. "You did well. Thank you."

Alfonso smiled and sat back in relief. He looked proud. Laura smiled back and sipped again, not letting go of his gaze. She felt her desire for him return. She wanted him. She wanted to be with him. She wanted to know everything about him. Who was he? How was he as a child? Did he have many girlfriends? Was he a good lover? She looked away in shame, placed her glass back on the table, and noticed the time on her watch. It was getting late.

"Would you be interested…" Laura looked up at him, and he continued. "How would you feel…Would it interest you to…Do you want to stay here?"

"What do you mean?" Laura asked. Was he asking her to stay the night with him? She wasn't sure. How would she respond? Would she want to spend the night with him? *Yes. Absolutely—*

The server broke the conversation with the next course; a grilled white fish and a simple green salad. The moment passed as Alfonso and Laura dug into the fish and ate in a semi-silence, with just a sprinkle of "how delicious" and "glad you like it" in between bites.

The swerving road of the Amalfi Coast ended in the coastal port city of Salerno. Alfonso turned down the main road, along the waterfront, and continued south, following the sign indicating Paestum.

"Just how far are these temples?" Laura asked over the roar of the passing cars.

"From here" Alfonso slowed down and pulled over. "It should be about forty minutes, give or take." He fidgeted with some buttons, forcing the car's top to close up over them. "From here, we'll take the highway, getting us there faster."

"I didn't realize we'd be so far from the city," Laura remarked.

"Well, taking the coastal road extends the drive, but we'll take the highway back to Naples. From there, it will only be an hour, max." He put the car back into gear and drove onto the ramp. "I know you will appreciate these temples," Alfonso continued. "After that, we'll pop on the highway back to Naples. Good?"

"Okay," Laura really didn't think she'd be gone all afternoon and into the night. She had no choice but to go with it. However, he had never mentioned they'd be gone for so long. More time with him wasn't a bad thing, though, was it? She was actually surprised he hadn't pushed in asking her to stay the night. She was convinced that was what he was trying to do so at the restaurant. What had prompted him to not follow through?

The temples came into view on their right. One glowed orange, its light at the base, rising up and fading as it reached the top. Another was green and the other pink. Laura could see they were perfect examples of temples typically seen in Greece. Laura looked on in amazement as Alfonso drove the car around the archeological park.

"I believe that one is the temple for Poseidon," Alfonso indicated to the one closest to them. "Or Neptune, depending on what you prefer. And the others are Athena and…I think Hera, maybe…Yes, I believe it's Hera."

"I can't believe these exist." Laura rolled down her window as Alfonso slowed the car. "I didn't even know about this. How did I not know? And the lights, what's with the colors?"

"Well, maybe you limited your focus," Alfonso suggested. "Maybe putting the research only on Naples, itself, was an error. But this is why I wanted to show you. This whole region breathes ancient Greece. You should consider broadening your topic."

"I just might have to." Laura continued to stare at the temples. "I mean, I did note visiting Pompeii and Herculaneum, but never had Paestum on my list. What a fool. How could I just miss this?" She rummaged through her bag and pulled out her phone. She swiped it awake and saw a few missed calls from Nick. She opened the camera app and snapped some quick photos. Then made a note in another app. She turned to Alfonso, "I assume it's too late to visit the temples. Can people go see them up close?"

"Of course," Alfonso responded as he drove the car into a small parking lot to their left. "Let's go check it out."

The security guard post was empty when they walked past the gate. Laura followed Alfonso into the orange-lit temple—she couldn't believe they were allowed to walk within it, but she felt some comfort seeing shadows of other explorers from behind the columns.

She walked around one column, then another. She refused to touch them though—it was sacrilege to her—the idea of handling an ancient artifact. She rounded another and allowed her hand to "accidentally" brush up against it. It felt wrong. She didn't do it again.

A shadow crossed her, then another. She didn't see the people that made them. Four columns ahead, she saw something moving—a cloth in the breeze. She continued to stare at the flowing cloth until a woman revealed herself from behind the column. She was wearing a long, black dress with an oversized hood, or was it a wrap? It was like an image out of a magazine. Laura was entranced. She turned to Alfonso but couldn't find him. She looked all around her for him—still no sign.

She glanced back at the woman, who had walked behind the columns, continuing the ethereal vision. Laura was still staring when hands grabbed her and spun her around. It was Alfonso. He pulled her close and planted a passionate kiss on her lips. Laura wanted the moment. She kissed him back with equal passion. Her head began to spin, her knees became weak. She felt her body stiffen. She knew another vision was about to take control. She fought the energy, tried focusing on Alfonso's lips. She rubbed his shoulders, put her fingers through his hair. She didn't want to leave the moment. She grabbed his arm with more force than she had intended, and he responded with more passion. Images flashed.

It was the same scene—Alfonso making love to someone. Was it her? No. It was the woman with dark hair again. Naked flesh rolling around. The woman's slender arm extended, her hand caressing the professor's body. But what was dangling from the woman's wrist? Was that Nick's bracelet?

Laura shook the image away. Her head was foggy now . She toppled out of Alfonso's arms and onto the ground. She could hear Alfonso's voice, as if from afar, asking if she was okay. She opened her eyes, then blacked out.

Chapter 42

NICK AWOKE IN a small room. His head pounded. His neck sore. *What happened? What did Lavinia put in me? Where am I?* He glanced around and saw he was laying on a large bed. He sat up. When he tried to move and get off the bed, he noticed his legs were spread apart and restrained; each ankle tied to a post with a thick, black ribbon. His shirt was missing. His pants were still on, but unfastened.

He reached for his right ankle and worked at untying himself, but the ribbon was tied in multiple knots. He managed to undo the first two layers when he heard the door unlock and open. He paused and watched Lavinia walk in.

"What are you doing?!" he shouted. "Untie me! What the hell do you think you're doing?!"

"Relax, my love," Lavinia responded with a calming tone. "Are you feeling okay?"

He felt a sense of calm. He didn't understand why. Maybe it was a combination of her soft voice and the floral scent of her perfume. He felt weak.

"Untie me," he forced the demand out of his lips. "What are you doing?"

"Trying something different," Lavinia replied. Her voice continued to sooth him, and he smiled. "Lay back and relax. If you want me to untie you, I will. Do you want me to untie you?"

"What do you want to do?" Nick asked tenderly. He liked that Lavinia had turned their heat up to kinky. He leaned in to kiss her, but she retreated. "Where are you going?"

"Do you want some tea?" Lavinia asked and walked over to a table in the far corner, pouring a glass of liquid. "It's always better with the tea."

"Absolutely." Nick sat up again, although struggling to do so. He stopped abruptly and remembered the needle. "Did you drug me?"

"Oh, Nick," Lavinia replied and turned back to him with a cup in hand. "Drink this, and let's have some fun."

Nick accepted her offer and drank the warm liquid. It was room temperature. Its taste resembled a tea of licorice and maybe chamomile. It was bitter, but the scent of mint and lavender helped. He let it fill his mouth, wash his tongue, and fall down his throat. It was soothing. His body relaxed. He felt numb. His head a fog.

"I love this mix." Lavinia drank the rest, placed the glass on the side table, and guided Nick's upper body back down on the bed.

Nick looked around the room that was now spinning. He watched Lavinia lift her dress over her hips and climb onto the bed, straddling him. She lowered his loose pants, sat on him, and pinned him down while she worked her hips on him. He liked that she took the lead. He liked her controlling him. It enhanced his thrill. Lavinia held him down and looked him in the eye. Nick's head continued to spin as what they were doing was all a very real dream. He just closed his eyes and gave into the pleasure.

Chapter 43

LAURA AWOKE, TAKING in a deep breath of air. She heaved momentarily as she examined the room. It was a doctor's office. Unrecognizable. The sunlight beamed through the sheer curtains. She was parched.

She remembered she was at the temple with Alfonso. She had a vision before blacking out. A gentle knock broke her thoughts. She sat at the edge of the bed and rubbed her head. She needed water. The knock started again.

"Laura," Alfonso's voice called from the other end of the door. "Are you awake? May I come in?"

For a minute, she froze. Did something happen between them? She wasn't sure. *No*, she thought to herself. *Impossible. I'm still all dressed.*

"Alfonso?"

"Yes, are you alright?"

"Yes. Come in."

The door opened. Alfonso walked in with a bottle of water and a look of concern.

"How are you feeling?" He asked and handed her the bottle.

"I think I'm okay…" Laura rubbed her head again. "Just thirsty. Thank you." She opened the bottle and guzzled the water faster than she anticipated. She coughed. "Sorry," she said, handing him the empty bottle.

"Don't apologize. I'm just glad you're okay." Alfonso dropped the bottle into the wastebasket "The doctor said you'd be fine."

"Doctor?"

"Yes. When you collapsed, I carried you to the car and took you here. The doctor checked your vitals and assured me you were fine, that you just needed rest."

"Where are we?"

"I had to go inland, not far from Paestum," Alfonso responded. "I didn't know what to do."

"I'm so sorry," Laura said.

"Oh, don't worry about it. I'm just glad you're okay."

"Yes." Laura stood up and steadied herself. "I just need some sugar or something. That's usually what my body needs when this happens."

"This happens often?"

"Yes and no. It's been more frequent since I came to Naples, but it's nothing, really. I just need to put something in my stomach."

"Let's get you something to eat then." Alfonso offered his hand. "Let's get breakfast."

"Oh, I don't need your hand, thank you. I think I can make it on my own. I'll follow you."

"So, what happened to you?" Alfonso asked in between bites. "If it's okay to ask…"

"It's fine," Laura replied, sipping her juice. Her head had stopped ringing. The breakfast had helped. "It's just something that happens now and then. It's nothing to worry about, really. I carry chocolate or candy with me when it happens. That usually helps."

"It doesn't sound like nothing," Alfonso pressed. "You were saying something about danger...*he's in danger* I think was what you said, right before you collapsed."

"I did?" Laura blushed. She wasn't sure if she should tell him her issue. Would it scare him away to know he was sitting across from some mad woman who thinks she sees things? She typically hides this ability from people, just for that reason. Unable to keep a man for that reason. She didn't want to tell him, but she convinced herself that if he couldn't appreciate her for all she was, then she shouldn't consider any relationship with the man anyways.

"Yes," Alfonso replied. "It scared me, to be honest. I'm just glad you're alright."

And there it is, she thought. She had already frightened him. *Well, if I've already lost the man, I suppose there's no harm in telling him.* After some silence, she spoke. "I see visions," she blurted it out; just threw it on the table for him to react.

"Visions?" Alfonso smiled. "What are you talking about?"

"They just come to me. They always have, since I can remember. I can't control them—they just come. I try to understand them. I try to decipher their meanings, but I rarely get it right. I don't know what they are, where they come from, or what triggers them. They just come."

"My mother claimed to have visions or something like that," Alfonso said as he chewed his fruit.

"Really?" Laura didn't like his use of the word *claim*. She watched as he examined her. Maybe he was waiting for her to tell him she was joking. Laura remained silent.

"Yes," Alfonso continued. "It only caused problems for her." He put down his fork and looked at Laura again. "So, you had a vision last night? At the temple?"

"Yes."

"What was it of?" He asked her in a tone that was between disbelief and intrigue.

"Nothing," Laura blushed. "I don't really know."

"Oh, come on, now," Alfonso prodded. "Surely, you must remember something that you saw. What was it?"

"I'd rather not say. It was the first time something like that—"

"Was it sexual?" Alfonso asked with interest.

Laura didn't respond. She placed another strawberry in her mouth and chewed, hoping her face hadn't shown her embarrassment.

"It was sexual, wasn't it? Was I in it?"

"Alfonso," Laura whispered.

"It was me," he deduced. "Were we having sex?

Laura shook her head and looked away. She didn't want to talk about it with him. He seemed to be enjoying it a little too much.

"Don't be embarrassed," Alfonso said. "It's okay to tell me. I'm not ashamed."

Laura smiled. She thought about the image. The man rolled around with the woman. It was passionate. It was steamy. It was almost painful?

"It was a couple engaging in…" Laura replied. "I can't remember the details. I just don't know why it came to me. What did it mean?"

"Maybe it's repressed feelings? Maybe you were expressing your desires?" Alfonso suggested with a tone of flirtation.

Laura let out a small laugh and focused. She imagined the vision. She tried to call it back to her. *Flashes of naked flesh, rocking, wrestling…or were they fighting? It was hard to tell. The woman's head facing up toward the ceiling, calling out in ecstasy…or was she chanting? The man on top of her, beside her, behind her, underneath her…was it Alfonso? No!*

"Nick!" Laura blurted. "It's Nick!"

"What?" Alfonso replied, disappointed. "Who's Nick?"

"They were having sex, but he looked like he was in pain or…"

"Pain? Wow! Now, you're making me blush," Alfonso remarked.

"Will you shut up for a second?" Laura closed her eyes. "He's in trouble. He's in danger. Nick. It's Nick. He needs help." She jumped from her chair and ran back to the car.

"Laura, wait," Alfonso followed. "Where are you going?"

"I need my phone," Laura called back. "I need to call Nick!"

She found her bag in the back seat. She went through it all but couldn't find her phone. Alfonso came up behind her.

"Where's my phone?" She asked as she continued to rummage through her bag. "I need my phone."

"Phone?" Alfonso looked on the floor. "I don't know. I didn't see a phone."

"Alfonso! I had my phone with me. Where is it?"

"I—I don't know," he pleaded. "Maybe it fell somewhere. I don't know."

"I need to get back to Naples," she said, exasperated. "Can you take me back?"

"Yeah," Alfonso replied. "Sure. Of course. But first, let me just check with the doctor's office. Maybe it's there. Are you okay?"

"Yes, yes. I'm fine. Thank you."

"Alright." Alfonso opened the door. "I'll go check with the doctor. Be right back."

"I'm sorry, Alfonso. I'm just really worried for him."

"That's okay. Be right back." Alfonso left.

CHAPTER 44

NICK LAY ON his back, catching his breath. He was worn out. Lavinia had finally untied him and lay by his side, caressing his chest. It was nice.

"Thank you for helping me," Lavinia whispered as she circled his nipple with her fingers. "I knew you'd understand."

"I don't understand." Nick responded. "What are you talking about?"

"The bracelet," Lavinia said. "I think you understand now; that it belongs with me. So, thank you for helping me."

"Lavinia, you're talking in riddles," Nick propped himself up. "Tell me what you're talking about. You took that from me. Where is it? How did I help you?"

Lavinia rolled her eyes and slid off the bed. She wrapped her naked body in a black robe and covered Nick with the top sheet. She walked over to the table, picked up the telephone, and pressed a button.

"Lavinia, tell me what's going on!" Nick shouted.

After a few minutes, a knock was heard on the door. Lavinia opened it and let in a woman pushing a cart, holding a large bowl of warm water, a sponge, and a wooden box. To Nick's surprise, she was Silvia—the woman he met with at Castel Sant'Elmo.

"You?" Nick said.

"Hello, Mr. Terenzi," she replied. "I'm happy to see you've come to your senses."

"What are you talking about? Who are you?" Nick tried to get off the bed, only to realize that his left leg was still tied to the post. "What's going on here?!"

"Oh, will you calm down," Lavinia said to him. "Thank you, Silvia. I need to talk to him."

"Very well," Silvia said. "We'll see you later, Nick."

Lavinia locked the door behind Silvia and opened the wooden box. From it, she pulled out the bracelet and clasped it on her wrist. Nick watched her and seethed. She then grabbed the bowl and sponge and turned back to him.

"Now, sit back," she ordered him. She sat on a stool next to the bed and began to wipe his body down. He didn't want to enjoy it, but he did. The warm water, with Lavinia's gentle touch, relaxed him. He lay still on his back and let her bathe him.

"Nick, let me talk to you about this." Lavinia displayed the bracelet on her arm. "And about its purpose."

"That's my bracelet," Nick said in one final call of ownership. "What are you doing?"

Lavinia dipped the sponge into the water, wrung it, and brought it back to Nick's body. "You've made it clear that you have no idea what you had here," she continued. "So, let me start by telling you what it represents."

Nick didn't respond. He lay still, feeling her bathe him, and listened to her.

"The etchings on the bracelet are a representation of sorceresses." She showed him one of the etchings. It was of the flower Nick had asked her about when they first met. "You recognize this one here," she noted. "The trumpet."

"Angel's trumpet," Nick said.

"Actually, it's the devil's trumpet." Lavinia replied.

"What do you mean?" Nick asked.

Lavinia didn't respond. She stopped bathing him and walked back to the table. Nick watched as she pour more hot water from the kettle into a porcelain cup. She then reached for a pair of gloves set on the table, and gently put them on. Nick watched as she carefully caressed the plant to her left, picked off two leaves, then ripped and dropped them into the cup.

"What is that?" He asked.

"Don't you recognize it?" Lavinia replied as she stirred. She reached her left hand to one of the white flowers that perched up from the plant. "It's your flower."

"The trumpet," Nick remembered. "That's the Angel's Trumpet."

"No, no," Lavinia shook her head. "The angel sloops down. This one sticks up, as if from the ground. This is the Devil's Trumpet."

"It looks the same to me." Nick replied.

"This plant, Nick," Lavinia continued. "It's called Datura Stramonium," She removed her gloves and stirred the tea. "Some call it jimson weed."

Nick looked at the plant, then at his empty cup on the nightstand. Then back at the plant. Then asked, "It is poisonous?"

"It is believed to be the same herb used by the Circe," Lavinia continued. "The mythological sorceress of the Odyssey. You are familiar?"

"Yes, yes…the one that turned Odysseus' men into pigs or something…" Nick tried remembering the detail Laura had shared.

"Correct." Lavinia leaned forward. "But she was also the one that warned him about the sirens."

"Oh, right." Nick sat up, his shoulder still sore from the beating by those mysterious men. "The sirens! Yes, I think there was a siren…"

"There were three," Lavinia corrected him.

"Yeah, yeah, yeah. And one of them is the siren of Naples. I know, Lavinia. Why are you going through all this? Why do you think the bracelet belongs to you?"

"It belongs to us," Lavinia corrected him. "Silvia, me, and many other women. We belong to the Order of the Eye of Partenope. Established in Naples in 1888, by a secret group founded by Eusapia Palladino—renowned seer and the first woman of our Order to have been accused and exposed. Eusapia was a powerful seer that men refused to believe. Eventually, she was betrayed and labeled a fraud—again, by men who refused to let a woman have more abilities than them." Lavinia raised her hands and chanted out loud. "Honorable Eusapia, may Partenope protect you." Lavinia lowered her hands and looked back at Nick.

She smiled and continued. "Our members are in Naples and spread out through the Campania region, some extended to Le Marche, some to Umbria. Every year, we make a pilgrimage from Naples to here, in Benevento, by way of Caserta, to the banks of the Sabato river, where the legendary walnut tree once stood.

Where we perform what we call our 'Dance of the Sisters' and pray to the goddess Isis."

Nick's head spun. He didn't know if Lavinia's elixir was still affecting him, or if it was her convoluted story of Egyptian goddesses, Greek sirens, and Italian witches. What Nick did understand from her explanation was that Lavinia was some crazy loon, with fellow oddballs that have crazy, mixed-up beliefs. He was weakened by her elixir and by their sex, so he continued to lay still to regain some strength. He needed to get that bracelet and get out.

"Why are you doing this?" he asked.

"This bracelet," Lavinia continued. "Was forged by these women, who called themselves the Order of the Eye of Partenope. Their mission was to keep watch over Naples' people. It is said that under the eye of Partenope, these seers would expose any criminal or betrayer of women. This bracelet is from that secret Order—our Order that lives on in the shadows. We are the seers and guardians of the Partenopese, the Napoletani, the people of Naples. We protect and serve the people, in the shadows. We are everywhere. The bracelet itself is called the Eye of Partenope," Lavinia repeated.

"And it was made to be worn by the leader of our Order. The woman who wears this bracelet is the leader of the Order. Unfortunately, not long after the bracelet was created, it was believed to have been taken and never found. For years, we were searching for it, but nothing. Until it appeared years ago in Milan. We heard rumors, but there was no sign of it. That is, until Gaetano and his group of underground dealers indicated its presence." Lavinia looked at Nick, almost as if challenging him to interrupt her.

268

LORENZO PETRUZZIELLOLORENZO PETRUZZIELLO

"We later found it was discovered in Milan after all, and then in Naples. Through our own connections and dealings with Gaetano, we worked for a long time to find out exactly where the bracelet was being held. And that was how we found you. No, it was not a mere coincidence that we met at the bar that night. I followed you. I seduced you and took you home with me. I wanted the bracelet. It was by chance you came into my boutique that day. But we already had our eyes on you. We knew where you were. We knew where you went, who you talked to, and what you were learning. You were under our eye. When we have our target, we see all, we learn all."

Nick didn't know what to focus on first. To learn that Lavinia had been hunting him all along was a shock. "So, you did know who I was at the bar. How did you know I would approach you?" Nick asked.

Lavinia rolled her eyes.

"What is your goal?" Nick continued his questions. "What is going to happen to me?"

"I told you." Lavinia turned away and worked at mixing her drink. "You've fulfilled your purpose. You helped me get this bracelet back. And I must say, it was enjoyable."

"Stop!" Nick jostled his legs. "Stop saying that! You can't get away with this! Untie me! That's my bracelet. Do you think I won't go to the police?"

Lavinia burst out laughing. She turned to Nick and shook her head with a smile. "Come now, Nick," she scoffed. "You know you won't go to the police. You'd be walking into a situation you don't want to put yourself in."

"What are you talking about?"

"You do realize you could still be a prime suspect in your friend Gaetano's death, don't you?"

"No, I'm not!"

"Oh Nick…" She abandoned her mix, turned to him, and said, "Just you watch."

Nick cringed at her threat. It was the same threat as the men that beat him in the tunnels. "Did you get those men to attack me in the tunnels?"

"No," Lavinia replied as she mixed more of her tea. "But I have Silvia on top of that situation. To find out who they are, and why they came after you."

"They threatened me with the same, you know," Nick replied as he kept working on loosening the ribbon on his left wrist—his eyes still on Lavinia's back. "They threatened to frame me for Gaetano's death."

"What do you mean?"

"That they'd go to the police and tell them I killed Gaetano. That if I don't bring them the bracelet, they would turn me in."

Lavinia slammed the cup on the table and paused. Nick lay still and watched as she breathed in and then went back stirring.

"Lavinia," he softened his tone. "Please…just let me go." He watched Lavinia shake her head. He searched for a way to convince her. "Maybe I can help you again."

"Help me with what, exactly?"

"To find these men," Nick suggested. "They'll be coming to look for me soon. I'm supposed to be getting the bracelet back, and they were going to come to me to take it."

"You made a deal with these men?!" Lavinia slammed the cup again and turned around. "How could you? Who are they?"

"I—I—I don't know," Nick squirmed. "I mean, I didn't really make a deal…I just told them *yes* so that they would let me go. They were kicking the shit out of me. I had to find a way out."

"What did you tell them?"

"Just that I was planning to take the bracelet back and that—"

"Did you tell them I had it?"

"No." Nick laid back again. His mind was less foggy. "I just told them it was in a safe place and that I had to retrieve it. And that's when they told me they would come for me in a week. That I better have the bracelet, or they would turn me into the police— telling them that I was responsible for Gaetano's death." He felt his body regaining its strength.

"Did they tell you why they wanted it?" Lavinia asked.

"No. I didn't ask either. I just wanted to stay alive and get away."

Lavinia abandoned the drink and sat on the bed, next to Nick.

"So, what do you say?" Nick asked. "Let me go, and I'll help you."

"Why would I trust you? You just told me you lied to those men about helping them. How do I know you're not lying to me?"

"Because." Nick caressed her thigh. "You want me."

Lavinia burst into a laughing fit. It was maniacal and uncontrollable. When she stopped, she stroked his face and said, "My dear fool, I don't want you."

"But, the sex, the flowers…"

"I just wanted the bracelet, you fool," Lavinia continued to laugh. "Sure, I like to sleep with you. You're very good. Great moments of ecstasy. But, you're of no help anymore. I'm done with you, really." Lavinia touched his cheek.

Nick pulled away in disgust. He felt used. He was angry. He jostled again and felt the ribbon had loosened.

"When we learned you were trying to sell the bracelet," Lavinia continued. "Of course, we tried to buy it. But Gaetano kept negotiating—playing games. We were so close to getting it back, we couldn't let it slip away. So, we had to take some drastic measures. We gave Gaetano another chance to make the deal with us, but he kept refusing. Leading us on. We grew impatient. And when we learned he made a deal with the Egyptian buyer, we had to act fast. So, we found him and gave him one more chance to close the deal with us. He refused, telling us it was too late. We wanted him to break the deal with the Egyptians. He said no. So, we broke the deal for him. And the only way to do that—"

"Was to kill him," Nick finished her sentence. He sat still in shock.

"He gave us no other choice," Lavinia retorted. "If communication between him and the Egyptian buyer ended, then that deal would have been incomplete, dead. The buyer would grow frustrated and assume Gaetano's lost communication would mean a lost deal."

"That poor man!" Nick shouted. "You killed Gaetano over a deal? How? I saw him jump!"

"Well, some flowers can be poisonous, some deadly. Overtime, they can even mess with your mind," Lavinia replied with ease, as if she didn't care she was confessing. "I got him to a point of weakness and threatened him. Now, I didn't expect you to come to his apartment. I was there. I watched you go into his bedroom.

When I walked in, I stood in the doorway right behind you. Gaetano saw me approaching and just jumped. I didn't expect him to do it himself. But he knew he was a goner."

"Wait," Nick shook his head. "You were there?! I didn't see you there. And he jumped.... because of you?" Nick felt the fear rise inside him. "You poisoned him over time? For a bracelet? He would have sold it to you!"

"We couldn't let the bracelet disappear again," Lavinia snapped.

"But to kill a man for just doing his job?"

"He was in the way," Lavinia responded dismissively. "And besides, we were losing focus on you—the man who actually possessed the bracelet."

"But at that point, you already had taken it," Nick responded. "There was no need for any of that. There was no need for him to die."

"But there was," Lavinia interjected.

"Because he knew who you were," Nick deduced. "Because you exposed yourself to him. He knew what you were after. He knew he could expose you."

"He had to go," Lavinia said.

"I can't fuckin' believe this!" Nick shouted. He grew angrier. With that anger, he felt his body strengthen—or somehow his mind convinced his body that it was at full strength. He pulled and loosened the ribbon even more, giving him the ability to set himself free.

"Nick, you are not a woman, "Lavinia continued. "So, you cannot understand what we endured throughout history. We women learn early in life that the world is against us. That we have to look out for each other. We are here for each other. We are sisters. We protect each other. We watch and protect."

"Isis…Witches…You make it sound like you're in a cult," Nick remarked with a scoff.

"We are a sisterhood," Lavinia responded.

"Witches?" Nick continued. "Silvia too? So, there are more of you here. Like a coven? What the fuck is going on? Are you crazy?"

"Ha!" Lavinia let out an exaggerated laugh. "Of course, you would say that word. *Crazy*. Typical label given to us. But you will see, we are not *crazy*, my dear. We are just keeping a tradition alive."

"What am I doing here? Why are you keeping me?"

"I would like to keep around, Nick," Lavinia replied and caressed his sore shoulder. "You are very enjoyable. Are you feeling better?"

"Don't change the subject," Nick retorted. "You now have me here against my will. How did you get me here? You drugged me. There's a lot I can go to the police with. Oh! And you stole my bracelet!"

"It's not your bracelet!" Lavinia shouted back. "I've just finished telling you it belonged to one of us. It was missing for many years and now we have it back. It belongs with us. Not with some random artifacts in some museum in Greece. Not on a trophy shelf with some wealthy collector in Egypt. Not passed around by some random old men in the United Nations. This bracelet is the band of the sorceresses!" Lavinia rushed back to Nick and held the bracelet to him. "Do you see this, Nick?" she asked through her teeth. "Do you see it?"

"Yes," Nick stammered. "Yes, I see it."

"This, Nick, is for the Eye of Partenope! You had no fucking clue! Another foolish man with no clue." She walked to the other side of the room, turned back to him, and continued, "But now, you lost it. Lost what my people held sacred. There was no chance in hell we were going to let it get lost again."

"Lavinia, calm down," Nick softened his tone. He was scared. Lavinia sounded out of her mind. If she was really a practicing witch, and she was surrounded by other practicing witches, and they all had him tied up in the bed, what was going to happen to him? "Lavinia, please. Let's just talk for a minute. I get it. I understand. I see why it belongs to you. And I'm sorry. I didn't know."

"Of course, you didn't know," Lavinia chortled and turned to the table again. "You are another foolish idiot. I've told you that before."

Nick watched as she kept her back to him. He unfurled the restraint. When she turned back to him, Nick laid flat. He waited for her to approach. When she got closer, offering another drink to him with her arm outstretched, he grabbed her. The cup flew against the footboard and cracked in half. He grabbed one of the halves, while the other fell to the floor. He held the sharp end of the broken cup to Lavinia's throat. His other hand over her mouth.

"Let me go," he whispered in her ear. "Now!"

Lavinia didn't move. He pushed the broken cup into her skin, slightly cutting through.

"Okay, okay," she moaned in a muffled voice and untied his ankles. Just as he saw a spot of blood on her neck, he felt his arm knock away, the cup flying across the room. Lavinia fought back and attempted to pin him down again. Her robe ripped off one shoulder. He wrestled and flipped her on her back. His hand still covered her mouth. Her robe was ripped away.

He noticed the streak of blood now ran from her neck to her nipple. Another around her waist. Lavinia tried to jostle her naked body from under his, but his strength had come back to him. He wasn't going to let her win. She jostled again, flipping him to the side, and screamed, but he managed to grasp her and cover her mouth.

"It's over, Lavinia," he said. "Just stop."

She tried breaking free again but failed.

"I'm going to leave, Lavinia," he said to her. "Just let me go. It's over."

"No," Lavinia mumbled through his fingers.

He climbed on top of her and pinned her against the bed. He found the sponge and put it in her mouth to prevent her from screaming. Then, he proceeded to tie her wrists together with one of the ribbons. Lavinia flipped him off of her and fell to one side of the bed—her hands restrained together to one corner of the bed post.

"Where are my clothes?" Nick fumbled through the armoire and drawers. Lavinia didn't respond. He noticed a pile of clothes underneath the bed. They were his. "It's over, Lavinia," he said as he dressed. "It's all over." He reached for the door and opened it a crack. No one was in sight. He went back in the room and walked over to Lavinia. He crouched down and unclasped the bracelet.

"This is mine," he whispered and left the room filled with her muffled protests.

He closed the door behind him, standing with his back against the wall as he made his way to the staircase, down to a courtyard, where he found two women in deep discussion. They looked at him in disbelief and asked what he was doing in the castle. He didn't respond. Did they not know? Instead, he rushed out the open gate, onto the street, and ran.

Chapter 45

"**THIS IS VERY** intriguing," Alfonso said. "Would you say your visions became stronger when you got here in Naples?"

"Yes," Laura replied. "But I think it has to do with someone in particular. You see, it isn't visions, really. It's messages."

"Messages?"

"Yes, something will contact me to send a message or share a message."

"Like a ghost?"

"No...but a spirit, I guess. I don't really know. It's more like a feeling...it's difficult to explain."

"A feeling?"

"Right...You know when you just know something? Like you feel it in your gut? You have this instinct or hunch?"

"Yes..."

"It's sort of like that, but clearer. Like it's a hunch, but a hunch is not as clear...a hunch could mean 'maybe this is going to happen'...or, 'I feel like this going to happen'...."

"Okay..."

"This is like that—a hunch—but with a clear message. You know what it's saying. You know why you feel this way or that. You see it. And you see it because someone is sending the information to you."

"Someone who is dead?"

"Correct," Laura affirmed. "A spirit or something wanting to send information. I'm, like, the tool for them to send the message."

"A medium," Alfonso completed the thought.

"I hate that word, but yes. I guess I have the abilities of a medium."

"But you also said you have random visions."

"Yes, which I only assume are messages…to clarify things or point me to things," Laura replied. "For example, just recently, I had a random vision of this woman, and in it, she said 'tell my son to be careful, and that I love him'. But I have no idea who she was trying to reach."

"Interesting…and why would they be getting stronger here in Naples?"

"Not sure, but it could be that there was just someone close that I needed to send the message to." Laura purposely kept her response vague. Alfonso didn't need to know that she thought it was Nick who needed the message. Truth was, she really wasn't even sure about that herself.

"How far have you come in your research?" Alfonso asked.

"I'm still in the early stages. Why?"

"Have you heard of the name or seen the name Eusapia Palladino?"

"Eusapia? No…Why?"

"Well, I think you need to look her up," Alfonso continued. "You see, Eusapia Palladino was a renowned medium, here in Naples. Known worldwide."

"What? Really?"

"Yes. I want to say late eighteen-hundreds, early nineteen-hundreds...She amazed so many. She was even invited to England and Harvard in the United States to debunk her abilities. Eventually, many had...including Houdini himself."

"What? No way!"

"Yes. When people won't accept the unexplained, they are always ready to tear someone down." Alfonso looked down solemnly, then continued, "She was an interesting character, really." He turned back to Laura. "You really had no idea?"

"None!"

"Hmm...Interesting..."

"What's interesting?"

"I just find it hard to believe...a research student here, in Naples, studying...what was it? Greek influence...and you happen to be a medium? But claim not to know about a famous medium that lived here? No. Impossible."

Laura was confused. She didn't understand if Alfonso was teasing her or if he was serious. He sounded the latter. "I don't know why that's hard to believe..." she said with a polite chuckle.

"It doesn't make sense, that's all," Alfonso quipped.

"What doesn't make sense?"

"I need to get gas," Alfonso said and pulled into a rest stop.

Laura stayed in the car and thought about Nick. She hoped her vision was not accurate, hoped it hadn't already happened, hoped that maybe it was a warning of things to come, and she had time to correct it. She changed focus to her phone, trying to think back to how she may have lost it. It must have happened when she blacked out at the temple, making it possible that it was still there. *Or*, she thought, *maybe it fell out of my bag in the car.* She unblocked her belt, searching the floor and peeking in the rear, but saw nothing.

Alfonso replaced the gas nozzle and closed the car's gas cap. He then wiped his hands on one of the free disposable sanitizer cloths and climbed back into the car.

"You do know that there is a group here that follows the ways of Eusapia, right?" he said as he buckled his seat belt. "Maybe you should connect with them."

"What do you mean?" Laura asked, refastening hers.

"There's a group of women that maintain Eusapia's legend, seeing her as a powerful woman who had unexplainable abilities. So, they worship her, in a way…"

"You mean like a cult?" Laura asked. She was intrigued.

"Well, no. Not really. They are like a sisterhood. They claim to be the guardians of Naples. They look out for people—mostly each other."

"How do you know all this?" Laura asked.

"Laura, did you forget I study the history of witches?" Alfonso said with an air of condescendence. "I come across these topics a lot."

"How do I find this group?" Laura asked. "If this group actually exists, and they are in Naples, maybe meeting with them or someone from that group could help me…"

"Help you what?"

"Well, understand my visions," Laura replied. "And maybe find…"

"Find what?" Alfonso asked as he took the highway exit that led into the city. "Are you looking for something?"

"Well, yes…" Laura stumbled over her response. She didn't want to mention that she was helping Nick find his bracelet. Part of her did want to talk about it, though. "I mean…find meaning."

"Meaning to your visions?" Alfonso surmised.

"Yes, what is the overall meaning? And who is sending them to me?" Laura turned to face Alfonso. "I told you how it's usually some sort of spirit talking to me, sending a message."

"You did," Alfonso responded, but his focus was on navigating through the chaotic traffic that is Naples.

"Well, it's been a while that the focus of my visions was on a particular item," Laura continued as she wrapped her fingers around the door handle. "Alfonso, you're driving really fast."

He ignored her, beeped his horn several times at another car, a couple on a scooter, and even a delivery truck.

"Whoa," Laura quipped and braced herself to the door handle.

"What item?" Alfonso asked, ignoring her concern.

"A piece of jewelry," Laura said, trying not to notice the speed Alfonso was driving in the city streets.

"Jewelry?" he asked when he was stopped at an intersection. "What jewelry?" He continued to the next light.

"I don't know what it is, really. It's a bracelet of some sort, but it's not about the jewelry. It's about the person who is sending me the message. Are you okay?"

Alfonso ignored her and sped through a yellow light, cutting off three cars. The drivers shouted obscenities at him. He shouted back.

"Alfonso, please be careful," Laura said.

"You have to be aggressive here, Laura," Alfonso replied while maintaining focus on the narrow streets. "Otherwise, you'll never get through this place. The people just go. They take the road from you. They don't care."

"Okay, but your car…"

"Don't worry about my car," Alfonso retorted. Laura was surprised by his change in tone. It had a sense of anger. He added, "My car is made for this," then changed gears with even more aggression.

"Are you in a rush?"

"Don't you want to find your friend?" His question came out curtly.

"Yes," she snapped back. "But I want to be alive when I find him. Please, slow down."

"Tell me more about the bracelet," Alfonso ignored her comment. He was focused. Laura couldn't tell if it was on the road, or on her story.

"It's just some piece of jewelry," Laura responded dismissively, with a tone to end the topic. "Not important, really."

"Was it definitely a bracelet?" Alfonso pushed. He slowed the car and turned onto the street off the waterfront. He pulled over and stopped the car. "There," he breathed out, then looked at Laura.

"Thanks for the ride back," Laura said and reached for the car door.

"Wait," Alfonso grabbed her arm, then let go. "Sorry."

"I should go," Laura said.

"Wait, please," he pleaded. "Please tell me more."

"That's it, really," Laura replied.

"The bracelet," he insisted. "What was it?" When Laura didn't respond, he added, "I'm just curious to know if it coincides with my research."

"Oh," Laura said with relief. "Of course. I *think* it was a bracelet. But we don't know for sure what it represents…yet. If I can meet with these women, maybe they can help me—"

"No," Alfonso said sternly. "Sorry…I just…I don't want you to get into any danger. Talking to random people about that, you know? Your vision, is one thing. The bracelet…"

"You think it would be dangerous talking to those women about the bracelet?"

"Well, sometimes, you need to be careful who you talk to about what. That's all," Alfonso said.

"Then, I'll just stick with the visions, Alfonso," Laura replied. "If these women understand this—understand the ability—then what harm could come from talking to them?"

"I suppose. Just, be careful," Alfonso said. "I'd like to see you again."

Laura blushed. He was putting on the charm again. With it, he managed to put aside everything she was focused on, including the idea of Nick in danger. Nothing mattered but the way he looked at her. "I should go," she responded, even though what she really wanted to do was give him a kiss. She opened the car door and turned back. "Thank you, Alfonso."

"It was my pleasure," he replied, leaning in and kissing her.

The moment his lips touched hers, she felt numb all over. She took in the euphoric sensation of his warm lips massaging hers. Flashes of scenes popped into her mind. She fought them—focused her mind on his lips instead. But the sparks continued to invade her thoughts.

Egypt. Airport in Cairo. Camels. Hotel lobby. Watermelons? All over a road? A gun! A shot! A man running in the desert. No, overlooking the desert. A car crashing. Pyramids…

She felt Alfonso pull away.

"That was nice," Alfonso's voice broke her vision. "I'll see you later?"

Laura tried to bring back the scene, but it was gone. "Yes," she mumbled.

"Are you okay?"

"Huh?" Laura shook her head. "Sorry. I…"

"You had another vision, didn't you? Just now?"

"Yes," she exhaled. "It made little sense, though."

"What was it? May I ask?"

"It was more flashes of things…I think?" Laura tried recalling the scenes. She wanted them back.

"Like what?" Alfonso pressed.

"A desert…I saw pyramids, so I think it was Egypt?" Laura winced to try and force the vision back. "A hotel in Egypt? But…"

"What?"

"There was a gunshot? Possibly?" she continued. "Or maybe a car crash? A loud bang."

"Where in Egypt?"

"I saw Cairo...the airport..." she responded. "But the pyramids. It was like a view from a rooftop..."

"Giza," Alfonso said.

"Giza? Oh, right...where the pyramids are located."

"Did you see any details on the roof...Where it was?" Alfonso pressed on.

"No...but I felt...or somehow, I knew, it was a hotel," Laura breathed out, fatigued. "Sorry, I think I need some chocolate or something..."

"Sure, sure." Alfonso started the car again. "Let's go get you some chocolate."

CHAPTER 46

THE DOOR TO his apartment was unlocked. Nick turned the knob and opened the door wide. No sign of anyone. He went inside and locked it behind him. He rushed to his bedroom and found his phone by his bed where he had left it. He was surprised no one had gone into the unlocked apartment, that no one had taken anything. He swiped the screen awake and saw texts had come in from Laura—the day before.

Been trying to reach you.

We'll catch up later.

Going to the coast with a friend. Will be gone for the rest of the day.

Catch up later tonight or tomorrow.

He tapped on her name and let it ring. No answer. He hoped she wasn't in any danger—that he hadn't put her in any danger. But he felt more at ease that she had left the city and was with a friend. He made himself believe that she must be safe. That she'd call when she could.

He ripped off his clothes, realizing Lavinia had dressed him after she had drugged him in his own home, leaving his money and wallet on his bedroom bureau. He had run from the villa she had held him captive in and reached a train station just outside of

Benevento. He managed to sneak onto a train that was heading to Naples.

He was sure Lavinia would come for him. He had to get out of his place. Find somewhere to hide. He went into the bathroom and glanced in the mirror. Looking back at him was a disheveled man who looked like he had had a rough night partying. He washed his face, rubbed cream on the bags under his eyes, wet his hair, combed it, and brushed his teeth. It was a quick routine he had mastered for the late nights he used to have when he could stay up past ten.

He rushed back into the bedroom, put on some clean clothes, and pulled the bracelet out of the pocket of his other pants. He sat on the bed and examined the band. Immediately, he felt violated and angry. He wanted to get rid of the damn thing and every memory that had now been attached to it.

He contemplated contacting the UNESCO office again, but if that Silvia woman really was involved with the organization, he didn't want her to know he was contacting them. He then thought about reaching out to someone connected to Gaetano. Someone that worked with him. But he didn't really have a way to reach any of them. How had he found them the first time, he couldn't remember. The attaché case!

He rummaged through the bottom drawer in his armoire. It was still there—Gaetano's leather portfolio. He opened it, looking for names and numbers…anything that would indicate an affiliated dealer, but his search came up empty. The case only held the notes on the Egyptian buyer—the purpose of Gaetano meeting with Nick at the time.

Nick remembered seeing something about a hotel in Giza… there it was. The contact's name and location. But there was not a set meeting. At least there were no notes on an appointment or instructions on how to make contact.

He pushed the papers back into the portfolio and zipped it shut. He didn't know what to do. He tried to think who he could talk to that would possibly have any dealings with Gaetano, or anyone in the underground market. He has to know someone—

"Of course!" he said aloud. He rushed to his bureau and grabbed a handkerchief. He wrapped the bracelet and slipped it into his inside pocket. He then splashed on some cologne, grabbed his watch, wallet, passport, and keys and rushed out the door.

———◆———

He knocked on the frame shop window and got the attention of the owner. The man's face lit up when he saw Nick and unlocked the door.

"Mr. Terenzi," he exclaimed. "It's nice to see you. Are you back for your painting?" He gestured to his front window.

"Oh, my painting," Nick responded. He had forgotten he left the depiction of the flower meadow there. The gold frame with the green matte really was beautiful. "Uh, no. Not yet, that is. I see that you're closed for the day; I'm sorry to disturb you."

"Not a problem," the owner replied. "Please, come inside. I want to lock the door. I don't want any other customers to think the shop is still open."

"Oh, yes," Nick obliged. "Sorry."

"It's okay," the man responded and locked the door behind Nick.

"I've come to ask you a favor, if that's okay," Nick said.

"A favor?" the man asked. "Sure, if I can be of help, of course. What is it?"

"I'm sorry to be so forward with my question, but I'm hoping you can help me find someone."

"How can I help?"

"Do you deal with, or have you ever dealt with, anyone in the black market? Here in Naples?" Nick asked.

The man didn't say anything. Nick could see he was contemplating how to respond.

"Why don't we talk in my office?" he finally said. "Please, come in the back with me."

CHAPTER 47

LAURA FOLDED THE empty bag of chocolates and sat back as Alfonso drove her around the posh Posillipo neighborhood. He slowed the car when he reached a quiet, well-manicured street. "There's the house." He pointed to a large villa overlooking the cliffs of the bay, but didn't stop.

The house was gorgeous, well maintained, and not overly sized. It stood up a hill inside the gated grounds. Its maroon and white walls stretched up four floors. Its top three floors were over the gates, allowing an unblocked view of the sea.

"Stop, stop," Laura suggested. "It's beautiful."

"Laura, I can't stop," Alfonso responded and drove past it.

"Why not?"

"I've tried communicating with these women," Alfonso explained. "But it didn't go very well. I don't think it's wise for them to see you with me."

"What happened?"

"Just misunderstandings...about my questioning. Silly, really." Alfonso drove back on the villa's street and stopped the car. "Just remember the house, and come back on your own when you're feeling better. Just don't mention my name. Don't mention that I gave you this address."

Laura opened the car door.

"What are you doing?" Alfonso asked her.

"Why wait?" Laura said as she stepped out of the car. "I'll just go now. I want to know if they can help me."

"Laura, wait," Alfonso said to her as she shut the car door. "Laura!" He put down the window and called out to her, "Laura!"

"I'm okay, Alfonso," Laura said. "Thank you."

"I'll wait," he said. "I'll wait and make sure you're good."

"Okay, fine," she replied and walked up to the gate.

She rang the buzzer and the gate opened without an exchange of words. Laura walked up the white stone stairs, bordered by lush plants on both sides. The door opened.

An older woman appeared from inside. Her hair was full, gray, and glamorously curled. Turquoise clips held it all up in a plump bun that flopped slightly as she spoke.

"Who are you?" she said, her voice velvety. Her accent was thick. Her tone: neutral.

"Hello," Laura's voice cracked with nervousness. "I'm sorry to trouble you. My name is Laura. I am a student researching here, in Naples, and I was hoping you could help me with my research."

"What research?" the woman asked condescendingly. "Why my help? Who sent you here?"

"No one sent me," Laura replied. "I came across this address in my research—"

"Where did you find my address?"

"In some document, in the library," Laura responded with a dismissive tone. She hoped it made the answer sound insignificant. "It was with the topics I was researching…about Greek influence here, in Naples—"

"I don't know anything about Greek influence," the woman replied and adjusted her hold on the door that she still had not fully opened.

"Well, I'm not here for that, really," Laura continued. "I've come here to talk about someone in my research. Eusapia Palladino—the medium."

"Palladino," the woman repeated. "She had nothing to do with Greeks…"

"No, I know," Laura stammered. "If I could just talk to you…it's not about the Greek research."

"What is it you are looking for?" The old woman grew impatient. "I don't like to receive guests."

"I'm very sorry." Laura stepped back. "I've come here because I thought it was the only place I could go to for help. I'm confused and don't know what to do."

"Well, I'm sorry," the woman said. "I cannot help you with your research." The woman started to close the door.

"I'm a seer!" Laura blurted.

The woman stopped the door from closing and opened it, wider.

"A what?" she said.

"I'm a medium," Laura breathed out. "I mean, I have the ability. I just don't know how to—"

"You can see?" the woman asked. Her tone had changed to that of interest. "What can you see?"

"Visions," Laura responded. "I don't usually know what they mean, or who they come from…I just see them. They come to me at random. I don't know how to control them. I don't know how to recall them. I don't know how—"

"Come inside," the woman interrupted her. "Let's have some coffee."

Laura looked back at Alfonso's car and watched it drive away. What she didn't know was that her lost phone was buzzing from within his glove compartment.

CHAPTER 48

THE INTERIOR OF the house was even more luxurious than outside. The floors were white marble with a scattering of light blue and gold accents. The walls were pale lavender with pink and white curtains flowing in the breeze that floated in from the sea.

Laura looked out one of the windows to get a look at the fantastic view. The water was a deep teal. Small boats scattered the little bay. She watched people swimming from a beach that she could see in one corner.

"Lido Sirena," the woman said.

"What?" Laura forgot where she was for the moment.

"That beach down there," The woman explained. "Lido Sirena. That's what it's called."

"Sirena," Laura repeated. *Siren*, she translated to herself.

"Come sit," The woman said. "Let's talk."

Laura followed the woman to the left, into a large sitting room with pale yellow walls with black borders and white sofas. At the woman's invitation, Laura sat in the green armchair by one of the sofas and shared what she remembered of her visions. The woman listened intently. She hemmed and hawed at parts and opened her eyes in surprise at others.

The coffee was delivered by another woman. She was younger, silent, and wore a large, gold and turquoise necklace. She placed the tray on the walnut coffee table and smiled.

"Grazie, Silvia," the old woman said.

Silvia smiled again and walked out.

"I'm very pleased you've come to us," the host turned back to Laura. "And, yes, we can help you."

"We?" Laura asked as she accepted the coffee.

The woman added sugar to her own espresso and sat back.

"I am Amalda," she said. "This is my house."

"Lovely house," Laura said and sipped her coffee.

"Thank you. It's been with my family for many generations. I hold meetings here for my cause, and I think my members would be pleased to meet with you. We can help you."

"May I ask." Laura placed the empty cup on the table. "Who are you, exactly? How can you help me?"

"Oh, forgive me," Amalda said. "I thought you knew who I was."

"I don't, unfortunately," Laura replied. "Your information was with stories about Eusapia, but no other connection or details—"

"I see," Amalda interrupted. "I am the elected leader of the Order of the Eye of Partenope. We are the guardians of the culture and history of the renowned medium Eusapia Palladino. Some of us, like you, also have the ability to see…Some of us have other abilities."

"You mean, you are a group of mediums?" Laura asked.

"Not just mediums," Amalda answered. "Some of us are mediums. Some support the seers—watching in their space and reporting or helping find what is needed, if needed." The woman looked Laura up and down and asked, "Would you be interested in being interviewed by our members?"

"Interviewed?"

"We always welcome new members," Amalda explained. "And it appears you have an ability that fits here. Based on the visions you just told me; I might be able to get our current leader to come as well. You're very impressive."

"I am?" Laura asked. She had never felt as comfortable as she did in that chair, in that house, with the old woman. She never really felt comfortable with her ability until that moment. "I think I'd like to—"

"Be one of us?" Amalda asked.

"Yes, I think I do."

"Wonderful," she said. "Let me make some calls, and we can get something together. Maybe tonight?" She reached for the phone on the table to her left, then turned to Laura again. "Oh, do you have a place to stay? Do you need a room? I'd be happy to have you here, if you'd like."

"Really?" Laura was surprised by the offer. The woman barely knew her. She looked around the opulent living room and imagined the elegance of staying in the villa. "I am staying in an apartment in the center, but—"

"Well, tell me where it is, and I'll send someone to get your things," Amalda said to her. She then she spoke into the phone, calling Silvia back into the room.

"I really appreciate your help," Laura added.

"I'm happy you've come to us," Amalda responded with a smile. "Silvia will take you up to your room. It has a private bathroom. Please make yourself at home, and we will call for you when everyone arrives. Sound good?"

"Oh, okay," Laura agreed without thinking. "Thank you, really."

"Please," Amalda replied. "The pleasure will be ours. I'm sure of it."

Chapter 49

"I'VE ALREADY LOST Gaetano over your bracelet, I'm not going to put more of my dealers in peril over it," the man said. He was Gaetano's partner – a large, sweaty man that exhumed a sense of wealth and cleanliness. He had gestured for Nick to sit in the empty chair across from him and sat down in his oversized, leather one.

"I—" Nick stammered.

"I don't want to hear it," the man interrupted. "You have a lot of balls to come here asking for anything. Especially after what happened to Gaetano."

"I didn't know there was any danger involved," Nick insisted. "Believe me when I say that."

"Right." The man looked in the top drawer of his desk and pulled out a folder. "Gaetano was almost done completing this deal—your deal. And, to be quite frank, all of us here are concerned that this operation will be exposed."

"It won't be," Nick assured him. "I can fix this. I can help."

"So, what do you have to offer us? How do you want to help?" The man asked.

"Well, what if I go make the exchange? What if I deliver it?" Nick asked.

"Ha! And lose out on that commission? Not a chance," the man responded. "They've already paid us. They have been harassing me for the money back. Do you understand how our reputation has been stained?"

"Well, what if we can fix it?" Nick asked.

"You think you're the one to fix it?" the man said sarcastically.

"Yes," Nick continued. "I'll run it down there. I'll meet with your contact. I'll deliver the piece."

The man scoffed.

"You'd still get your commission," Nick reassured him. "Afterall, you guys found this buyer. You made the connections. You made the deal. You've got the money."

"And you want to deliver it?" the man asked.

"I want my money," Nick replied. "You have it, and I want it."

"And why would I trust that you won't make your own deal while you're there?" The man leaned in.

"Because you guys already handled the monetary exchange," Nick responded. "You have the money. You pay me when I get back. I'd just be your runner or delivery man or whatever you call it."

After some silence, the man relented and opened the folder. He flipped through some documents and proceeded to give Nick instructions on meeting his contact in Giza.

CHAPTER 50

AFTER AN UNEXPECTED nap, Laura was ushered back down to the living room on the main floor. The room was now filled with several other women drinking champagne and socializing. The room's layout was rearranged. The white sofas were against a far wall. In the center of the room, was a large, round wood platform covered in cloths. Laura followed Silvia to Amalda standing with a small subset group of the women.

"Ah, Laura," Amalda said as they approached. "Welcome back." She turned to her companions and said, "This is Laura, our new hopeful. Laura, this is Lucia, Benedetta, Maria, and Angelica."

"Pleased to meet you," Laura said to the group.

The women all murmured friendly welcomes in return. Silvia reappeared with a champagne cocktail and handed it to Laura.

"Welcome to our meeting, Laura," Amalda said and lifted her glass. The women followed, as did Laura, and they all sipped in unison.

"Excuse me, ladies," Amalda said to her group and led Laura to the center of the room. "Are you good?" she asked Laura.

"Yes," Laura replied. "I'm fine. I apparently dozed off. I didn't realize how tired I was."

"Actually, your absence worked out in your favor," Amalda said.

"It did?"

"Indeed," Amalda lowered her voice. "I was able to talk to all the members here before you arrived. Told them your story. Everything you told me…about your visions, your abilities. They are looking forward to witnessing it."

"Witnessing it?" Laura asked in shock. "But I told you, I don't know how to control it, how to call a message. They just come to me."

"My dear," Amalda leaned in. "That's what we're here for… We're here to guide you. Help you harness and call them to you. Don't you worry."

"Help me harness them?" Laura was confused. "I don't understand. How will you help me do that?"

"Just follow our lead," Amalda replied and turned to the room. "Everyone! Everyone!" As the chattering dissipated, Amalda continued, "Some of you have already been introduced. But, I'm sure the rest of you have surmised this is Laura—the hopeful I spoke of earlier."

The crowd all murmured hello to Laura and listened.

"Will you all agree to commence Laura's reading?" Amalda asked.

The crowd agreed and closed in on the platform.

"Laura," Amalda said softly. "You will need to lay on the platform here—your head on the blue pillow. You can use these steps to get up there."

"What are you going to do to me?"

"Oh, don't you worry, now," Amalda responded. "We will stand around you in a circle and guide you to call a vision."

"How—?" Laura asked as she followed Amalda to the small steps and climbed on top of the table.

"Don't be frightened Laura," Amalda continued. "We are your sisters. Come now. Up, up."

Laura lay flat on the platform and watched as the women encircled it. She watched as they held each other's hands. She watched each of them looking at her, including the ones she hadn't yet been formally introduced to. She watched them start a low chant.

"Laura, just focus on a vision you want to see," Amalda instructed. "Focus on a person. Or a place. Anything."

"Should I close my eyes?" Laura asked.

"Of course," Amalda responded. "Whatever you think may help." Then, she joined in on the low chant.

Laura closed her eyes and focused. The women around her kept chanting softly. Laura opened her eyes again and looked at each of them, still holding hands. Some had their eyes closed, some looked down at the platform. None had their eyes focused on Laura. Except for one. Laura saw the woman staring straight at her. She looked familiar; her dark, wavy hair. Her distinctive face. Where had she seen this woman? *The vision! It was the same woman fighting with Nick! The woman with the bracelet!* She looked at the woman's wrists—no bracelet. The woman glared at her, then looked down at the platform.

Laura wanted to say something. But what? She attempted to sit up, but it happened. Her head spun. Her eyes went out of focus. And a vision came...

A colorful chandelier. Piles of lanterns hanging over a fountain…a hotel lobby. Hallway of doors. Elevator. Fourth floor. Brown, leather shoes. A feeling of fear. Scared. A bird. Endorphins. A death?! An escape! The bracelet! …darkness. Was that her phone buzzing?

CHAPTER 51

Cairo, Egypt
Present Day

NICK HAD FOLLOWED the man's instructions; found the concierge at the airport in Cairo, who then put him in a van driven by another man named Mehmet.

When Mehmet made an unplanned stop in an alley near a bustling outdoor market, Nick grew suspicious. Under the guise of wanting to offer Nick a soda, Mehmet convinced him to get out of the van. Nick wondered if Mehmet knew what he was carrying. That Mehmet was working for someone involved and was after the bracelet. That Mehmet was planning to kill him.

Nick held onto his bag and stood in the alley between the van and the open market. He contemplated throwing himself into the crowd, and as Mehmet approached, calling out to him, Nick did it; he slipped within the crowd in the street market and didn't look back.

The stands were closing for the day, so only some remained opened. He avoided several hanging fabrics. A shelf half full of pottery, the stand owner in the middle of locking them up for the evening. He bumped into a grain vendor who had just finished loading his cart. He apologized and swept past him toward the end of the street. He didn't know what was there, but he saw activity. He hoped it was a center plaza, where he would find a taxi.

"Mr. Nick! Mr. Nick!" Mehmet's voice carried toward Nick as he continued pushing forward. "Mr. Nick! No, Mr. Nick!"

Nick walked into a small table, forcing it to slide forward off a step and tip onto the floor. Fortunately, it was empty. Nick paused and saw a few men stand up, concerned over the commotion. Nick gave a sympathetic look and lifted the table.

"Mr. Nick!" Mehmet said from behind.

Nick thought about taking hold of the stool and swinging it behind him.

"Mr. Nick…Soda!" Mehmet said.

Nick turned to him and saw the man standing there with a big smile. Mehmet patted him on the back and spoke to the men in the eatery. He held up two fingers and gestured to Nick and himself.

Nick felt some shame in thinking the man was going to kill him. He felt shame that he had run off like he did. He felt shame for thinking everything he thought about Mehmet since he first saw him. The nice man just wanted to show some hospitality, and Nick assumed the worst. Nick apologized to Mehmet with a half-smile. Mehmet laughed and handed him one of the glass bottles. They drank the soda, thanked the owner, and returned to the van.

Continuing toward Giza, Mehmet turned the van onto the highway ramp and climbed onto the elevated road. The highway was surrounded by apartment buildings, which were no taller than the ornate steeples of the many mosques scattered throughout. In-between the buildings, Nick noticed the immense size of the deep orange sun setting beyond.

The view was accompanied by the chime of mosque bells. Among the sounds of the bells and cars passing, Nick heard the muffled sound of a muezzin calling all to prayer. At closer examination of the details on the steeples passing by, Nick spotted the large speakers from which, he realized, the announcements had come. He didn't understand the words that echoed, but the monotonous tone was a soothing and continuous chant.

Nick finally sat back and allowed himself to believe everything was just fine. He didn't want to believe this kind man, Mehmet, was suspicious. But he had let himself believe it. Partly from the fear that both Gaetano's man and the concierge at the airport had given him.

He pulled out a map from his carry-on bag and looked for the airport, familiarizing himself with the layout of Cairo. His finger ran on the map. Cairo—over river—through what looked like a small island or archipelago…Giza—then Pyramids…

"Mr. Nick," Mehmet called.

"Yes," Nick looked up to meet the driver's eyes in the rear view again.

"Neel," Mehmet said as he pointed out the window.

"Neel?" Nick repeated, then realized they were crossing a bridge over a river. *Wait—that's…that's…that's the Nile!*

Nick had never seen the Nile. It was his first time in Egypt, and to see one of the most popular bodies of water in the world was incredible. A river one hears of as a child, in school, on TV, in the movies, in books, and well, the Nile comes up in conversation in some way or another. Nick was actually seeing it with his own eyes. It had been a while since he felt this new-first-time experience. It was refreshing.

He sat in awe, staring at the serene and grand Nile, seductively laying there underneath the now dark night sky. The city lights reflected on the river's width and curves. *Cleopatra—the Pharaohs, the Egyptians, the Romans, well, just about everyone sailed along this river. This is* the *most popular river in the world, and I'm passing over it. I am looking at the actual Nile River!*

The van descended off the bridge and onto a wide, five-lane raised highway—the Nile snaked away from view. Nick referred back to his map following the river and tried to figure out where they were and the distance to the hotel. He looked at the 'X' marking the hotel and the winding river but had no idea what road they were taking.

"Mehmet," Nick said, looking at him again in the rear view. Nick pointed out the window to the road and asked, "Name?" Swiping his finger in the air, back and forth, to signal the road. "Name?" he repeated.

"Ahh," Mehmet nodded and mimicked the finger pointing. "Fey-zal, Fey-zal."

"Fey-zal," Nick repeated, and Mehmet nodded in agreement.

Nick looked down at his map and found King Feisal. "Ahh, Feisal!" he confirmed.

Mehmet nodded with a smile, appearing to enjoy their drive.

They pulled up to the hotel, decorated with black, metal vines all along the top floor. Mehmet turned back to face Nick and smiled again. Nick returned the gesture when the side door had been slid open.

"Welcome." The hotel steward offered to take Nick's bag. Mehmet said something to the steward, causing the man to respond curtly, all while ushering Nick to the hotel steps.

Nick looked back at Mehmet, who had been calling out to him. Nick's smile diminished as he watched the steward and another hotel employee force Mehmet back into the vehicle, shouting at him until he drove away.

The two men brushed off their burgundy jackets and, as if the scene had just not occurred, they looked up with a pleasant smile and signaled for Nick to head on through the metal detector and into the hotel.

The matted brass accents on the exterior glass doors were chipped and trimmed with what appeared to be rust. However, the hotel was not near any water; it was odd to see rust along the trim. Maybe it was caused by whatever chemical they use to clean the glass. Nick stopped caring and went inside.

CHAPTER 52

COLORFUL, STAINED-GLASS LANTERNS hung at different heights, spreading bold red, blue, and yellow colors throughout the hotel lobby. The bulbs appeared hand-blown, hung from brass-colored chains, twinkling in sunset light that had begun to trickle in through the octagonal skylights. The lantern colors accentuated the ornate mosaic tiles that lay on the floor and continued half way up the high walls, before they were cut off by white stucco that continued up to the high, sculpted ceiling.

Large, leafy plants surrounded the space, which was commanded by a giant fountain in the lobby's center. Water flowed through spouts inserted into meticulously scattered jugs, which laid in haphazardly, perfect piles that reached just below the lowest of the hanging lanterns. A decorative and colorful stained-glass dome, revealing the sky, hovered above this massive flowing sculpture.

Nick walked past the few people gathered among high-back bamboo lobby chairs, toward the quiet reception desk. He passed the brass elevator doors when he noticed the sign for the hotel business center. He avoided the reception area and followed the arrow, just as he had been instructed. The shipping area, he was told, would be nearby. He found the glass doors, but, of course, they were locked.

A young man appeared from behind the counter, seemingly cleaning up for the evening. Nick knocked on the glass and waved. The man pointed to his watch and made a gesture that Nick translated to mean *tomorrow*.

"I'm sorry," Nick said through the glass. "It's very important."

The man gestured that he could not hear him, clearly trying his best to politely shush him away.

"Please, sir," Nick pleaded.

The man relented, walked around the counter, and unlocked the door. "I'm very sorry, sir, but the business center will open again tomorrow morning at 7:00 a.m."

"I know, I know. My apologies, but I'm looking for Mo."

"I am Mo." The man pointed to his name tag.

"Oh! Right," Nick said, embarrassed. "I was sent to give you something."

The man immediately changed his face to concern. He looked up and down the hall and whispered, "Not here. Meet me upstairs. Thirty minutes. Room 425. Just below the rooftop bar." Mo looked around again and continued, "Take the elevator at the front lobby. I'll be there soon."

Nick retraced his steps back to the lobby and called an elevator. To the right was a sign promoting the Pyramid View Rooftop Bar. It was then he realized how close he must have been to the ancient Pyramids. He stepped inside and was about to press the button with the number four, but his eyes were drawn to the "Pyramid View Bar" button instead. He pressed it, thinking he might as well catch sight of the historical wonders while he waited. Sure, he had been instructed not to get distracted, but Mo needed some time to arrive to the room. Maybe just one photo.

The elevator opened to a small hallway that had one door to the left and a brass sign holder, with the name of the bar and an arrow pointing to the stairway straight ahead. Nick followed the direction of the arrow, up the stairs and turning the corner, and saw the glow of the lights that shined on the massive pyramids.

At a small table to his left, sat a couple holding hands. They stood up and left the terrace. Nick was alone. It was just him and the fantastic view. From where he stood, he could only see the top half of the pyramids. He would have to get to the railing to see their complete beauty. Instead, he remained in the doorway, staring at them, and breathed in the Egyptian air. His Nile-induced goosebumps returned. *This experience*, he thought, *is just as glorious.*

He stepped toward the railing, pulled his phone out, and tapped on the camera app. He positioned the camera, framing the pyramids, and moved his thumb over the button. Just before the camera snapped the photograph, the lights on the pyramids went dark. Shocked and disappointed, Nick turned around to look for some sort of explanation. No one was there. He quickly reviewed his last photo and saw nothing but blackness.

A server appeared and began clearing the table behind him.

"Excuse me," Nick got her attention.

"Yes, sir," the young woman replied without stopping cleaning the table.

"The lights." He pointed at the blackness behind him. "Does that happen often? Will they go back on soon?"

"Yes, sir. And, no, sir. You see, the lights are turned off every night at this time. The pyramids are closed, sir."

"Closed?"

"Yes." She placed the tray of empty glasses on one of the plush seats and proceeded to wipe the table. "No more visitors."

"Oh." Nick scratched his head. "Well, why don't they leave the lights on, at least? It's a beautiful view."

"Yes, it is, sir," she replied with a hint of frustration in her voice. "At this time of night, everything is closed. There is no place to view the desert. Our terrace has just closed as well."

"Oh." Nick got her hint. She just wanted him to leave. It made sense why Nick was the only one on the terrace.

He missed it. He didn't catch the view. He saw it for one quick second and then, *poof*, it was gone. Defeated, he thanked the busy server. He stepped down the stairs, past the elevator, through the glass door, and continued to the floor below.

Nick knocked again on the door to room 425. He thought maybe he knocked a little too gently the first time. The door opened, and Mo quickly ushered him inside.

The room was basic; pale gray walls, red ornate blanket on a king-sized bed. A yellow couch sat with a blue patterned armchair by the two windows at the far end of the room.

Mo motioned for Nick to sit as he pushed aside the pile of magazines that sat on top of the small, round coffee table. Nick sat at the edge of the plush armchair.

"Do you have it with you?" Mo's eyes shifted as he asked. The man looked suspicious or nervous, Nick couldn't really tell.

"It's here," Nick replied, purposely keeping his response vague. He wanted to make sure Mo was legit. He waited for Mo's response to gauge him a little longer.

"Do you have it with you?" Mo replied with a little frustration, but with a hint of concern seeping through his words.

"Can I ask you something?" Nick said and leaned in. He had been instructed to stall. Make sure the man was truly the man he was supposed to meet. He didn't know how to stall, though. He couldn't think of what to say. He blurted the question, "What is so special about it, exactly?"

"Rumors, really," Mo responded and took a breath. "Well, it was once said to have been something important, but no one in the historical arena would give it any credit, anyway." He looked away, at the window, then turned back to Nick.

"I don't understand."

"There's just too much involved here," Mo offered the dismissal. "Do you have it with you or not? Can I see it?" He looked Nick in the eye.

Nick didn't respond. He could see Mo's mind working, reading him, gauging him.

"Where is it?" Mo was curt. "Give it to me," Mo demanded and stood up holding out his hand.

"Relax, Mo," Nick sat up again. "I'm just curious to know what it is I am carrying. I mean, it just looks like a bracelet. I did do some research on what it could be, but I'm not a scholar of such items. I'm sure I can find someone to tell me what it is."

"You don't need to know what it is." Mo's frustration was growing. "Just hand it to me, and go on your way, as you were instructed to do." He then reached into his pocket and pulled out a pistol.

Nick's eyes widened. He didn't think he would meet a gun on this delivery. "Okay, okay." Nick raised his hands. "There's no need for that."

"Give it to me," Mo commanded. His hand shook nervously as he pointed the gun.

"Yes, okay," Nick replied. "Please, just put that down."

"I'm sorry." Mo put his gun away. "I'm just really nervous. I don't want to do this anymore. I need the bracelet, and I need to go. You need to go."

Their discussion was broken by a knock on the door, followed by the sound of cars screeching from the street below. Mo and Nick looked at each other in confusion. There were voices of men on the streets shouting at each other in Arabic before being met with a scream. They looked out the window and saw the commotion happening at the hotel entrance below. A silver taxi had collided with a white van. One man lay on the ground, surrounded by a small crowd. It registered to Nick that it was his soda-obsessed driver, Mehmet. *What the hell was he...?*

The knock on the door continued.

"We have to get out of here," Mo pleaded. "Shit! Shit! Shit!"

"What's going on?" Nick secured the bracelet, that he was about to hand to Mo, back into his inside pocket.

Knock. Knock. Knock. The sound was louder and more aggressive.

Mo looked at the window and pointed.

"Go!"

"What?" Nick resisted. "Where?"

"Just step on the ledge. I'll get rid of them. It will be quick. They mustn't see you."

"Who are they?" Nick asked.

"Just go!"

"I'm not going out the window," Nick said.

The knocking was again accompanied by shouting in Arabic, to which Nick did not understand.

"Go." Mo pushed Nick to the window. "Hurry."

Nick looked down, seeing the commotion still in action. He examined the ledge. It was wider than he had thought it would be. The outer walls of the building were decorated with black metal bars that he would be able to hold onto as he stood on the ledge. He swung his leather bag over his shoulder and gently climbed out.

Mo waited for Nick to secure himself on the ledge and took a deep breath. "Don't move until I tell you," he said, then popped his head back inside and opened the door at the other end of the room.

Out on the hotel window ledge, Nick could feel a bird approaching his feet. At every breeze, his pantleg ruffled, making him wonder if one of them had reached his leg or if it was just the wind. He wanted to look down, but the height was too much for him. Granted, he was on a wide ledge, holding onto sturdy, decorative metal bars, but the idea of falling weakened his knees, and the damn birds were not helping.

His bag was strapped over his shoulder. The weight of it hindered his focus to maintain balance against the exterior stucco wall. A loud flapping invaded his left ear—one of the birds had landed on his shoulder. He shrugged, but the bird didn't budge.

He had to focus on remaining quiet and unseen, while listening to the chaos that ensued in the room through the window to his right. But the bird still stood on his shoulder, cooing in his ear. Another shrug, and the bird finally flapped its wings. It eventually leapt off of him and fluttered further down the ledge.

Nick breathed in and turned to his right, leaning for a peek inside. He had a view of the lower left corner of the vanity mirror. In it was the reflection of a beige, linen pant leg—overly wide— that, with every slight movement, revealed the brown-auburn top of a man's leather shoe.

He stood still and listened. *What language was he speaking?* He leaned in further for a better view but immediately froze at the sound of a gunshot from inside the room. Nick became wide-eyed with shock. He had never been close to a gunshot. He had heard a gun from afar, but never this close. He felt himself shaking. He breathed in and composed himself.

He carefully leaned in and looked at the mirror again, seeing the man he had been meeting, Mo, fall to the floor. His body was still as the beige pant leg walked over him and disappeared from view. Nick stayed in place, listening. Eventually, the sound of the hotel room door closed.

He breathed in, shaking with disbelief. What mess had he gotten himself into? He had to get out of there. He shuffled closer to the window and looked in. The room was still intact, no signs of the scuffle he heard from the ledge. In fact, everything appeared to be untouched, except for the body that lay by the yellow couch. Mo was dead.

He tightened his grip on the metal vine, closed his eyes, and breathed. He had to get out of there. And he had to find a way to do it unseen. He listened for any noises in the room, but the noises on the street below started again. A man walked out of the hotel below and shouted back at the small group of people comforting Mehmet, who seemed to be alive but in pain. Nick focused on the man. He was dressed elegantly. He resembled the same man that had attacked him in the tunnels in Naples. *Could it be the same man?* He watched the man step over Mehmet's leg, his white linen pants flowing in the breeze. He ignored the crowd's insults as he stepped into an idling luxury car and was driven away.

CHAPTER 53

NICK STOOD BY the door, staring at Mo's dead body. He didn't know how he managed to climb back into the window or how he stopped himself from vomiting while he stepped over Mo's body to reach the door.

He listened for any noise out in the hallway, while avoiding looking back at Mo. While he had been close to a dead body before, never had he spent so much time with one.

Was he safe? He surveyed his belongings—leather bag in hand and bracelet in jacket front pocket. He was ready for a quick getaway. He stepped closer to the door and looked out the peephole. No one was there.

He sat back down on the bed, contemplating leaving the hotel. He almost forgot about Mo's body lying on the floor. Someone may know he was there. Someone may know what he had. Someone may try to attack him or kill him for the bracelet. His plan to complete the delivery was ruined. He still had the bracelet. He had no back up plan. No one else to deliver the bracelet. Would the men come back? He needed to get out. He needed to get on his flight back to Italy.

The room telephone rang. Nick almost picked it up out of habit but stopped himself and let it ring. He had to get out of there, and he had to go now.

He grabbed hold of his bag and rushed to the door. He still didn't see anyone through the peephole. He opened the door to an empty hallway. He took the staircase down four flights to the lobby and immediately went for the front door.

The doorman stopped him. "Should we call a taxi for you? Where should we tell him you are going?"

Nick was about to respond with "airport," but held back.

"Oh, I don't need a taxi just now. I'm meeting a friend down the street."

"But sir, it's very late."

"Yes, I know. I'm sorry, but I have to go." Nick opened the door himself.

"Sir, are you sure you don't want a taxi?" The man called out as Nick stepped past him and through the glass doors.

The crowd grew around Mehmet still on the ground. Nick looked through to see his condition. One of the men looked at him with suspicion. Nick crouched down behind a few of the frantic people and then stepped back, turned, and ran down the street.

It was almost four in the morning; the main road was now desolate, the desert stars shining through the dim street lights, and still, no sight of the pyramids to the left. Nothing appeared to be opened, not even a late-night eatery. He walked up the street, headed toward King Faisal Street, which he knew led to the airport. But he also knew he wasn't close enough to walk. He needed to find a taxi.

A rush of footprints swarmed from an alley to his left. A herd of confused camels rushed onto the street, with their herder calling to them. Nick stopped in his tracks in disbelief. The spectacle was such an extreme stereotype on display, no one would believe him. But he was not hallucinating. It was happening right there in front of him, and so late at night (or was it now early in the morning?).

The herder shouted at the bright lights that followed his small caravan, until a little, gray car turned out of the same alley and abruptly stopped. With the lights still shining and his window rolled down, the plump driver exchanged words with the herder, who was now calming his camels on the side of the street. The driver was probably wondering what kind of man moves his herd at that time of night.

In the kerfuffle, Nick noticed the car was actually a taxi! The herder made a hand gesture, ending the exchange, then turned and led his camels down the street. The driver got out of his vehicle and shouted something back. Nick didn't know what the man had said, but surmised it to be some sort of insult toward the angry herder.

The driver stood with one leg still in his vehicle, looked around in disbelief, and inadvertently locked eyes with Nick—the only other person in sight.

"Taxi?" Nick called out to him and smiled. "Are you a taxi?"

The plump man smiled through his carefully stylized, barbell mustache, exposing a gold tooth in the right corner of his mouth. He nodded and happily gestured for Nick to get in the car.

The interior was surrounded in mustard yellow from top to bottom. Nick bounced onto the plush seats, covered in a velvet-like fabric, typically seen on an old sofa. The ceiling was lined with a trim of soft yellow balls that rocked as the driver plopped into his seat. The man adjusted his purple turban, put his hands on the wheel, and asked for the destination. Nick was convinced these drivers purposefully exaggerated their look. He decided this man cleverly played the role of a cartoon character for the tourists.

"*Lil Mataal,*" Nick uttered, hoping it was the correct way to say it. Just in case he had messed it up, he repeated it in English, "Airport."

"*Mashi,*" the man replied with enthusiasm and put the car into gear.

"How much?" Nick called to the driver.

The man looked at him through the rear view, confused.

"*Be Kam?*" Nick hoped he had said it correctly. "How much?" Nick handed him two-hundred pounds.

"*La,*" the man refused and shook his head.

Nick didn't have time to haggle. He handed him another fifty pounds and instructed, "Fuh-y-sal." The name of the highway to Cairo; which he had remembered Mehmet had told him.

"*Mashi,* okay." The man smiled and made the vehicle jolt up the main road.

Nick knew that further up the road, would be the ramp for the main highway, King Faisal Street, that would take them to the Cairo airport. He knew they were headed in the right direction.

He turned and looked back at the hotel getting smaller and smaller as they drove away. No one seemed to have been pursuing him. Maybe he was still under the radar, no one knowing who he was, nor what he was carrying. He reached into his inner front pocket and confirmed the bracelet was still with him. He tended to do this every so often, making sure he knew where it was at all times.

The car suddenly jolted as the driver took a quick left onto a narrow street and came to a complete stop. The street resembled more of an alley, squeezed between two low, white stucco buildings. Nick's heart jumped to his throat. He had not expected the driver to turn off the main road, and especially not with such urgency. What was his plan?

"Faisal," Nick ordered. It was the name of the main street that led to the highway. The only street he knew. He had to get the driver back on track. Just where was he taking him? "Faisal!"

"*Alaikhtisar,*" the man pleaded, or said something of that nature, but the car remained stopped.

"Faisal," repeated Nick. "Faisal!"

The driver turned in his seat, looked back at Nick, and gestured for him to calm down. Nick maintained his angry glare and shook his head. The driver turned back to his wheel and, again, honked the horn.

Nick looked beyond the windshield and saw what the issue was. The abrupt stop was to avoid hitting a group of men taking a short cut to the main strip—early day workers of the hotels or cafés that aligned the main street.

"Thank you," Nick repeated in a calmer tone. "Faisal."

The driver relented, put the vehicle in reverse, and continued up the main street. The pre-sunrise traffic had begun to fill the strip. Nick allowed himself to be swallowed by the back seat when he understood the driver was only trying to take a short cut.

The car turned onto the ramp, leading to the highway that crossed the Nile. The driver swerved away from a small truck that carelessly sped past them and honked his horn. He shook his head and continued. "El-Rawda," he said to Nick, pointing down at Rawda Island below them.

Nick looked up and locked eyes with him in the mirror. He smiled and nodded—a look of gratitude that he had brought them back on track. The driver smiled back and continued driving.

Nick felt justified he had not wasted his time examining the Cairo map before the trip. He always took time to gauge the layout of a place that was new to him.

He tapped his mobile phone, looking up flights out of Cairo. The first to Italy was set for Naples—perfect. Flight departs Cairo at 06:25 a.m.—that works. His watch confirmed the time to be 03:18 a.m., which left him plenty of time. He entered his details and confirmed the ticket.

However, he still felt a sense of pursuit. Who had been knocking on that hotel door? And just what in the hell had he agreed to? Was someone going to look for him? Did they know who he was? Would they find him? Did they know where he was headed? He had to get inside the airport, pass through security, and the, and only then, would he feel somewhat safe. Well, he would feel much better once he was on a plane, but at least past security would be a barrier to open space—where he could easily be approached.

Nick looked out the window and noticed they were over the incredible Nile. He was looking at the lights glistening on the black water, when he felt a sudden deceleration and turned to the front window. A flicker of red lights ahead forced the driver to slow the vehicle again, behind the other cars, right in the middle of the highway.

As they approached the scene, Nick saw that same careless truck from before now on its side, and its contents of watermelons spilled and rolling across all the lanes. The cars ahead honked their horns, some drivers getting out of their cars and standing around in disbelief, some arguing with the truck driver, while others rushed to help clear the road.

The far-left lane was the first to be cleared. One or two cars squeezed by, leaving the commotion behind. Nick's driver maneuvered his taxi between other vehicles and squeezed through the lane as well. He laughed and honked as they continued toward Cairo.

It was still dark out. The driver turned off the highway to the airport terminal. Nick watched in shock as they approached another chaotic scene before them.

Security was trying to control the crowd fighting their way into the airport. The men in uniform shouted at the chaos, directing orders to form a line. Nick had no idea how the hell he was going to get through that mess. *Maybe the airport was not yet open?*

Nick looked at the driver, and the driver looked back and winked. He turned the vehicle to the left side of the main entrance, where three men guarded a roped area. The driver called out to one of them, and gestured for Nick to go to him. Nick looked back at the driver who took his money and encouraged him to go.

Nick nodded, took his bag, and got out of the taxi. He watched the friendly driver and his little car drive away, then turned to the man now standing to his right.

"Forty pounds," the man said immediately. "This is first class entrance." He pointed to the roped area and continued, "If you want to go this way, I can take you. Forty pounds."

He had a salesman's stance. Well, he was more like a conman working a swindle. Nick looked back at the main entrance and the continuous chaos.

"We go in this way," the man said, pointing past the ropes, at the steps that led to the glass doors. "Straight to the ticket desk."

Nick followed his point, seeing ticket agents quietly waiting for passengers to approach. There were no passengers yet inside.

"Forty pounds," the man repeated.

"Okay," Nick replied. "But I give you twenty now. Then twenty once I get inside."

"Forty pounds," the man repeated.

"Twenty now, twenty later," Nick said, this time with more confidence.

The man scoffed, rolled his eyes, and reluctantly accepted. Nick handed the man twenty pounds and followed him to one of the men behind the rope. The two had a few words, a quick exchange of money, and the man opened the rope to let Nick through.

Nick smiled at the man and turned back to the swindler, who was holding out his hand.

"Twenty pounds," the man said.

"No," Nick responded and made his way toward the steps.

"Hey," the man called out after him. "Twenty pounds!"

"Thank you for your help," Nick replied, turning away once again, and approaching the doorman holding the handle to the glass doors.

"Welcome," he said and pushed open the door.

"Twenty pounds," the swindler's voice called again, but this time, it was met with shouting from the doorman and the other men behind the rope.

Nick didn't look back. Instead, he continued into the airport hearing the voices disappear as the doors closed behind him.

For a moment, he felt good about out-swindling a swindler. And for another moment, he felt awful for swindling a man who was just trying to make a living. His small moment of guilt was interrupted by the ticketing agent, handing him back his passport.

The feeling followed him as he crossed through the metal detector and picked up his bag from the scanner belt. The feeling disappeared when he heard loud voices approach the security area. He turned and saw a glimpse of the swindler again. He was shouting at him and at the security guard blocking his way. More guards arrived, grabbed the man's arm, and escorted him away.

Nick picked up his pace away from security. When he found his gate, he sat down, away from the other five people already there, waiting. No airline worker was yet at the gate. There was still a lot of time before boarding was to begin. The café before him was not yet open, either.

As he waited, Nick realized he had made it. He escaped whatever potential danger was about to reach him in Giza. He had made it to Cairo, through security, and was in a now somewhat safe space, until he was on that flight, headed back to Italy.

Should he contact Gaetano's man and find out what the danger was? No, he decided to wait until he got to Italy.

He continued to look at the café, hoping someone would open it up soon. He eventually sat back, let down his guard, and rested his eyes—knowing the aroma of coffee would awaken him should he fall asleep.

CHAPTER 54

STILL NO ANSWER, nor a callback from Laura. Nick rushed to her place immediately from the airport. He rang her door buzzer to no response. He began to think Laura was in some sort of danger.

Did those men come looking for him again and got to her instead? Had they connected him to her? How had they found him in Egypt? How did they know he was there? Who was the man that killed Mo? His mind circled on theories, questions, ideas, and fears. But ultimately, where was Laura?

He had to get into her apartment. What if she was inside, hurt, or worse? A woman came to the main door and explained she was the building manager. He apologized for loitering on the steps, but said he was supposed to meet his girlfriend (people always let their guard down when the story is romantic), and she wasn't responding. He told her the apartment number, but she informed him that the *Signorina Laura* moved out.

"Moved out? When? Where did she go?"

"Somewhere nearby, I believe. I'm sorry, I don't really know where," the woman replied. "She just called and had movers come to pick up her things. It was yesterday."

"Yesterday?" Nick repeated. That confirmed Laura was alive… but where had she gone, and why hadn't she mentioned it to him? And why wasn't she answering her phone? He thanked the woman, apologized for the inconvenience, and left before she could respond.

He walked away from the building, not knowing where to go next. The bracelet transaction had failed. He still hadn't registered Mo's dead body, nor the mysterious man that had killed him. He thought it was probably best to go back to Gaetano's colleague and tell him about the whole thing. But would he want the bracelet? Nick didn't care anymore. The bracelet, the money… none of it was his priority now. He needed to find Laura. He needed to make sure she was okay. Once he knew that and could clear his conscience, he would focus on the bracelet again. *The library! She was probably working on her research.* He headed south toward the university.

His phone buzzed. He took it out of his pocket and saw a number he did not recognize. He let it go to voicemail.

The phone buzzed again. Same number. He answered. "Pronto?"

"Hello, Nick," Lavinia's voice invaded his ear, his mind, his thoughts. He had to keep her away. He pulled the phone from his ear and ended the call.

The phone buzzed again. He ignored it.

Once again, the phone buzzed.

It was clear Lavinia was not going to stop calling him. He didn't know how to stop it, until he remembered; he denied the call, went into call list, and blocked the number. He had to figure a way to get her to leave him alone. He wanted her to stop. He kicked a trash bin that stood on the sidewalk, making it roll onto the street.

His phone buzzed again. He looked at it. It was another number he did not recognize.

She wants the bracelet, he thought. *And she won't stop until she gets it again.*

He needed to find a way to make her stop. To give up. *How?* He decided he had no choice but to answer again. That's how he would make it end.

"Hello," he said into the phone, ready to tell Lavinia to fuck off.

"Nick! Nick!" It was Laura's voice. "Nick, are you okay? Where are you?!"

"Laura!" Nick exclaimed. "I've been looking for you. I sent you a text—I was in Cairo."

"Cairo?!" Laura repeated. "Why? Never mind. I don't have my phone. I lost it."

"Well, that makes sense as to why I didn't hear from you," Nick responded. "It's a long story. I'm back now. Where are you?"

No response.

"Laura?"

Still, no response.

"Hello?"

"Hello, Nick," Lavinia's voice took over.

"Lavinia!" Nick shouted. "What are you doing? Are you with Laura? Leave her alone! Where are you?!"

"I will send you the address to where we are," Lavinia's voice commanded. "You will bring the bracelet to me, and you can come get your girl."

"Don't hurt her!" Nick shouted into dead silence.

His phone pinged with a map. Location: Reggia di Caserta.

CHAPTER 55

THE RIDE TO the palace was filled with anxiety. The thought of having to confront Lavinia again made his body tremble with fury. He wasn't sure if it was revenge anger or anger at himself for putting Laura in jeopardy.

He pulled the rental car up to the palace-turned-museum and followed his instructions. The museum was closed for the night, but he was instructed to walk up to the door and wait for entry. He stood under the portico and waited.

A small door to the right creaked open. Behind it, a tall, slender man allowed him to enter. Nick crossed the threshold and found himself surrounded by a group of men dressed in black. Immediately, he realized they were the same men that attacked him in the tunnels.

One of them held a woman against her will—a gun to her head. Nick noticed it was Lavinia's cohort, Silvia. He looked around the opulent marble foyer for some sort of escape but saw that he was surrounded.

Nick recognized the scar on the man that approached and frisked him. The man patted Nick all over until he felt the bracelet in his inside breast pocket. He reached in but Nick stopped him by grabbing his arm. Another man pointed a gun to Nick and clicked the safety. Nick paused, looked around again, and let the man pull the bracelet out.

The sound of footsteps trickled in from around the corner. A new man appeared with a smile on his face. The sound of his accent was clear. It was Spanish.

"I promise you guys," Nick stammered. "I was planning to hold it for you."

"Of course, you were," the man's thick Spanish accent was a sheathed threat. "Unlike my men here, I don't trust you. So, I had you followed." The man closed in, glared at Nick, and continued, "You see, I knew you had the bracelet for some time now, and I knew you weren't waiting for me."

"But I was—" Nick interrupted.

"Silence!" the man interrupted in return. "Don't bother sparing me with some foolish story. I know you weren't waiting for me. You were seen at the airport. You were seen getting on a plane to Cairo. I had no choice but to try and intercept you. Apparently, I just missed you…that poor, young man," he turned back to Nick. "You didn't have to do that, you know. Kill him like that."

"What?!" Nick was in shock. "You followed me? You were the one that killed him? Why did you do it?"

"I think it's a better story to say that you killed the man at the hotel," the man looked at Nick again with a false, exaggerated look of shock, and replied, "We have evidence that tells that story."

"You mean tells the story you want to tell!" Nick shouted.

"Will you please be quiet?" the man seethed. "You're going to make this more difficult than it has to be." The man then nodded to the one that held Silvia hostage.

At the signal, he led her through the massive hallway, out into the gardens.

"What are you going to do with her?" Nick asked.

"She's done her job," the man replied, but stopped as his man came rushing back.

"Señor Millàs," the man called to him. "Ella escapó! A los jardines!"

The elegant man scolded him in Spanish and demanded he follow her. "You're coming with me," he ordered Nick, then pulled him through the hallway, out into the back gardens.

"Where are we going?" Nick asked.

"Where are you supposed to meet her?" the man asked in response.

"You mean, you're not working with her?" Nick said. He wondered how he knew he was to meet Lavinia.

"Where are you meeting her?!" the man repeated and continued to pull Nick toward a group of parked four-wheeled pedal bikes.

"I—I don't know, really," Nick stammered. "I was just told to knock on the door. I assume that woman, Silvia, was supposed to—"

"Shut up!" the man shouted.

A woman's scream echoed from somewhere down the long path of gardens behind the palace. Both men looked toward the direction and saw a faint glimmer of a flashlight far off in the distance.

"Get in," the man commanded. Nick climbed onto the front bench of the cycle, but assessed an escape as he did. "Pedal!" the man shouted. "Pedal!"

Nick put one foot on a pedal, but before swinging his second leg in, he took his chance. He jumped out and ran into the thick hedges to the far right. He continued up toward the direction of the flashlight but stayed out of sight in the hedges. From a distance, he heard the Spanish man shouting to his men.

Nick didn't stop running until the sound of a gunshot stopped his pace. Nick dropped to the ground, then crawled to the closest hedge to hide. Another scream followed; it was the scar-faced man. Nick remained on the ground and shuffled closer to the opening on the main pathway. He peered between the branches and saw Silvia's body lying motionless by one of the large basins that collected fountain water. He was startled by the man groaning in the distance.

Nick remained still and listened to one of the quadricycles *whoosh* past him, further up into the gardens. He peeked and saw that the Spanish man was accompanied by another one of his men.

"Come out, Lavinia…" the man called out and shone his flashlight haphazardly along the hedges and the fountains. Nick noticed some of the fountains were not running.

Another gunshot in the distance. Nick flinched at the sound. He heard the cycle crash and the elegant man shouted, "Levantarse!"

Nick looked out again and spotted the cycle on its side, the driver writhing in pain. The elegant man struggled as he crawled over him and onto the path, crossing to the hedges on the right side. It looked to Nick like the man was in pursuit.

Nick was startled when his phone buzzed in his pocket. He was surprised the men had not taken it from him. He pulled it out and pulled up the text. It was from Lavinia.

Stop what you're doing! You will not succeed.

It's not me! Nick replied. *I thought they were with you! Where are you?*

Lavinia didn't respond.

They have the bracelet. Nick added. *They took it from me.*

Lavinia didn't respond.

Nick heard a motor in the distance. Maybe a vespa…He didn't know. Then he heard a woman shout, "Nick! Nick!" It was Laura's voice getting further and further away.

Another gunshot followed. Two. Nick lay still in shock. He hoped it wasn't Laura. He got up, stayed in the shadows, and followed the noise. He reached what looked like a bridge but was actually the face of another fountain that looked over the large basin of water. The façade appeared to have arches—a potential spot to hide. He ran across the path and found the opening to a cavern hidden within the façade. He stopped and listened, but the sound of the water splashing into the basin drowned out any noise.

"Don't move," her voice crawled up his spine. It was Lavinia. "Show your face in the light." She waved the gun in the ray from the spotlight over the fountain.

Nick trembled with fury. He wanted to say so much to her. He wanted to attack her. He wanted to take her gun and shove it in her fucking face. He leaned into the light, allowing her to see him.

"My beautiful Nick," she said in a soft tone.

It made him cringe. Her tone. Her words. He was boiling with fury.

"Oh, Nick!" Laura said with relief.

"Laura?" Nick called out to the darkness. "Are you okay?"

"Shut up," Lavinia shouted over to her. "Stop talking!"

Laura said nothing. Nick was relieved she was alive.

"You led them to us, you know," Lavinia said to Nick. "Whomever is chasing us; you caused this."

"They just wanted the bracelet, like you," Nick said. "They have it."

"Then what is all this chasing, shooting…" Lavinia asked.

"He's looking for you," Nick said. "He wants you."

"Me?" she replied in shock. "Who is he?"

"You know who I am, Lavinia," the elegant, Spanish man's voice broke through the darkness.

"Professor?" Laura interrupted. "Alfonso?"

Alfonso didn't respond.

"Alfonso?!" Lavinia said with, what Nick saw, a look of anger mixed with shock. "You caused this commotion? You don't give up, do you? The bracelet doesn't belong to you!"

"Thank you, Lavinia," Alfonso replied. "My persistence was worth it. I now have what was due to me." He held the bracelet in the light, letting it shimmer.

"That is not yours and you know it," Lavinia replied and aimed the gun at him.

Nick saw his chance and grabbed her wrist. That forced the gun out of her hand and into the basin. She pulled him off and forced herself onto Alfonso, who flipped her over the railing and into the water.

"My bracelet!" Alfonso shouted and looked over the railing.

Nick heard Lavinia splashing in the water. He grabbed Alfonso and struggled to force his gun to the ground. Alfonso then punched him in the jaw and ran out of the cavern.

Lavinia had pulled herself out of the water. She was leaning onto the edge of the basin, catching her breath. On her wrist was the bracelet clasped and shimmering in the moonlight. Upon seeing her like that, Laura felt a sense of déjà vu. *Wasn't this in one of my visions?*

"Get over here, Lavinia," Alfonso shouted from the end of the cavern. He lunged at her.

Lavinia groaned and pushed him away. She keeled over and held onto the edge of the basin.

"Alfonso!" Laura appeared behind him with the gun in her hand. "Let her go!"

"Laura!" Nick shouted. He saw Alfonso lunge at Laura. "No!" He ran to her at the other end of the cavern, out onto the path where they were, when he heard the gunshot. "Laura!" Nick stopped just behind her. He reached out. Her shoulders trembled. "Laura, are you okay? Put the gun down," he said.

"Oh, Nick," she cried. "What have I done?" The words came out of her as she hyperventilated.

"Laura, drop the gun," Nick said again as he approached and gently embraced her.

Laura looked at the gun, then at Alfonso's bloody head. She lost her composure, sobbed, and dropped the gun into the water.

Nick held her tight as she shook in his arms.

Lavinia groaned further down the basin. She held onto its outer wall and lifted herself to her feet. She reached an arm down to her torso and grumbled in pain.

"Lavinia," Nick called to her.

She looked at him, her eyes giving him a look of pain. She was not well. She lifted her arm, saw the gore, and let out a blood-curdling scream.

CHAPTER 56

NICK CARESSED THE grooves of the satin and velvet as he brushed off the crumbs he let fall onto the expensive armchair. They were freshly-baked, flaky biscotti with a chocolate and cherry filling. Nick couldn't stop at just one—they were too good.

"You like?" asked Amalda, the kind and kooky woman sitting across from him.

"Delicious," Nick mumbled through his chews. He lifted his hand to his mouth and apologized for talking with his mouth full. "Sorry."

The woman chuckled and sipped her coffee. Nick blushed and continued to inconspicuously brush any leftover crumbs.

"As I was saying, I'm truly sorry for what you've been through," Amalda shook her head. "Lavinia lost her way. I'm sorry that happened to you. She thought she deserved to be leader. A sad, misguided sister."

"I appreciate that," Nick said. He really didn't know how else to respond.

"We will have to deal with her, of course," Amalda continued and poured more tea. "Once she is out of the hospital, and after the police do their required duties. And Silvia...may she rest in peace, even though she used her position at the United Nations to participate in all of that." Amalda set down the tea pot and focused her attention to the hallway. "Laura," she exclaimed.

Laura had finally come down from upstairs. Nick stood up politely—he remembered gentlemen doing that in those period films. He didn't know why he felt he needed to do it. Laura had a small bandage on her forehead.

"Hello," she said softly to the room, then turned to Nick directly. "Nice to see you, Nick."

"Same," Nick responded and sat back down after Laura took her seat. "I'm glad you're okay."

Laura smiled back.

"Laura is in good hands here," Amalda said. "We will take good care of her. She is one of us now." She leaned into Laura and added, "No pressure. Whether you stay with us or not—you are now family."

"Thank you," Laura replied, then looked at Nick.

"Oh, right," Nick responded to her look, then sat forward and spoke to Amalda. "Signora…"

"Amalda," she said.

"Amalda, right," Nick repeated. "Laura and I had a long talk, and we decided that this belongs to you." He reached into his pocket and pulled out a long jewelry box.

"For me?" Amalda asked and accepted the gift. "Why for me? I don't deserve a gift." She turned to Laura. "Laura—"

"It's really from Nick," Laura interrupted. "He was the one that found it. I just helped him find where it belonged."

Amalda looked at them both, confused. She untied the green ribbon and undid the lavender box. Her eyes opened wide in shock and wonder. She breathed in and opened it further. "It's beautiful," she finally said. "It looks just like it. What made you—"

Nick looked at Laura, confused, then smiled.

"I was told it belongs to the Order of the Eye of Partenope," Nick explained. "That it's been lost—"

"Lost?" Amalda interrupted with an insulted tone. "What do you mean *lost*?"

"Well, you see..." Nick said. "I found it at a market in Rome, and—"

"You found this in a market?" Amalda interrupted again. "Well, it looks just like it. Like my legendary Eye of Partenope."

Nick and Laura looked at each other again.

"You mean, it belongs to you, right? That it should have been with you all along...?" Laura asked.

"Well, I was voted to wear it," Amalda replied. "It's only to be worn at the annual rituals, of course. I keep it in my safe, upstairs."

"Wait, what?" Nick asked.

"The original," Amalda responded. "I have it upstairs."

"You mean, *this* is the original," Nick insisted. "The one that was missing. Lost."

"Mr. Terenzi," Amalda scoffed. "I'm certain that the one *I* have is the original. We've had it in our Order since inception. This one is a beautiful replica, though. I would still like to have it, if I could."

"Of course," Nick stammered. "But I don't understand."

"Don't understand what?"

"Well, if this was not the original, then—"

"Lavinia and Professor Millàs were chasing a fake all along," Laura finished his thought.

"Lavinia? Millàs? Alfonso!" Amalda sat back in shock. "Alfonso Millàs? He was back?"

"You knew him?" Laura asked.

"Yes, yes." Amalda caressed the replica bracelet. "Tragic story, really. Almost pathetic. One moment." Amalda reached for the phone and asked the person on the other end to bring her the bracelet.

"Alfonso came to us a few years back," Amalda explained. "With claims that he was entitled to the band of Partenope. Of course, we refused him."

"How did he think he was entitled?" Laura asked.

"Alfonso claimed his mother was the rightful leader of the Order," Amalda continued. "We realized who she was—a poor actress who had joined the sisterhood around the same time as me. But she was excommunicated from the Order. This happened years ago."

"Excommunicated?" Laura asked. "Why?"

"Well, she believed she was next in line to receive the honor as the wearer of the Eye. Similar to Lavinia's way of thinking, really. She was not elected leader, but she tried to take the position anyway. She didn't agree with the results. She had no choice but to leave. It was quite a scandal.

"Anyway, Alfonso came to us with this cockamamy story that his mother must have fed him growing up, and he believed it. He believed the Order was unfair to her, that it was all orchestrated to get her out. That she had been unfairly excommunicated by the

Order. Well, I can assure you, the scandal was not orchestrated. There was no scandal, really. It was all ego. That woman," Amalda scoffed.

"Actress!" Laura sat up. "I had a vision about her."

"Just now?" Amalda asked.

"No," Laura replied. "It was recent, though. She was backstage…I felt she was sad…hated by her peers…"

"Well, I'm not surprised by that," Amalda responded.

"She said something," Laura added. "She said: *tell my son I love him. Tell him to be careful.*" Laura looked up at Amalda. "Was it his mother? Was she trying to send a message to Alfonso?"

"Your skill may be stronger than you think," Amalda commented and smiled.

A tall, slender woman appeared in the room with a yellow box. Nick watched as she walked over to Amalda and handed her the box. He watched the wisps of her straight, pitch-black bob caress her cheeks as she bent down to lift the empty coffee cups. Laura kicked his shin and forced him to look away.

"Grazie, Beà," Amalda said to her. "Would you guys like anything else? Water maybe? Beatrice, here, will get it."

"No, we're fine—" Laura started to say.

"Water," Nick blurted and looked at Beatrice. "Please. Thank you."

Beatrice nodded and left the room.

Amalda opened the yellow box to reveal a brightly polished, exact copy of Nick's bracelet.

"You see," she said to them. "This is the original Eye of Partenope. It's made of gold. Designed by the Order and forged right here in Naples. It has never left the Order."

"Well, then how did this one get made?" Nick asked. "Someone clearly had the designs of the original to make a replica."

"Could yours be the replica?" He cringed as the words came out. He knew they sounded accusatory.

"I can assure you," Amalda chuckled. "Mine is no replica. But I will take this one, if you don't mind, and have it appraised and looked at. Just to be certain."

"Yes," Nick replied. "Of course. As you should. It's yours. I don't want to see it again. It's only brought me misery and bad luck."

Amalda chuckled again.

"About Alfonso thinking he deserved the bracelet," Laura interjected. "About his mother…"

"Yes," Amalda responded. "As I was saying, Alfonso came to us years ago. He claimed we had taken his life from him. When his mother was removed from our Order, she was left to live the life of a poor actress, traveling from country to country, and finally, settling in Spain. There, she managed to find a husband, and she found a like-minded Order of women who practiced witchcraft in northern Spain. She convinced them to take her in as a member. I can't imagine what trouble she put them through. Anyway, Alfonso was born. When his mother passed, he came to us and told us he believed she was the one who should have carried the Eye. That he had a right to our Order. Of course, we refused him."

"And when he found out the bracelet—the Eye—was back in Naples, he felt it was his chance to get it back," Nick deduced.

"That's how he found me. Through the black market…And what about Lavinia?"

"Lavinia," Amalda scoffed again. "Well, I am actually surprised by her actions. She knew how the Eye is passed on in the Order. I don't understand why she did all that. Especially, since what you had was not even the real one."

"Or maybe it is," Nick said. "Please have it checked. Either way, keep it."

"I will," Amalda replied. "Thank you for bringing this to me. And for stopping Alfonso. He would have come for me. I'm sure of it."

"That was Laura, really," Nick replied.

Laura sank into the couch.

"Don't be ashamed, Laura," Nick said to her.

"I wasn't expecting to do that," she said. "But I'm glad we helped."

Beatrice returned with a pitcher of water and three glasses. She set the tray onto the coffee table, removed all the contents, lifted the empty tray, and walked back out of the room.

"You think this bracelet brought you bad luck?" Amalda asked.

"Absolutely," Nick replied. "It's cursed. Or maybe I was cursed. Either way, I don't ever want to see it again."

Amalda chuckled and got up from her seat. Nick stood up out of politeness and sat back down. Amalda stepped over to a small cabinet and opened the mirrored doors. She pulled out a small box. She then sat back down and opened it. "This is for you," she said to Nick and handed him a small, velvet pouch.

"For me? No," Nick said. "What is it?"

"Open it," Amalda said.

Nick opened the pouch and turned it over his open palm. Out dropped a deep red devil's horn. The Napoletan symbol found in trinket shops all around the city.

"It's protection," Amalda said. "This one is made of coral from the sea. And it has the protection of our Order—The Eye of Partenope. With this particular horn, called a *cornicello*, you will be protected. And you will be protected under us – the Eye of Partenope."

Nick admired the horn and caressed the yellow ribbon Amalda had tied to it. He looked at Laura, then at Amalda, and smiled. He looked back at the horn and rubbed his thumb along its blood red curves.

EPILOGUE

January 1891

UNBEKNOWNST TO THE relatives of the late renowned archaeologist, Dr. Heinrich Schliemann, some of the contents belonging to him travelled to Berlin. The woman carrying the contents knew they did not belong to her, but she felt she had to take them. Otherwise, she would have been found out. She held onto her handbag tightly, as the train continued past the border and out of Italy.

She knew it looked suspicious when she abruptly quit her hotel job, but she was tired of catering to the wealthy travelers. The job didn't pay much, but it allowed her access to many valuables. It started with a small earing left on the lunch table. Eventually, it led to her taking a ring someone had left on a side table on the hotel veranda. She knew who the ring belonged to, but she remained silent as she wiped the abandoned table and let the ring slip into her pocket. Over time, she accumulated enough to allow a comfortable life back in Berlin.

Her last assignment had unexpectedly given her the opportunity to take something that she would keep for herself.

She was to care for the elderly man that had collapsed while on a stroll. He was Dr. Schliemann—the famed archaeologist known to have discovered the renowned treasures of Helen of Troy. When he fell ill, her role had become almost nurse-like. She was to be at his side all day, and sometimes, at night. She jumped at the opportunity to get access to whatever treasure the man could be holding in his room. And, as she thought back, she realized she did appreciate their time together.

She remembered her first day bringing him his lunch. She knocked gently to not startle the man, as instructed by the medical doctor.

"Ja," the man responded from inside.

"Herr Schliemann," she spoke softly as she opened the room door.

Dr. Schliemann sat, propped up on his bed, with papers scattered all around him. He was examining his journal while adding details to his sketches.

"Ah, Danke, Greta," his voice was weak, but focused. He finished tracing a sketch of a flower and placed his pencil back in a leather case. Greta placed the tray of food on the table by the window and went back to the bed to assist the man. She helped gather his notes and sketches, then held his left arm as he shifted out of the bed and shuffled to the table. As he ate, Greta returned to the bed, and returned the papers to their place on his writing desk.

"Greta," the man called to her. "Might I ask you for a favor?"

"Of course, Dr.," Greta replied and continued to straighten his papers.

"Would you mind delivering a letter for me? I would go myself, but…" He gestured to himself. "As you can see, my old body won't allow me just yet."

"Yes, of course, Dr.," Greta replied.

"Thank you." He slurped a spoonful of soup, then added, "It's on the desk there. Addressed to Palladino. Do you see it?"

Greta found an envelope addressed to *Signora Palladino, Eusapia.*

Greta felt slightly remorseful for never delivering that letter. She had forgotten, really. Soon after he had given it to her, the archaeologist had passed away. Right there, in the hotel bed.

She had made sure to be one of the staff assigned to gather his belongings, and be the first in that room once his body had been removed. She had rummaged through his trunk and found the only treasure that he had in his belongings—it was an antique bracelet. *It has to be worth some value*, she had thought. She had slipped the bracelet into her pocket and left the room before the other members of the staff had gone in.

The train traveled through another tunnel. The view out Greta's private cabin window confirmed she had left Italy and finally entered into the German countryside. She was almost home. She was relieved.

Greta zipped open her bag and looked for her pocket mirror. She looked at her face, checked her makeup, and adjusted any hair she may have had out of place. When she returned the mirror to the inside pocket of her bag, she felt something else in there. It was an envelope. She pulled it out and saw that it was the note the archaeologist had asked her to deliver. She had forgotten she slipped it into her bag.

She ripped open the envelope and unfolded the note.

For Signoria Palladino...

Thank you for talking with me about your skill and reading my aura. I appreciated learning about your history and witnessing your ritual. I was happy to connect with you over Greek mythology and learning about your fascination with the legendary sorceress Circe. I was quite surprised to learn that her infamous island was believed to be off the coast of Italy. Ponza will be on my travel list.

I was intrigued to learn about you and your group, the sisterhood. I am grateful to learn that there is a secret group that maintains the old traditions and to learn about Naples' connection to the siren Partenope.

And thank you very much for showing me your bracelet— the Eye of Partenope. It was beautiful. And I appreciate you allowing me to handle and examine the precious piece. I wanted to let you know that my sketches helped me get a recreation made. I'm looking forward to gifting it to my wife, who is waiting for me in Athens for our Christmas holiday.

I look forward to returning to Naples very soon. And to introduce you to my wife and family.

All the best to you and to all the sisters of Partenope.

Dr. Heinrich Schliemann

Distraught, Greta read the letter over again, hoping she had misread the words. However, it was all there. The bracelet she had taken had no value. It was a recreation. A fake. But she thought if it was made of gold or some other valuable metal at least, she would still be able to sell it. A consolation, though, was that she still had all the other valuables she had stolen during her time at the hotel.

She folded the letter, slipped it back into the inside pocket, then reached for the narrow jewelry box that was wrapped in her silk scarf. She flipped open the box and stared at the polished bracelet with a look of disappointment. Although, it did look like an expensive artifact, knowing it was a fake was deflating.

She picked up the piece and wrapped it on her wrist. She admired its shine reflected on the wall across from her. It looked very expensive. Maybe she would wear it. Maybe she could tell people it was expensive. Priceless. A family heirloom? It would help in keeping up an appearance of wealth. It could be her talking piece. She was convinced the wealthy loved people talking about their heirloom pieces. She would make sure it would be seen on her as often as she was seen. She decided she would not sell it. She would keep it. She would grow old with it. And she would pass it down within the family she planned to create.

She wore it when she met her husband—a successful textile salesman from Munich. She wore it when she hosted several parties at her grand home, the one her husband had built just outside of Berlin. She made sure to showcase her bracelet to all the guests. When a guest brought a photographic camera to one of her parties, she reveled in showcasing the bracelet again—capturing it for eternity.

She wore the bracelet when she announced the arrival of her first child—a daughter she had named Claudia. She made sure it was seen and sometimes made off-hand comments, claiming that it brought her luck. When it was time, she left her bracelet—*her* family heirloom—to her daughter, who she hoped would pass it down from generation to generation.

But what Greta didn't know was that her precious and worthless heirloom would eventually be stolen from her granddaughter's Berlin apartment and end up in the hands of some incompetent thief.

THE END

ACKNOWLEDGMENTS

Thank you to my parents and grandparents for giving me the opportunity to spend a lot of my childhood – my summers – in southern Italy. The experience was a very important part of making me the man I am today. I will forever be grateful for giving me the opportunity to connect with and learn about my family background, culture and history. My books are my tribute to all of it. It is because of you that I am inspired to tell my stories and share my knowledge of culture and history, and whatever stories I imagine.

Thank you to my beta-readers for being the first to read my story and to giving me your quality and important feedback. Faye, I appreciate your input on my Greek history, and other myths I touch upon in this story. Your input was important in enhancing my points. And to Kelly, I appreciate your focus on details and the characters. Your input and suggestions allowed me to give these characters more depth and reality.

And thank you to all you readers out there that continue to support my work. It's always a treasure to hear it when my story has touched or fascinated you. And please remember, the best way to support a book by an independent author is to help with its ranking: purchase the book, write a review, and recommend it to your friends.

Purchase. Review. Recommend

With love,

Lorenzo

AUTHOR'S NOTE

Thank you for reading my final book in what I call my "Italy Trilogy." What started with a challenge to myself to write a book, turned into promising myself that if I write one, then I can write three. This project started in autumn of 2011, when I left my job in television and temporarily moved to Rome. If you have followed my talks and interviews, you know that in all the summers I spent in Italy as a kid and teen, I'd never really gotten to know Rome. So, I took my days to walk and explore the Eternal City. At the same time, I had made my promise to try and write a book—something I had thought about for a long time. As I got to know Rome, I thought about potential stories. Soon, the setting for my story had been decided. Next, I chose the tone for my story—it was going to be inspired by Fellini, with a mix of romantic comedy. And during my time in Rome, the first draft to my first book *The Love Fool* was born.

After many reiterations, rewrites, edits, and beta reading sessions, *The Love Fool* was finally published in March of 2013. I took my time in learning the process of writing and publishing a book. After some fundraising campaign, I successfully got *The Love Fool* published via a hybrid publisher.

I began the fun part of the process: promoting the book. I reached out to any book blogger, interviewer, or independent bookshop to help promote my indie-book. My ultimate goal for *The Love Fool* (or this whole project), was to see my written work on a shelf in a bookstore. My goal was Barnes & Noble. So, I researched and found out how to do it, and I got it done. My book was on the shelves in three or four B&N stores in Massachusetts, and still available today via their website. I even booked events at a couple of their stores. The major highlights of promoting *The Love Fool* were a talk over dinner and drinks at EATALY Boston, and book club discussions at an indie bookstore and private homes.

After a couple of years, I removed the middle-man hybrid-publisher (they weren't really providing me with anything other than what I myself was doing anyway), and took full control of the rights. Soon, I re-released/self-published *The Love Fool* under my own publishing name, Magnusmade, and continued to promote my book.

At this time, I had begun writing my second book, *A Mistake Incomplete*. This story was set in Milan and inspired by noir films—my favorite movie genre. I looked to Hitchcock style, and stories by Hammett, Woolrich, and Patricia Highsmith. I removed the detective and focused on the characters. The result was a dark caper with elements of mystery, crime, and broken hearts. The intention was to incorporate details about the city of Milan, like I did with Rome in *A Mistake Incomplete*. I had been going back to Milan once a year and took notes here and there. I watched bartenders mix their drinks, mapped out routes my characters would take, and noted some sights that would be incorporated into my new story.

As I wrote more of my story—knew more of where my characters needed to go in Milan—I had one more trip to take to get all the details and make Milan part of the story. The trip was booked for April of 2020. That dreaded pandemic hit the globe and the world had shut down. I cancelled my trip. All had been put to a halt. Work on *A Mistake Incomplete* (that had no title yet, at the time), was stopped.

Home alone, I soon finished the story to *A Mistake Incomplete*, without waiting for that final trip. I finished the plot, but not enough setting details like I wanted. Eventually, I decided to not delay the release any longer. So, I took my time locked up at home to edit, polish, and release my second book. I came up with the title *A Mistake Incomplete* as it fit the plot, but also fit the writing process—a book that was missing the details (of Milan) that I wanted to have in it.

A Mistake Incomplete was released in December of 2020. I promoted it online as much as I could, but nothing beats in person events, meeting readers, and chatting about the writing process. I'm sure I could have done better with promoting it, but *A Mistake Incomplete* was out in the world. And those who followed me and waited (patiently) for it, enjoyed the story—or that is what I was told, at least.

In late winter of 2021, the world had not yet opened. I was home, wracking my brain, to get working on book three. I knew I wanted to set the story in Naples, but I couldn't think of a plot that inspired me. I eventually realized why I struggled—I wasn't traveling. I understood travel sparked my creativity but didn't truly grasp how much I had relied on it—how much my writing hobby relied on it.

I tried ideas, made notes, lists of characters, potential outlines, but nothing inspired me. Would I write a sequel to *A Mistake Incomplete*? I did like my new character. But did he die in that book? Or did he live? I tested stories with him dead. I tested stories with him alive—continuing his adventure. I convinced myself I would write a direct sequel with Stef, again, as the main character. With excitement, I announced it to my readers: I am writing a sequel. I'm not done with Stef. I was inspired.

I had a plot, I had a theme, I had a mission. But after writing a good chunk, I decided to test it out with a totally different character. And I liked it. This book is still a sequel of some sort, but it was not through Stef; it was through something else. I focused on the bracelet. The object I had never really explained in *A Mistake Incomplete*—used it as a McGuffin (a nod to Hitchcock). But, why not give the bracelet a purpose and make book three about discovering what that was. So, I apologize to overzealously announcing a Stef continuation, but the bracelet won that struggle, and this story continues with it.

Naples was another hurdle for me. Although I spent a lot of my summers in Southern Italy, only about forty-five minutes away from Naples, I rarely went to visit. When I did visit, it was only for half a day—grab a pizza, walk around, and leave. So, I never got to know the city well enough to write it into a story. I promised myself I would incorporate the city into my story, but I wasn't inspired enough by Naples—or what I knew of it— to do so. I wanted more. I wanted something special. I wanted something more interesting than pizza, tomato sauce, religion, or anything that had been glorified on TV and film, including crime. I wanted something different. Something that intrigued me. And I discovered the fascinating legend of Partenope—the siren of Naples. For those of you who are not familiar, I won't tell you more—I'd rather you discover it along with my characters in this story.

Thank you again for picking up *The Taste of Datura*—my third book. Although it completes my personal promise for an Italian trilogy, it doesn't mean I'm done with writing.

Lorenzo

Printed in the USA
CPSIA information can be obtained
at www.ICGtesting.com
JSHW020317111123
51664JS00003B/17

9 781735 065441